Lessons Learned

A Mission Mercenary Novel
Marie James

D1521106

Copyright

Mission Mercenaries

Lessons Learned
Mistakes Made
Bridges Burned
Depravity Delivered
Redemption Refused
Confusion Cleared

Other Series in the Same World

Cerberus MC
Blackbridge Security
Ravens Ruin MC
Hale Series

Prologue

Angel

The sunlight streaming in feels out of place.

Days like today are meant to be shrouded in darkness.

Bad things only happen in the black of night.

That's how things are supposed to be.

The limited amount of cartoons I've watched tells me so.

My experience has been different.

Time of day doesn't factor into the traumas I've endured.

The cartoons lie.

Unlike the bird that gets up and runs away after being hit in the head with an anvil, Momma doesn't move.

My eyes dart from the pool of red spreading across the floor to the hammer.

Maybe that's the difference.

Daddy didn't have an anvil like the coyote had.

Wetness drips down my cheeks, and I swipe at it repeatedly. If Daddy sees, he'll be angry.

Making Daddy angry is never a good thing.

He's always angry, though.

At me.

At the world.

But mostly Momma.

Women will never learn.

She had it coming.

If she'd just done what she was told...

Correcting her is the only way she'll learn.

But Momma never learns.

As her skin turns ashen before my eyes, I know her lessons end today.

"What a fucking waste," Daddy says with a chuckle, his foot lashing out and hitting Momma's side.

She doesn't move like she normally does. She doesn't cry out in pain. She doesn't beg him to stop.

The silence is as strange as the sunlight coming in through the curtains.

It doesn't belong.

"See her?" Daddy snaps. "See how useless women are?"

I nod. I've known women are useless for as long as I can remember.

Good for only one thing, Daddy always says.

I don't know what that one thing is.

Momma wasn't good at cooking, nor cleaning, nor raising me the way he saw fit.

As the red continues to grow, I still don't know what Momma was good for.

"Fuck!"

My eyes snap to Daddy, watching as he runs rough, irritated hands over the top of his head.

Wild eyes dart around the room, but this is nothing new. Daddy always looks a little frenzied, a little out of control.

"I have to go," he snaps. "I'm calling Poppa. He'll come get you."

I tremble with the news. His father, Poppa, is worse than Daddy.

Daddy only taught lessons to Momma.

Poppa likes to teach *me* lessons.

But when I learn, the lessons change. I can never get it right.

Silence swims around me, the soft swish of the ceiling fan the only thing I hear.

The sun rises further, casting shadows over Momma.

The red pooled around her turns black before I'm yanked up from the floor by rough, calloused hands.

"I fucked up with your daddy," Poppa says, his dark eyes wilder than I've ever seen. "I won't make the same mistake with you."

I was born Benito Corea.

That person died the day my mother did.

The man I became later is much worse.

Chapter 1

Angel

Numbness.

Most people feel it at some point in their lives.

They try to chase it away.

They medicate.

They seek happiness.

They seek pain.

Anything to just... feel.

I live in a constant state of emptiness.

It's the only way I feel at home.

Silence.

Solitude.

Seclusion.

Only the constant itch of needing *more* pulls me from isolation.

More pain.

More violence.

More *lessons*.

This is what I fill up on.

This is what I devour.

All things I learned from birth.

My father taught me lessons.

My grandfather taught me lessons.

It's my turn to teach, to punish.

William Varon is my latest pupil, and the sight of his ostentatious home makes my skin crawl.

The landscaping, the welcome mat, the flimsy curtains that are always pulled back in invitation. It's all smoke and mirrors. What lies behind the walls would make any normal person sick to their stomach.

It's a good thing I'm not normal.

From the outside, the man looks like a model citizen.

He smiles and laughs at all the right times and greets people by name when he sees them on the sidewalk.

He donates to charity, buys girl scout cookies, and drops money in the iconic red kettles during the holidays.

He's *normal*, a successful businessman, a philanthropist.

That's what others see.

That's what he *wants* them to see.

People can't see past the gleaming smile to the darkness inside of him.

They don't know what happens in the dark, what he's capable of behind the fancy double doors of his home.

They don't have a clue that he's a third-generation abuser, a sex trafficker.

They would be surprised to discover he has a woman enslaved inside, that he's purchased a little girl meant for unmentionable things.

They would probably be appalled, disgusted, downright sickened by the lessons he's taught to those he has owned over the years.

If she had just done what I said.

Women will never learn.

As those thoughts invade, my heart kicks up a notch.

It's not that he's teaching them that bothers me.

It's that they aren't *his* to teach.

The woman's husband hired me, contracted me for my skills.

I need my wife back, he'd said to me after I found his plea online.

I don't care that he sold her in the first place because he was disgusted with her. It's not my business.

Women will never learn.

Sometimes you have to cut your losses. Trade up. Replace.

Out with the old and in with new and all that.

The husband isn't even happy about his request. He's being forced into it. Greta Murphy gone is more of a problem for him than when she was at his feet, begging to be set free.

Greta's family has the money, and without her, his coffers are running dry.

I guess he has learned his own lesson.

His money is as green as the next person's and staying on the right side of moral issues has never been my thing.

Green is my thing.

Green is my favorite color.

It speaks the only language I know fluently.

It's my *more*, the only thing I answer to now.

The little girl isn't my concern.

I wasn't hired for her.

She doesn't provide me with *more*.

Greta, however, took pity on the child, carrying her bruised body out of the house and to the hospital, despite the lessons she'll be taught for intervening.

I've been watching William Varon for the last two weeks, waiting for the perfect time to grab my paycheck so I can move on to the next job.

He's the ultimate teacher, confident in the education of his pupils. He manages to keep his lessons hidden, keep his students from speaking, keep his marks hidden.

He's so certain of his skills that he allows others into his home, unafraid that his purchases will ask for help.

Several days ago, he had lunch with an old friend.

Sylvie Davis, a former resident of Telluride, Colorado, entered his house and left unscathed, unbothered by what she saw inside.

It seems Varon is picky, selective in his endeavors. She must not have qualified.

Or maybe he was aware of Sylvie's connection to the Cerberus MC, a club of do-good bikers from Farmington, New Mexico. The man who accompanied her to town didn't hide who he was. His leather cut with the three-headed dog on the back was on his body every second he was in public.

Cerberus MC is known for rescuing trafficked women. They aren't big on the same type of lessons that William Varon is.

Soft touches, compassion, and shelter from harm are more their style.

I've kept in the shadows, postponing my payday to avoid Cerberus.

If they have their sights set on Greta Murphy and the little girl, I know to keep my distance.

I've been tangled up in their messes before and it left with me with two holes in my chest.

I learned that lesson quickly.

Sylvie and her Cerberus escort, Dylan "Spade" Pratt, left days ago, and they haven't been back.

The club must not be as good as everyone thinks because two potential clients were right under their noses and they walked away.

Their loss is my gain.

I watched Greta reenter the house last night after leaving the girl on the sidewalk outside the hospital.

She could've kept on walking, could've easily jumped on a bus headed out of town, or walked into the police station and told her story, opening the eyes of the town to who William Varon really is.

Maybe here is better than home.

It doesn't matter to me.

Greta Murphy isn't paying me. Her husband is. I follow the money. Always.

Varon returned home not long after Greta reentered the house, leaving a few short hours later. She didn't leave with him.

I didn't follow him this time.

My paycheck was left inside.

I waited.

And waited.

Even as the sun rises, he hasn't returned.

His routine is off.

For the last couple of weeks, I've observed. I know his schedule as well as he does.

Yet, I still wait.

Getting sloppy only means trouble.

A lesson that took me a few tries to learn.

Midday sun beats down on my back, the leafless trees providing only minimal coverage.

It isn't until afternoon that I move, ignoring the ache in my muscles for standing still for so long as I inch closer to the home.

If Greta feels like she's better off here than back in Wyoming with her husband, it could mean trouble for me, but I'm always prepared. A kicking, screaming, crying woman isn't new to me.

I go over the list of items concealed in my pockets. I'm all stocked up on tape, rope, and a mild sedative just in case she isn't agreeable.

The back door doesn't make a sound as I push it open. It not being locked doesn't concern me. Varon is so assured of his teachings, he doesn't have to cage his pupils. They know not to wander too far from their master.

Silence, exactly the way I like it, engulfs me as I step inside, and I take a moment to breathe it in.

The kitchen is spotless, as I would expect it to be.

The foyer, dining room, and formal living area are just as pristine.

Greta looks like a goddess on the marble stairs, hair fanned around her shoulders like a blonde halo.

With her eyes wide open, I wonder for a brief moment what her last thoughts were, what she saw before being taught her final lesson.

Did she beg or accept her fate for breaking his rules?

Did she wish she'd kept going after dropping the little girl off at the hospital, or was she grateful that her education was complete?

I pull out my phone, my teeth grinding as I type out the message. *Wife dead, transaction refunded.*

My skin crawls with irritation as I go through the steps of sending Henry Murphy his money back, each second spent hating the bullshit *satisfaction or your money-back guarantee* promise that comes with each of my jobs.

What kind of educator would I be if I didn't suffer from my own mistakes, if there wasn't punishment for my own errors?

Sunlight from the expansive windows casts Greta in a radiant glow, glinting off the knife sunk deep in her chest.

There's a certain kind of beauty in death.

The silence.

The splashes of red were a magnificent contrast to the gray of her skin.

Pretty blue eyes open and knowing.

"Women will never learn," I mutter, before turning and walking out the front door.

Chapter 2

Lauren

I've perfected the art of being who people expect.

I'm an excellent FBI agent for my handler and those at the Bureau above him.

I'm skilled at my job, impressing those around me.

Terrified and fearful? I can be that woman in the blink of an eye, trembling with tears running down my cheeks.

All it takes is channeling memories from my past to make me a little insane and emotional.

A hard-ass who won't take no for an answer? Step back and watch me work.

Somber and grief-stricken? *I'm so sorry for your loss.*

All of it is easy as pie.

What I struggle with is misplaced pity. People with opinions they're too couth to speak out loud.

The only problem is their eyes can't hide it as well as they think they can.

Several pairs of those eyes watch me as I mingle around the Cerberus clubhouse. Of course, they have smiles on their faces. Tonight is a celebration, after all.

Cheers to a new year, new me.

All of it bullshit.

These people.

This place.

As fake as the designer fingernails on a debutante.

As fake as a housewife's orgasm, thirty seconds into her husband's rooting.

I fucking hate fake.

People who pretend everything is perfect make my skin crawl.

This can't be real. This can't be the paradise they all try to convince me it is.

Yet, when the women look at their men, I don't see that familiar fear I've learned to read when I'm working.

They don't flinch when one of the guys hoots and hollers.

I don't catch them with contemplative looks, as if they're dreaming of a better life when they think no one is watching.

Even Cara, who was one of the trafficking victims I helped rescue a few years ago in El Salvador, leans against former FBI agent turned Cerberus member, Thumper.

She thought the man raped me the night she and I were pulled from the back of a truck and sold.

Maybe he told her the truth. Maybe she knows I came hard on his dick that night, overcome with pleasure at his violence.

Is that why they pity me?

They think I'm damaged, broken somehow for enjoying the things I do.

I chuckle as I look around the room. Maybe they are as happy as they try to make people think they are.

Maybe vanilla is the only fucking flavor they can stomach.

They'd look at me with more than just pity if they knew the things I've done, knew of the things I seek while working.

Pain, degradation, humiliation. I feed off of it. Welcome it. Yearn for it.

Mommy issues? Daddy issues? Sister issues? Hell, Grandmother issues. I've got it all, not that I would ever speak of them out loud.

I know I'm different. I know most people would read my full story and use it to commit me to a mental ward. The women would want to help me get better. No sane person would seek such things out, right?

The men, on the other hand? They know more. Hell, I provided the video when I showed up on their doorstep years ago, in a bid to help Thumper after the FBI refused to help him because it would compromise another case.

They thought he was the villain, a man who infiltrated their sanctuary. They were actively searching for him so they could end him for the betrayal.

The video showcased the second time I met Thumper that night I arrived with Cara. It was more graphic, more violent than I'm sure many of them had seen before. It also had my voice begging for more.

I explained my prior relationship with Javier Sosa, aka Thumper, along with providing the video evidence. It didn't take long to believe what they had wanted to all along, which was that Thumper wasn't the epitome of what they despised. He was undercover, in need of their help, not the monster they were led to believe.

Fucking do-gooders.

Movement across the room catches my eye, and I give one of the wives a quick smile before moving on.

Spade somehow looks irritated and happy all at the same time as he watches a woman standing across the room. They may not be together yet, but I know he'll end up attached to the first woman who doesn't bend to his will. The man thinks he needs a little push back to be happy.

He puts on a good front, wants everyone to believe he's a tomcat on the prowl when deep down he's a teddy bear needing his head scratched. That's why he ended up tied to a chair the night he wanted to hook up with me.

He thought he was a badass. I had to prove that I was worse.

His eyes dart away the second they meet mine.

I think I've left the man traumatized. The thought makes me smile, and I chuckle as I lift my beer to my lips.

I could deny the real reason I'm here, but I've spent years internalizing why I do the things I do. It hurts, which is my goal in life.

Pain is familiar, needed, a requisite for me in life.

But even I need a reprieve sometimes.

I'm here because Cerberus is safe.

The men don't leer at me.

The women, although they pity me, don't talk shit behind my back. I don't catch them gossiping or sneering when I enter a room when their men aren't around.

I don't have to worry about the lock on my door being busted in the middle of the night because one of the guys just couldn't help himself. They don't see me as something to take without permission.

I guess I'm a masochist because the refuge hurts as much as the uncertainty my job entails.

I benefit in a way from how fearlessly these men protect the ones they claim to love, the possessions they've earned with their compassion and care.

They're safeguarding them, not me.

I'm unworthy of that shelter.

I will always be unworthy.

If they had to choose, it would be no choice at all.

It's them... always.

Happiness and laughter surround me. It echoes off the walls.

Nothing but good cheer and joyous celebration for these people.

Despite what they've seen, despite what they know happens outside of these walls, they manage to find jubilation.

Maybe we're all just pretending, waiting for the other shoe to drop, and it will.

It always does.

Someone will cheat or be unable to hide their anger. Someone will lash out, get violent at the wrong time, get caught with their pants down.

Bliss never lasts forever. Sustaining it is impossible. Those that think they can hold on to something as tenuous as contentment are bigger fools than they'll ever realize. The wool covering their eyes will be pulled back eventually. The slap in the face will be harsh, leaving behind a mark nothing can erase.

But I've been here multiple times, off and on for several years, and I can never find the pain, the abuse.

I don't see bruises left behind by the men.

I don't see the women plying their men with more drinks on the off chance that they'll be able to fall asleep without having to succumb to their partner's desires.

I've never walked into a room and seen one of the men angry and backing away from his partner in an effort not to be discovered for the monster they truly are.

Maybe they're better than me at playing their parts, but I know the darkness always rears its ugly head.

The pain always manages to bubble over, spilling on the floor at your feet.

Liana was the best actress of them all.

My sister was a champion at hiding her truths.

I close my eyes, the memories of how her red-tinted pain flowed from under the bathroom door, hitting me out of nowhere. She was always braver than I could ever be. She took matters into her own hands.

It took grit, a certain fearlessness, and fortitude to face her demon.

It took courage to know she'd never get over what had been done to her.

She destroyed her monster.

Then she destroyed herself.

I choke down my weakness with another sip of beer, getting rid of those thoughts of her before opening my eyes once again.

With my smile back in place, I search the room for an outlet, a way to put me back on an even keel.

I come up empty.

It looks like it will only be me and my incessant need for pain tonight.

But that's okay.

We've always been great bedfellows.

Chapter 3

Angel

People are pawns.

A means to an end.

Their fears aren't my problem.

I learned that long ago.

My father taught me.

My grandfather taught me.

I was a great student.

But every once in a while, the ghost of my mother haunts me.

Every once in a while, she tries to slip that white cape over my shoulders.

It doesn't cover my black heart for very long. It burns away into ashes quickly.

Tonight, as I sit outside the hospital where Greta took that bruised little girl, I'm struggling to untie the knot around my throat.

It's choking me, cutting off the air and circulation.

It refuses to burn, and I hate my mother a little more because of it.

I don't deserve this. I'm a good wife, a good mother.

I blink away the image of her on her hands and knees, a cut on her jaw as she cleaned up the broken vase my father threw at her because he had to wait a few minutes for dinner to be ready.

Women will never learn.

I sneered at the thoughts of her.

It's your fault, I told her at five years old.

The words were hard then, but by seven, they flowed easily from my mouth. Those words earned me praise from my father, and I learned quickly that praise would always be better than what my mother was getting from him.

White knuckles grip the steering wheel as I battle the two men inside of me.

One man doesn't give a shit. That little girl is only one in millions that doesn't have a perfect life. Who cares what happens to her?

The other man, the one that rarely pokes his head out of my subconscious, screams at me that she deserves better. He places blame on me for not acting sooner, for not putting a bullet in Varon's head the day I showed up in Telluride.

Most days, he's easy to silence.

Tonight, he's louder than he's ever been, and I hate him more than ever.

Decision made, if only to ease the internal battle, I climb out of my truck and head inside the hospital.

I knew this was coming. I knew when I went back to my hotel and dressed in slacks and what many consider a nice button-down shirt that this was the direction I was heading, and I hate the time that I've wasted debating it. This problem could've been solved hours ago if I hadn't fought so hard against it.

Dutifully, I head to the gift shop, voicing my thanks when the clerk tells me they were about to close, but she'll give me time to pick out a gift. Thankful for shopping during business hours despite them not being scheduled to close for ten minutes is expected, so I offer it. Telling her that the sign on the fucking door says open wouldn't go over well. It would draw attention, and that's the last thing I need tonight.

I don't speak as I pay cash for the small, stuffed cat.

The goal is to always be as unremarkable as possible. People shouldn't remember me.

Average height, average build. I look just like everyone else.

Brown hair. Brown eyes. Boring.

I'm not worth a second glance as I climb off the elevator in my plaid shirt and chinos. My shoes don't even make noise on the linoleum.

I don't fidget or let anyone catch me looking around. I don't make eye contact with anyone.

When questioned what time they went on break and if they saw anything suspicious, the nurses and other hospital staff won't even be able to remember they saw me.

The placard outside her door lists two patients—*Katie Matson and Jane Doe.*

Bingo.

Like I suspected with the influx of flu cases every medical facility has seen since Thanksgiving, I'm easily able to slip inside her room unseen.

The other little girl in the room might pose an issue as she watches me walk past her bed, but I won't worry about that until she becomes a problem. I'm not one to look for complications before they occur. Wasting energy won't do me any good.

Blue eyes, one encircled by various shades of purple and blue, blink at me when I pull back the curtain separating the two beds in the room.

To her credit, she doesn't jolt or look terrified.

She also doesn't smile when I hold out the stuffed animal.

She takes it dutifully, her fingers barely clasping the faux fur.

She's been taught not to cherish things, not to show emotion until she knows what's expected of her.

Varon was an excellent teacher.

I hold my hand out.

She takes it bravely, but the tremble in her tiny fingers betrays her fear.

The stuffed animal is forgotten on the bed, and I make no effort to retrieve it.

Security cameras will explain exactly what happened here tonight.

"Is that your daddy?"

My eyes snap to the other little girl in the other bed as we walk toward the door.

What I wasn't yet worried about has now become a complication.

The little girl standing by my side squeezes my hand, as if telling me not to hurt anyone because she'll take care of it. Her bravery stuns me for a second. I never would've chanced pain or punishment at her age for anyone.

"Yes," the little girl at my side answers before looking back up at me.

I smile down at her, the action foreign on my face before I urge her out of the room, looking toward the nurses' station to make sure the coast is clear.

She's slow, her injuries making her little face scrunch in pain, but she never complains. Not a single hiss of discomfort leaves her lips, not even when I sweep her up in my arms in the elevator because she's moving too slowly, not when I shove her into the back seat of my truck.

She's brave. I'll give her that.

Bravery is stupid, however.

Bravery can get you killed when facing your teacher.

Do your worst.

Those were my mother's last words. She challenged my father.

It was the only time he obeyed her.

"Seatbelt," I snap when those blue eyes just stare up at me.

Taking a little girl from a hospital isn't even close to the worst thing I've ever done. Hell, I don't think it makes it into the top ten, but my own hands are trembling as I pull out of the hospital parking lot.

The shake doesn't ease until I'm heading south.

"Do you need something to eat?" I growl.

Blue eyes blink at me in the rearview mirror before her little head shakes.

"Do you need something to drink?"

Another shake of her head.

"Bathroom?"

Those blue eyes widen slightly before she shakes her head this time.

Varon may be one of the best teachers I've seen, but the fear in her eyes, the bruises marring her skin, makes me rageful.

Children are meant to be taught, not hurt.

Those words came from my father.

His father didn't have the same mindset.

The itch to kill grows with each passing mile, and I only start to feel relief when the little girl closes her eyes, exhaustion winning against her desperate need to anticipate what's coming next.

I refuse to analyze why I do it, but I slow down, cautious of the dips and bumps in the road.

I know what it's like to sleep with one eye open.

I've done it my entire life.

She deserves a little respite from the pain she's suffered.

The cape knotted around my neck eases a little with what I've done tonight.

Chapter 4

Lauren

If I were alone, I'd throw my cell phone against the wall when I look down and see it void of call and text notifications.

I sent a text to Alan Moore, my FBI handler, three days ago. When he didn't respond, I sent an SOS text.

I'm not in danger, despite my skin feeling like it's getting sticky around all the sweetness here at the Cerberus clubhouse. He's supposed to get back to me immediately after an SOS call. What if I was really in trouble?

The FBI would replace you in a second.

I know that may be partially true, but the FBI doesn't have many agents like me.

I do things, work cases, most men are too afraid to touch.

I welcome the depravity, the punishment, the real threat that I may enter a house and never see daylight again.

It makes me feel alive.

I feel like I'm dwindling here, and although he's not saying it directly, Diego "Kincaid" Anderson, president of the Cerberus MC, thinks it's time for me to move on.

"Still haven't heard from him?" Diego asks.

I shake my head and shrug. "It's New year's Eve. He's probably letting loose a little for the holiday."

"I can put in a call," he offers.

Translation—the sooner you're gone, the better.

He's too mannered, too polite to tell me that I make people feel uneasy, that he, along with everyone else, can't truly understand why I am the way I am.

I guess I should be grateful he hasn't offered to help me other than giving me a place to crash for a few days.

I'd be out the door faster than anyone could blink if he mentions Dr. Alverez, the psychologist the club uses regularly when one of the members drags home some stray victim they couldn't cut loose on a job, or when one of the members themselves struggle with something they saw or had to do in the field.

I understand the idea of it, but the whole healthy mind, body, and spirit bullshit makes me want to roll my eyes.

Feeding the demons is the only way to control them. Fighting them keeps the power exchange tipped in their favor.

Talking about it with an overpriced doctor and cleansing your mind of it may work for them, but I've got no damn interest in all that woo-woo shit.

"He'll get back to me soon," I assure Diego. "If I don't hear from him tomorrow, I'll head to the office."

"I'm not trying to rush you out, but—"

There's always a but, and statistically, it means everything said before that one three letter word is complete shit.

"We're thinking of expanding."

"More guys?" I ask, choosing to focus on that part of the conversation rather than the half lie he's just told.

The man has been overly generous to me. So much so that I'm suspicious of him. It's the reason I keep looking for the bad in all these people and hating when I come up empty. I don't get bad vibes from any of them, and that's suspicious as fuck. Everyone gives off at least a little menace because, as humans, we're all capable of evil shit when pushed to our limits.

"Maybe."

"But you can't offer up a room that isn't empty," I explain for him.

He gives me a soft smile. "We have an empty room at my house, and Misty and Shadow have space as well."

"That's very kind of you, but not necessary."

I give him the smile he expects before walking away.

Unwanted.

Unwelcome.

Familiar feelings for me.

I should be working, not getting the boot from Kincaid. I should be chained up to a wall, looking for a way to save the women chained up beside me, not sipping on beer, wishing I was as brave as my sister.

"Not long before the ball drops," Emmalyn, Kincaid's wife, says as I approach the long table with every finger food one can imagine.

"Not long," I agree, my smile a little more forced after speaking to her husband.

Feeling unwanted and practically being told I am, are two very different things.

I embrace the minimal hurt it brings, knowing I'll need it to fall asleep.

I contemplate causing problems as I look around the room.

Emmalyn doesn't take long to busy herself with something other than being forced into niceties with me, but I imagine it's a skill long mastered, considering she's the very first woman to come to the clubhouse and be kept for the long haul. Once a domestic abuse victim herself, rescued by Kincaid, she's now the mother hen around here with children and grandchildren of her own.

I'm still deciding on what type of trouble I want to stir up when the front door opens.

Rather than another gaggle of women hoping to wake up in a Cerberus member's bed, a ghost enters, one just as tall if not slightly more haggard than the one I met years ago.

My breath catches, my heart pounding a mile a minute in my chest as his eyes dart around the room.

"Angel," I whisper, but no one notices.

They're all too shocked at the sight of him to pay any attention to me. Good thing because the sight of him leaves me more than a little vulnerable, and that's not something I want anyone to witness. Vulnerabilities are always used as weapons later on.

I look around the room, knowing I'm not the only one seeing him, but unable to understand how he's standing in the room.

Grinch looks down at his woman, confusion marking his brow.

"Baby? Who is that?" he asks as he looks toward Angel, his woman growing more and more terrified by the second.

Angel has always been intimidating. His size, the constant snarl of his lips, would make anyone with an ounce of common sense back away. I've never been known to have such sense, and I pushed this man, tested him, played games with his head before stepping over his dead body without a backward glance in El Salvador years ago.

"He's... that's... when I was kidnapped. He was the leader." I expect the words to come from Cara, although her recollection of the details isn't very accurate. Thumper led the crew in El Salvador.

Grinch's woman Grace is the one who spoke.

It was another case Angel was on. Had to be.

He was working a job in El Salvador, a mercenary looking for a certain woman so he could get paid. He didn't go out of his way to hurt the women. That's not what he was hired to do. He had a single focus until I crossed his path. Somehow the hired gun felt the need to intercede, to step in and shield me from my job. The memories still annoy me, but deep down there's... relief.

He didn't die, despite the lack of effort I put in to making sure he was okay.

The amount of blood pooled around him after he'd been shot twice in the chest meant death. At least I thought it did.

Legend and Grinch both position themselves in front of Grace, a wall of muscle shielding her from even seeing her captor.

I do my best to hide a smile, grateful no one is looking my way. I wouldn't be able to explain how my black soul is feeding off the chaos unfolding.

Thumper inches closer, the same look of confusion on his face that I must be wearing. He was there in El Salvador, but he was taken by the men that shot Angel. I have no doubt, had he been left behind, that he would've attempted to save the man.

"Are you fucking kidding me?" Thumper snaps before wrapping his arms around Angel in a bear hug.

Angel stands stock-still, his eyes still roaming around the room, assessing any threats as he endures the embrace.

It's Kincaid's turn to step forward, the man tasked with regaining control of his clubhouse. The man doesn't look impressed with Angel being in such proximity to the ones he loves, but instead of asking him to leave, he turns and arrows toward the huge conference room at the back of the clubhouse.

Like the trained soldiers they are, every Cerberus member moves in that direction, circling Angel and forcing him to join them.

Muffled sobs come from Grace. Faith, Legend's woman, has taken his place and comforts Grace with light pats on the back and whispered words I'm unable to hear.

Cara, the only other person in the room that recognizes Angel, looks around for answers she will never find.

I wait until the conference room door slams closed before making my way to it.

I knock, only for Dominic, Kincaid's older brother, to open it.

"This is club business," Kincaid snaps from the front of the room.

A split second later, the door is closed right in my face.

Chapter 5

Angel

"You need to calm down or you're going to be asked to leave," a guy snaps as he holds a Cerberus member back.

If I had to guess, the pissed-off man has staked a claim on that crying woman.

I recognize her from a job a while back. I guess I shouldn't be surprised to find out that she ended up here after I sold her.

She wasn't part of my job, and sometimes I have to play the role I'm given. Selling women, being uncertain of what will happen after they're gone, doesn't normally bother me, but the angry man looks like he'd give his life for her, and that makes me feel a little guilty in the role I played in her demise.

"That man—" he snarls.

"Didn't fucking touch her," I hiss back.

I hate nothing more than wasting fucking time, and if we don't get to the point quickly, I'm liable to lose my fucking cool.

"Maybe not, but you watched her fucking shower after abducting her," he rages. "You did nothing to help her. Fucking sold her to some fucking creep and just went on about your fucking day."

"Someone better start fucking explaining," another man yells, seemingly just as angry as the first guy.

"He's a mercenary," Kincaid says.

My eyes snap in his direction. I don't like being on anyone's radar, much less the president of some desert do-gooder club.

"I was working a case. What I do isn't any different from what—"

"That's not going to help your case," Thumper interrupts.

"We're nothing like you," someone else spits. "Cash doesn't control what cases we take. We don't hurt others to get the job done."

"Angel," Thumper says. "Why are you here?"

I take a deep breath. Being hated isn't a new thing for me. I seldomly meet a person who walks away much less walks away with a good opinion of me.

"I was working in Telluride," I explain, wishing I'd just dropped that little girl off on their front doorstep and drove away. But if she died because of the temperatures outside, that would be on me. I don't like blame. It makes my skin itch.

The atmosphere in the room changes some, but I continue. I don't know how long these men will let me explain before all hell breaks loose and one of them tries to put an end to me.

"I thought your man was there for the same reason, but he left before getting anything done."

"I thought you were dead," Thumper says, digging up shit that has long been buried.

But how is he to know that the Angel he thought he knew is dead?

I can't think of El Salvador, or the way my heart jumped at seeing Lauren Vos in the fucking living room.

I don't often let betrayal seep into my bones, but that fucking woman makes me see red.

Had Thumper not been taken, I know he never would've left me bleeding out on the floor like she did.

He wouldn't have left me for the cleanup crew to discover. It took me eight months to get away from that group of deranged assholes.

"I saw you go down. Lauren said you were still on the floor when she left with Cara, Penny, and Amanda," Thumper continues.

His words confirm what I already knew, but they still somehow have the power to anger me.

Lauren *said*.

I bet Lauren said a lot of fucking things.

But I'm not here for Lauren.

"Everyone, sit the fuck down!" Kincaid roars, and the men in the room move like the robots that they are, pulling out chairs and dropping their asses down.

It seems Kincaid is a good teacher as well. I respect the man for it.

Wielding such power over a group of testosterone-riddled men can't be easy.

Even the pissed man who feels the need to defend what happened in his woman's past takes a seat, but he never drops the rage from his eyes. He's twitchy with it. I know without question if we were left in a room alone, he'd try everything in his power to rip my throat out.

Good for him. Having goals is important.

"What's your full name?" a guy in the corner asks, his fingers hovering over a keyboard.

"You're not going to find shit on me, techie," I say, smirking when the man lifts an eyebrow in challenge.

"Angel Guerra." The man I became the day my mother was taught her final lesson.

His fingers fly over the keyboard, and it only takes a second for his eyes to lift back to mine, brow scrunched.

"As I was say—"

I clamp my jaw closed, and I take a deep breath to calm the irritation forming in my gut when a knock at the door echoes in the room.

The door is opened by the same guy who held the man back who wants my head on a spike.

"This is club business," Kincaid hisses, and the door is immediately snapped closed.

Without even seeing her, I know it was Lauren Vos who knocked on that fucking door. The woman plays her parts very well.

In El Salvador, she was the perfect victim, acting scared around the men, assuring the women they would be fine when no one was watching. She didn't hesitate to insert herself in both mine and Thumper's way once it was disclosed that she was also working a case and the house in El Salvador was her way of getting to whatever location she was ultimately aiming for.

I am surprised that another knock doesn't sound throughout the room, that she doesn't barge in here and demand to be involved.

Her presence here throws me off a little, but I do my best to remain stoic. I'm the cat walking along the fence that's keeping a pack of wild dogs at bay. I'd be a fool to think any different. I'm good at my job but being cocky and overconfident will cause problems. I knew I wouldn't be welcome here, but I have a problem in my truck I'm not going to deal with on my own.

"You were dead," Thumper says again as if he can't believe that I'm in the room with him.

He hugged me when I first arrived, but as he looks at me now, it's not with relief.

That job wasn't my last job, and his teammate glaring at me right now, sucking in rapid breaths, is proof of that. I doubt he can reconcile the two.

I fucking blame Lauren for that as well.

I was a dark and dangerous man before El Salvador, but being left for dead and subsequently held captive myself because she couldn't be bothered to press her fingers to my throat to check for a pulse turned me into the monster I am today.

Before, I'd make sure that undue stress wasn't suffered by the women in my care.

Before Lauren Vos discarded me like trash, I was ready to kill Thumper for what I thought he did to her.

I operated under the guise that broken women don't bring as much money before finding out he was FBI. I knew I couldn't always stop the abuse. I knew they'd endure more once they were sold, but I never wanted to bear witness to it. Out of sight, out of mind kept me from fucking up my own jobs.

I'm different now.

Now the paycheck is all that matters.

I no longer look out for others because there's no one looking out for me.

I'm not some goddamned martyr.

I shove all that shit down and lift my chin another inch, my dark eyes scanning the room.

I knew what coming here meant. I knew Cerberus thought I was dead. I knew Lauren thought the same thing. I just never thought she'd be here.

I pictured her dead herself, carved up by some sick fuck, because as much as she liked to pretend to be the victim, that fucking mouth of hers always got the best of her.

"Takes more than two to the chest to get rid of me," I tell Thumper before turning my attention back to the leader of the group.

It's a warning for all of them. I'm not easy to kill, and I'll pop up and invade at any given fucking time.

Be warned, motherfuckers.

"Can someone start from the top for those of us who have no fucking clue what's going?" a guy to my right asks.

The club president runs both hands over his slick bald head before answering. "Angel is a mercenary that was on the same job that Thumper was on when he worked for the FBI. Traffickers showed up, shot Angel, and took Thumper. It was revenge for the death of another trafficker. Thumper killed one of the guys who raped one of the women in his care. The brother wasn't happy about it."

That has to be the simplest explanation to so much tragedy, bloodshed, and torture I've ever heard.

It's succinct. I like it.

"I'm working a case," I say.

"Earning a paycheck," the angry man counters, making me wonder just how much control this man has over the group.

I don't even bother looking toward the other man. He isn't wrong. Money is the only thing that feeds me. It's the only thing that keeps the real demons at bay.

"Enough," Kincaid snaps.

"That job took me to Telluride. When I saw your man there and his cut…" I point to the man I researched and discovered as Spade. "I figured maybe we were working the same case. I know better than to get in Cerberus's way, so I stayed back, waiting for the dust to settle, only it didn't. He left and didn't take the woman with him."

"What woman," Spade hisses.

"Greta Murphy," I answer. "She was abducted from Wyoming fourteen months ago. I tracked her to Will Varon's house in Telluride."

Kincaid's eyes dart to the man on the computer, and I can instantly tell someone fucked up. The club president drops into his seat at the front of the table as if he's been shoved.

A chill settles over several people in the room, and I take an easier breath for the first time since arriving.

"You guys won't find shit on him either," I inform them.

On paper, William Varon is picture-fucking-perfect. I only know different from what I observed for the two weeks I was watching and waiting to make my move to get Greta back to her husband in Wyoming.

I had time to dig a little deeper after leaving Greta looking like a fallen angel on the stairs, and the information I discovered was only by chance after coming across an old news article about a missing woman from years and years ago. It took hours to link the disappearance to Will's family.

"Varon is a third-generation trafficker, running his family's business out of Telluride, although they keep their abductions a couple of hours away in neighboring states," I explain.

"I'm glad you were able to solve your case," Kincaid says as he stands. "Now you need to leave. I don't want to see you on Cerberus property ever again. If you need to give us a heads-up, you can call. I vow to keep everyone here safe, and that includes their emotional well-being. There's no justification in how you handle business, and I just can't allow you to be here any longer."

That would sting if I had a fucking heart or gave an ounce of a damn where these men are concerned.

I nod, knowing when I'm being dismissed.

"I'll go, but what do you want me to do with the girl?"

As if an arctic breeze has floated into the place, everyone in the room freezes.

"The girl?" Kincaid asks.

"Two days ago, Greta took an abducted girl to the hospital. The little girl had been beaten pretty badly."

"You took her from the hospital?" the angry man snaps, jumping up from his seat as if my words are the final fucking straw and his president's demand to stay seated be damned.

Two guys grab him and hold him back. My fingers itch to teach the rude fuck a lesson of my own, but I know when I'm outnumbered. Kincaid has already made it very clear that it's time for me to leave, but I won't be taking that damned kid with me when I do.

"Greta was found murdered this morning in Varon's house. He's in the wind, and there was nothing in the house that I could find that identified the girl. She's the entire reason I'm here. You fucking do-gooders are more cut out for this shit than I am."

I didn't exactly look around the fucking place to gain any new information. While I was there, my only intention was to leave town and head home before finding another fucking job to busy myself. I had to make up for the loss of income from Greta getting killed.

Several men growl as if the death of a woman means anything in the grand scheme of things. Bleeding heart fucking fools. They'll never learn.

Spade looks sick to his stomach as Kincaid storms toward the conference room doors.

Spade had to have voiced his opinion about Varon only for it to fall on deaf ears after their man in the corner didn't find anything on him. Regret swims in his movements as he locks his eyes on the table in front of him, and I can only feel glad I don't suffer from that emotion. It would surely get in the fucking way.

The guys start to file out of the room, and I follow suit. The closer I get to outside, the closer I am to leaving.

"Em, Colton," Kincaid hisses as he strides toward the front door of the building.

They follow just as obediently as the wall of muscle I'm moving with.

I point to my truck, and Kincaid doesn't hesitate to open the back door.

Being the obedient thing that she is, the little girl is just lying there exactly where I left her, curled up and asleep. She didn't take the time alone to run or hide.

It's an ode to Varon's training and will be her fucking downfall.

Her eyes pop open when the chilly breeze from outside hits her face, but instead of crying, she simply sits up, pushing a tangled mess of blonde hair from her face as she watches him.

I grin a little when Kincaid inches in further and she shifts back a little. Where I'm unassuming until angered, Kincaid, the tattooed fucker that he is, looks scary all the damn time.

Maybe the little girl isn't as hopeless as I presumed.

A woman automatically steps into her view, Kincaid taking a step back as she takes over.

"Hi. My name is Brynn. What's your name?"

The little girl shakes her head, refusing to answer.

"Has this man hurt you?" Brynn asks her, pointing toward me.

The girl looks to me as if deciding how to answer before looking back at Brynn and shaking her head.

"Do you feel safe with him?"

She doesn't hesitate to shake her head once again.

Smart fucking kid.

"I'd like you to come inside with me," Brynn says.

Taking inventory of the situation she's in, the little girl once again looks all around, refusing to budge from her position in the backseat.

Nearly a dozen scary dudes are standing around the truck.

As if receiving some sort of silent command, the guys disperse, Kincaid included.

I'm left standing there because I refuse to let some little kid dictate what I do. Besides, I can't leave until she gets out of my fucking truck, and I'll be damned if I go hide in the shadows with members of Cerberus. It's likely I'd never make it out alive.

Time ticks by, seconds turning into long minutes, before Brynn is able to convince the little girl that she's going to be safe, and no one will ever hurt her again. Lies I'm certain, but, shit, whatever it takes.

When the girl slides out, Brynn lifts her and holds her against her chest before walking away without a word.

"Good fucking riddance," I say, closing the back door and making my way around to the driver's side.

Before I can put the damn thing into gear, the passenger door opens.

Lauren locks eyes with me, a split second of indecision on her face, before she tosses a small duffel into the back and climbs inside.

I take ten breaths before I'm able to drive off, fighting the urge to wrap my hands around her throat instead.

Chapter 6

Lauren

"You're alive," I whisper, feeling like an idiot for stating the obvious.

He doesn't turn his head in my direction.

That bad vibe, the one I tried to locate but couldn't find in the Cerberus men, is radiating off him in waves.

It's what made me pause before climbing into his truck.

I can't count his silence as acceptance of me being here though.

From the curl of his lip and the way his right eyebrow keeps twitching, it's obvious he's not happy to see me. It's more likely he's driving just far enough away to slit my throat and roll my body out onto the frozen ground.

I wouldn't use the word happy to describe the way I feel about seeing him either.

I could speak of the guilt I feel for what happened to him in El Salvador... his dying that is, but it wouldn't solve anything.

He doesn't seem like the type of man that would even care, but something is bothering him.

"You're rescuing little girls now?"

Nothing.

The lights of town grow brighter, the streets busier now that the countdown has ended and we're a half an hour into a new year.

I'm pissed, too, but that isn't on Angel.

Alan, my handler, gets most of that irritation right now. I could be working, could be helping, could be living in my own pain and retribution. Holidays always have an uptick in crime, especially trafficked women. Drunk men like to fuck, and there's an endless supply of those that get off on taking things that aren't offered. They're loose with their morals and cash.

I was drunk has been used as an excuse for them doing the shit they wished they were brave enough to do sober since the dawn of time.

Tonight's celebrations are wasted with sitting in this truck with him rather than being in South America or some dank torture chamber in Mexico.

"Not talking to me?" I ask as he pulls up outside a gas station.

We both sit and watch as a woman wobbles on too-high heels as she returns the gas handle back to the machine.

The store is closed, only offering credit-paid services, and it's obvious that she's past the point of being safe to drive, but neither one of us say anything or attempt to stop her as she drives away.

"I wanted to—"

"Get out of my truck, Lola."

I don't know what's worse, the hatred in his tone or the fact that he's using the name I use when I work undercover.

Lola.

What a fucking joke.

"Lauren," I snap, needing to remind him exactly who I am right now.

I'm not the lost girl I pretended to be in El Salvador. I've got teeth and will use them to tear him to shreds if he pushes me too far.

Slowly, he turns his head to me, and the man I taunted years ago is nowhere to be seen.

His eyes, as dark as they've always been, are now soulless and empty.

I revel in the frigid chill that starts at the center of my back, radiating out until my arms and legs are covered in goosebumps. It's thrilling, dangerous. Just what I've been looking for.

"Get. Out." There's a warning in his tone, one any person other than me would heed.

This man was a pawn. As an FBI agent, I couldn't believe that he was there to protect the women, that he was truly upset with what he saw happen between Thumper and me. He was fair to the women in captivity with me. His eyes didn't linger any longer than he had to in order to get his job done. He was livid when one of the men raped a girl after getting the keys from him, and proud when Thumper shot that man in the head for what he'd done.

I kissed him, turned him on, stroked him off in the hallway of that house in El Salvador, and like the good little boy he was, he let me, begged me to stop without forcing me to do so. He enjoyed what I offered, drank it up like a kitten lapping at milk. He wasn't the kind of guy I needed to feel whole, but he was a means to an end.

The man staring back at me now isn't a kitten any longer.

He has either changed or he played the game much better than I ever could.

This man is the one I need.

I'm staring into the eyes of a cold-blooded killer, looking at the face of a man who could wipe my existence from the face of the earth and not even blink an eye when he washes my sticky blood from his hands.

It's electrifying, the frantic beat of my heart making me feel more alive than I have in months, years possibly.

As a mercenary, he goes against everything I've done in my years as an FBI agent. He should be behind bars, rotting away in prison for the things he's undoubtedly done, not working another job, and collecting a paycheck.

Yet, I have no intention of making that happen. I don't want to stop him, and that either means he's not all bad or I'm not as good as I like to claim.

The man I wanted to bend to my will, to play with while bored in El Salvador, while waiting to transition to the real job I'd set out to do, isn't watching me right now.

His jaw flexes, drawing my attention to a faint scar there. I don't remember it from before, but I don't know if it's because I felt sorry for the bastard after leaving that house and have tried—and failed—to forget him.

I haven't spent long amounts of time wondering about him—death is final in that way—but he has crossed my mind. The man was shot trying to protect me. He bent to my will exactly as I had intended. He wasn't the first man it happened to, and he hasn't been the last since then. I know it'll happen again. There are only so many shields you can put up in those types of situations.

The first goal of working undercover in some of the most dangerous places on earth is to stay alive. Everything else comes secondary to that.

A mercenary dying so an agent could live is seen as a good thing. A lot of training, time, and money has gone into creating who I am. The pain I get in return, that feeds my demons, is just an added benefit to me.

"I had to get away from Cerberus," I say when he refuses to blink or back down.

I hate the confession. Playing meek and in need of help really isn't my style while I'm not undercover.

"Bus station," he says, throwing his thumb over his shoulder without breaking eye contact.

The words are harsh. He has no problem telling me exactly like it is, unlike Kincaid who seemed to want the exact same thing but wasn't asshole enough to just come out and say it.

"I remember how your lips felt on mine," I whisper, biting my lip in a way that makes me feel ridiculous.

His eyes don't drop to my mouth the way they did years ago when I spoke. He doesn't shift in his seat or seem uncomfortable with what I'm clearly offering him. He isn't questioning whether he should take me up on it or not.

It delights me in ways I can't explain, his indifference.

"We could pick up where we left off," I tell him, snaking my hand up his thigh.

"Don't fucking touch me," he growls, his hand gripping my wrist to the point of pain.

I wince before I can stop myself, my body threatening to catch on fire at his rough touch.

He releases me just as quickly, throwing my arm back into my lap, but instead of insisting I get out again, he shifts the truck into drive and pulls out of the gas station parking lot.

Neither of us speak as he drives to the shittiest part of town, pulling up outside a motel that's less than half a step above a hovel. He grabs a duffel from the backseat before stepping out.

I wait, watching the front office of the motel for him to exit to head to his room, but he never does, despite the row of rooms being outside entry.

Enticing men has never been hard for me. I learned early in my teens that men turn into idiots when propositioned. My body, my words, the slightest hint of cleavage turns them into desperate blobs with only one thing on their mind.

Most men grovel and beg, plead for a taste. It doesn't matter if they have a wife at home or if I'm asking for more money than they have. They're willing to give it all up for me.

It's not even just me. Men will burn down their entire worlds, forgo their perfect fucking wives, turn their backs on their children with just the promise of hot sex. Maybe it's innate, something they learned watching Eve sin in the garden and think they missed out on something delicious—just one bite of that apple she made look so fucking delicious. Now they're unable to turn down any offer that comes their way. They're desperate for a taste of the forbidden.

It's not my fault I use that, manipulate them into getting what I want.

I shouldn't single out men. Women can be just as easily tricked. They're just more likely to give in to the sob story, the *my kids are hungry* bullshit, than sexual desire, but easy to manipulate, nonetheless.

I thought Angel was that man.

I've never been happier to have been wrong.

Chapter 7

Angel

Wasted time.

Wasted energy.

That's all the last two weeks have been.

A solid fucking waste.

Much like the way I have to stay in this fucking town.

I know how William Varon thinks. I've trained myself to be him without crossing certain lines unless absolutely necessary.

I know he'll somehow convince himself that Sylvie Davis is responsible for his actions, that Cerberus is the reason Greta was brave enough to blow his cover and take that injured girl to the hospital.

He'll never be able to reconcile that she mustered enough bravery to defy him. He's too narcissistic for that, too convinced that he's the ultimate educator, to ever admit his own faults.

That means he's coming after her. He'll never be able to get back to normal until she's wiped from the face of the earth.

It also means Cerberus will realize the same thing.

I noticed Sylvie back at the clubhouse. If she stays there, it doesn't exactly make things impossible for me, but it does complicate the situation.

Being caught watching the clubhouse will bring on trouble I don't need. It would be much easier to watch her from her own house in town. I can only hope for the best outcome at this point.

Meaning, I have to stay in fucking Farmington, New Mexico until Varon is brought to his knees. It's his punishment for losing control, his sanction for making me lose a paycheck.

I can't leave until he's taken care of.

I hardly register the cool temps of the water as I shower because my thoughts are focused elsewhere.

Lauren fucking Vos.

My skin itches as I scrub at it, but the images of her standing, looking shocked when her eyes first landed on me, just won't dissipate.

I vowed to never see that bitch again because doing what I wanted if I did makes my stomach twist.

Darkness and the stench of rancid sewer infiltrate my mind.

Slices of a knife.

The poking and prodding.

The sinister laughs of Satan and his minions in the flesh.

The things I had to do to prove I was just as evil as them.

All of it washes over me, taking up the dark corner of my mind before I can shove it all back down.

She did this to me.

I was a saint back then compared to the man I am today.

I remember how your lips felt on mine.

The woman doesn't have a fucking clue.

Kiss her? I'd rather use my teeth to rip the fucking flesh from her bones.

I toss the thin towel to the floor before making sure my gun is on the bedside table.

I'd prefer sheets that weren't itchy, but nicer hotels don't let you pay in cash. They require a credit card for incidentals and shit. It's not possible to stay in the shadows if you're using your American Express card all over the fucking place.

It's not the irritation on my skin keeping me from sleeping. It's not thoughts of putting an end to William Varon or wondering what's going to happen to that little girl.

FBI Agent Lauren Vos has once again sunk her fucking claws into my subconscious, and it's getting more and more difficult to shove away the thoughts of revenge that kept me alive after getting pulled from that house in El Salvador.

A shadow cast by the streetlight outside passes in front of the window, but it doesn't alarm me. I know despite it being after two in the morning, crackheads keep irregular hours. It's nothing new to see people wandering around at all times around shitty motels like this one.

It's the attempted twist of the doorknob that makes me narrow my focus.

The click of the lock being disarmed sets my senses on fire, but I don't budge. I'm always up for a challenge. How close can I let them get to me before I reach for my gun?

Wil they be faster this time?

It thrills me to find out.

I turn irrationally angry, as the scent of her skin, the same spicy smell that invaded my nostrils in my truck, washes over me.

The woman has a lot of nerve and not nearly as much common fucking sense breaking into my room.

I don't move a muscle as I anticipate her coming closer.

I don't flinch when the bed dips and her weight settles on my lower body.

I don't pull away when I feel the cool blade pressed to my throat.

She's an FBI agent after all. Maybe she thinks she can arrest me, have me tried and convicted for the things I've done. There's not much she can use against me as far as El Salvador is concerned. The red tape involved in extraditing criminals from foreign countries is usually a deterrent. It's why I don't usually take jobs in the United States. Not to mention the fact that everyone and their fucking mother has a phone with a camera these days. They're more likely to record someone getting hurt or abducted than having the balls to step up and take actions. Americans live for that type of drama. It's hard to stay out of trouble, under the radar, with everything getting uploaded and going viral on social media these days.

But I did sell one of the Cerberus members old ladies here in the US recently, and earlier tonight, I'd abducted a little girl from the hospital. Maybe Cerberus sent her to do their dirty work?

I ignore the thickening of my cock as best I can.

"Are you going to kill me, arrest me, or fuck me?"

She chuckles, the sound sinister as it floats around us.

"Do I get a choice?" I growl, wondering what it will take to force her hand into action.

The first time I saw Lauren Vos, she was getting pulled off the back of a covered truck along with a handful of other women. They were captives, women with dollar signs, things to purchase and sell.

I was working that job because I knew one of the buyers coming for them was the man who also had the woman I was hunting for. It was a means to an end.

Thumper was challenged by the man selling them to us. He was forced to prove he was a sadistic fuck, and he did so easily, bending her over a vehicle and fucking her for the guy to watch and record for his own boss.

I was disgusted, enraged, and even more demented, it fucking turned me on a little. The sound of her screams, her pleas for help, got me hard.

I tried to convince myself it wasn't so bad after discovering they were both undercover FBI agents that had a sexually violent relationship years prior. That was back when I still took the time to justify my actions and reactions to certain shit.

The men who pulled me bleeding from that house in El Salvador beat that out of me.

With one hand gripping the knife at my throat, Lauren lifts just enough to slide her hand between us.

"Feel familiar?" she hisses, her hand stroking the thick length of me like she did in the hallway of that house years ago.

It is familiar. It does take me back.

"That's it," she whispers, her lips against my throat. *"Come."*

I smile up at her, my eyes opening for the first time since she broke into this room. I can see the fear in her eyes, but I don't give her time to prepare.

A pinch of pain at my throat drives me, gives me what I need to finally get my own fucking revenge. It clatters to the floor as wetness drips down my neck and I shove her back on the bed and pin her body under mine.

"Is this what you fucking want?" I hiss.

"No. Please don't."

A shadow of the man I was forces my hands off of her and I climb off the bed.

She scrambles to get away, but before she reaches the door, she looks back, the gleam of a grin on her face.

It's the biggest mistake she ever could've made.

I'm on her in the next second, uncaring of the way her body crashes to the door.

The cops won't be called. Crackheads don't give a shit what's going on next door. They mind their damned business because they want others to do the same.

I press every inch of my naked body to hers, crushing her until she's taking ragged breaths.

"Your safe word is El Salvador," I growl into her ear.

Chapter 8

Lauren

El Salvador.

The place we met.

The place he discovered what I needed.

He was never the man capable of offering that to me.

He's that man now.

Coming in here was stupid. Threatening his life was worse.

Two huge mistakes.

Two things I knew I had to do.

Two things I'm paying for now with the weight of him crushing me to the point I can only take very shallow breaths. Eventually, I'll pass out if he doesn't shift his body.

It terrifies me, but not because I'm afraid of what will happen if I do. It scares me because I don't want to miss a second of it.

He's going to hurt me tonight, his weapon of choice thick and hard against my ass. My blood sings, the chorus to the song he's going to make me scream tonight.

I yelp out in pain when he grips a handful of my hair and jerks my head back.

"Did you fucking hear me?"

"El Salvador," I confirm. "Got it."

It's not a real out. I have no doubt if I say it, he'll just use it to torture me further. The man is deranged. There isn't a hint of the man who begged me to stop touching him in that hallway long ago.

The only way this is going to end is with me bleeding and him exhausted.

"Pants off," he growls, not pulling back an inch to give me room, nor releasing my hair from his fist.

I do my best, tears streaking down my face as my knuckles scrape over the roughly painted door I'm pressed against. It reeks of stale cigarettes and musk. The entire room is dank and disgusting. It's the perfect setting for the shame that will engulf me later.

As I try my best to get my jeans down, he rips my shirt right up the back, his hot breath on my shoulder in an instant.

I don't have time to wonder what he'll do next because he sinks his teeth into my shoulder blade, and the pain radiates from the bite.

"Stop!" I scream, my hands freezing on my clothes.

He responds by pressing my face back against the door, his mouth near my ear.

"Move a fucking muscle and I'll make you bleed."

God help me, I believe him. I'm torn between wanting to prevent that at all costs and punishing myself further by forcing him to keep up his end of the bargain.

The sound of tearing fabric fills the room, my harsh breaths increasing as pieces of my clothing flutter to the floor at my feet.

A rough hand slips between my legs now that he's ripped away every barrier between us. My nipples scream from the rough texture of the door as tears roll down my cheeks.

Shame. Humiliation. Disgrace.

I feel all of it when his fingers pull away wet with my arousal.

I try to draw in deep heaving breaths, but he still hasn't relented an ounce of the weight he has against my back.

"Please," I beg, knowing I want him to stop, knowing I need him to keep going.

"Have you always been such a dirty fucking whore?"

I can't answer him. My sobs are taking over, making it even harder to breathe.

"How hard was it for your daddy to keep his hands off of you, Lauren? I bet you were his fucking favorite."

His words are disgusting and makes my skin crawl as if a million ants are taking tiny bites of my flesh. It's so far from the truth, I almost open my mouth to explain how I wasn't my father's favorite. I easily could've been, but Liana protected me from that.

I let the demons seep in instead, let his rough hands roll over me.

I take a deep breath, gagging on the sharp intake of air when he pulls back some, allowing a little room between the door and me. But the reprieve doesn't last long as harsh fingers twist my nipple, causing me to scream out once again.

"Fucking stop!" I roar, knowing it will do no good.

I fight, try to jerk away from him, but it only brings more pain.

"Angel! No!"

He doesn't hesitate, doesn't question what he's doing. His hands don't shake or tremble. He powers forward, my pain and humiliation his only goal.

It's what I wanted. What I asked for. What I needed.

And he provides.

"You'll fucking keep it there or I'll fuck your ass raw," he threatens as he lifts my leg, situating my boot on the doorknob. My torn and tattered jeans hang from my ankle, and the sight of it is strange to me as I glare at it, my brain not fully online at the moment.

There's no warning. No, *here it comes, baby… get ready* before Angel slams inside of me.

My jaw unhinges on a silent scream at the invasion.

Thick, throbbing, and fully seated, he growls in my ear.

"Fucking whore."

He doesn't sound pleased with himself. It's more like he's ashamed for letting me push him to this point.

That's his fucking cross to bear.

We all have them.

"Please, no," I beg once again when he pushes inside even further.

There's nowhere for him to go, but that doesn't stop him from trying.

Pain leeches through me, spreading from deep inside until it's enough to make me try and jerk from his arms.

"Don't. Fucking. Move." Each word is punctuated with a thrust of his hips.

A fingernail snaps back when I claw at the door, my boot slipping on the doorknob.

He notices it. Of course he fucking notices, taking a breather from ramming inside of me to watch it fall.

I stiffen, locking my leg so it stays in place.

The man isn't a liar. He'll do exactly what he promised, and as much as I pushed him to this point, I refuse to push him to the next. I wouldn't survive it.

"Well, that's disappointing," he snarls. "But I never said I wasn't going to take your ass anyway."

I cry out in terror when he pulls from inside of me and situates his cock at my asshole. Clenching is the worst thing I could possibly do, but at this point, I have no fucking control over my body. Everything tenses up.

His laughter is as demented as every other man who has had me exactly like this.

"Scared?" he challenges, and for the first time in my life, I don't know which road to take.

Either direction could still put me right in the same outcome.

"Please don't."

I don't know why he listens, but instead of hurting me in that way, he drops down an inch and reenters me.

I groan, the intrusion no less rough than it was the first time.

"Who are you pretending for, bitch? Moan like I know you want to."

I obey, the neediness inside of me bubbling out.

One rough finger drags over my clit before he pinches it.

It's euphoric, so painful, and perfect.

I must not be responding the way he wants despite demanding it because he grips my throat.

He doesn't do it on the sides to restrict blood flow. His entire hand is wrapped from side to side. No blood is getting to my brain. No air to my lungs.

Then the real fight begins. I shift and struggle, attempt to gasp, and come up on the losing side of all of it.

My vision blurs, those fingers still pinching my clit until I fear he'll rip the damn thing right off of me.

His hips never stop. They're relentless, pulling back, shoving forward, the pattern so brutal each shove must be tearing up the back of his own hand the way it did mine when he demanded I undress.

Blackness starts on the outer halo of my line of sight. It narrows, growing smaller with each passing second.

Then his hand pulls away.

The orgasm hits so hard, I still can't breathe.

My body convulses, every muscle jerking, drawing in the elements of life it demands.

Screams are no longer possible.

Begging will do no good.

I don't think slitting my throat at this exact moment would make things any different.

He broke me.

Made me love what he did if only for this exhilarating, intoxicating moment.

It consumes me, leaves me drained.

"Stupid fucking whore," he snaps, pulling from me so violently, I crumple to the floor as he steps back.

The sting of his hand in my hair barely registers, as does the hot spurts of cum as they splash across my face and tits.

Instinctively, I reach up to wipe my eyes.

"Touch it and I'll slit your throat."

I believe him. God help me, I believe this man will do exactly what he says.

My eyes remained closed, but I sense him backing away.

I don't have the strength to move, to stand or leave the room.

The crash of adrenaline controls me, the chemicals in my brain making my body tremble uncontrollably.

I hate it.

I fucking hate him.

My mouth pulls up at the corners as I start to drift.

Feeding my monsters has never felt so good.

Chapter 9

Angel

Everything is pissing me off today.

The sunshine.

The happy chatter around me in the diner.

Even the fucking perfectly cooked eggs on my damn plate make me livid.

After tossing Lauren's bag into the motel room and leaving her lying on the floor where she slept last night, I swore to put it all behind me.

I've tried. With each breath I've taken since walking away, I've attempted to just forget the fucking she-devil.

It's impossible.

With each turn of my head, the cut she made on my neck pulls, a constant reminder of her attempt at bravery.

Each time I pick up my coffee cup, the fresh scabs on my knuckles either flash in my line of vision or they sting when broken open again.

My cock threatens to thicken with every fucking move I make.

I haven't spoken except for ordering today, and even the gravel in my tone from growling things in her ear, degrading her, makes me want to go back to the room and do it all over again.

I won't waste the time or energy. She won't be there. I know I hurt her last night. Her blood was under my fingernails when I washed my hands this morning.

I have no doubt she ran straight back to Cerberus despite declaring last night that she needed to get away from them. I have no doubt she meant it. Someone deranged enough to come on my dick while being treated the way she was last night doesn't mix well with the likes of those at the clubhouse.

Lauren Vos isn't love and light and healing.

She wouldn't be caught dead talking about her feelings and sharing her traumas.

So maybe she won't go back.

If she was as smart as she wants everyone to believe, she would've hitched a ride to the bus station and found the fastest route out of town.

I stab at my eggs, the force of my fork hitting the plate loud enough to make the elderly couple at the table across from my booth look over.

I remind myself to get my shit together, be unremarkable.

"It's so good," I say, the smile I manage feeling foreign on my face as I shovel more food into my mouth.

The woman grins, giving me a light nod in understanding. Her husband isn't so easily convinced, but after another second, he turns his attention back to his own breakfast.

I don't have a fucking clue why seeing Lauren Vos again is bothering me so damned much. I knew she was alive. I researched her after my escape from El Salvador. I knew she moved on to the next case as soon as she could. She wasn't even an afterthought for me despite my hatred for the woman. I shoved down my thoughts of revenge the second I got back on American soil. Killing Lauren Vos, making her regret leaving me behind, didn't give me the more I needed.

Revenge on her because I slipped and fucked up, thinking she needed my protection was my problem, not hers.

Letting her live was my penance.

Right now, I'm second-guessing myself. I fucking hate it.

Now I can't even make it through the fried eggs and hash browns without her seeping into my fucking thoughts.

The waitress refills my coffee before skittering away just as quickly. I must be radiating with shitty energy.

Just one more thing I can attribute to Lauren.

I clean my plate as I was taught before sliding it back and draining my cup of coffee.

The gum comes next, the only thing that keeps me sane these days.

I bite into it, chewing slowly until it starts to taste like shit before letting it settle between my teeth and cheek.

There's nothing about this that makes it better than an actual cigarette. I don't even know why I decided to stop smoking in the first fucking place.

There isn't a reason on earth to worry about health issues later on in life. I'll never make it past forty.

Maybe I'm as much a glutton for punishment as Lauren is.

"Fuck," I growl in irritation as she wedges her way back into my mind

I don't bother looking over at the elderly couple because I can already feel their eyes back on me.

Instead, I focus on the last remaining piece of nicotine gum in the pack I'm holding. I'm going to have to hit the store before camping outside of Sylvie Davis's house.

She's back home, and of course Cerberus is also camped outside of her place. I wouldn't be surprised if there was a man inside with her. They're not exactly known for keeping their distance when one of their flock is threatened.

The atmosphere changes as someone settles across from me in the booth.

I know it's her before I have time to lift my eyes.

It doesn't matter that I'm clear on the opposite side of town from where I rented the room last night. She found me.

The woman who should be running for the hills tracked me down. Her skills in that department aren't surprising. I imagine she comes highly recommended as an agent.

What I did to her last night should be reason enough for her to keep her distance, or at least bring backup if she has intentions of arresting me.

I won't go down without a fight. I'm more likely to die in prison than out in the free world working. I'd never go there willingly.

The cut on my neck itches when she lowers her eyes to it.

My cock swells at the sight of bruises I left on hers.

My fingers itch to trace the blues and purples, to make them bigger, to squeeze it again.

I stare at her, my eyes locked on hers.

She doesn't flinch, doesn't back away, doesn't apologize, or admit she'd made a mistake by getting back in my line of fire.

"Can I get you something, sweetheart?"

Neither of us turn our attention to the waitress as she speaks.

Lauren doesn't rush to place an order. She takes her time, drawing unnecessary attention to the two of us. It's smart, tactical.

"Black coffee and two scrambled eggs."

"Toast or hash browns?"

Lauren slowly lifts her eyes, lip quivering slightly. "I'm not allowed to have carbs."

Her eyes dart in my direction, terror making them shiny as she slowly lifts her hand to her throat.

I nearly smile at her, only managing to keep my lips flat as the waitress gasps.

"It'll… umm… be just a few minutes," the waitress stammers before darting away.

No other words are spoken. Lauren doesn't say thank you when the waitress carries over a cup of coffee.

"Your eggs… they'll be here any minute," the waitress assures her.

Lauren nods, her eyes glassy as she once again makes eye contact with the waitress.

She doesn't wince when she takes a gulp of coffee despite the steam coming from the cup, but when she places it back on the table, I notice smudges on it.

Without warning, I reach out and flip Lauren's hand over.

"Fucking bitch," I growl as low as I can manage at seeing the words HELP ME scrawled on her palm in lipstick.

Lauren chuckles, and I realize when I thought she was drawing the woman's attention to the marks I left on her skin, she was actually flashing the plea on her palm.

"My eggs will be here any minute," she mocks, her voice low and taunting, her face still that of a terrified woman.

God, she's fucking good.

I stand, pulling money from my pocket. I drop it to the table and make my way to the front door of the diner.

The waitress looks like she wants to speak out, but I know she won't. There's nothing she can do to stop me.

The sound of distant police sirens fills the air, confirming that Lauren's ploy worked and the police are on their way to investigate.

The second I open the driver's side door, the passenger side opens as well.

I don't have time to argue with her, to demand she get out of my fucking truck.

I wouldn't put it past the devious bitch to tell them exactly what happened last night in that fucking motel room.

She's intelligent enough to take pictures and DNA samples before jumping in the shower and washing my cum from her skin.

She'd lie and say she came to my room to arrest me for kidnapping and in turn, I raped her.

She'd never mention the safe word—not that I would've listened if she used it. She'd never tell them that she came on my dick.

Her word, that of an FBI agent, against mine, a low-life scum who bounces from place to place, breaking the law.

I know exactly how it would go, but as I drive off with her in the passenger seat, I still don't regret a single fucking thing I've ever done.

Chapter 10

Lauren

"Fucking quit," I snap when Angel smacks my hand for the third fucking time when I try to reach for the power button to the radio. "It's too fucking quiet in here."

"I like it quiet," he says, his tone conversational despite the grip he has on the steering wheel.

I hate the fucking silence. It drives me crazy. It's too easy to hear all the shit in my head. I need a distraction, something else to focus on.

He doesn't allow it.

I'm going mad, riding around town with this man. He doesn't seem to have any real destination in mind, but he is sticking close to Farmington for some reason.

I want to question him, grill him about his plans, demand that he tell me why he isn't leaving town, especially after abducting a little girl and turning her over to Cerberus.

I know I would never share the details of my work with him, so it doesn't make much sense to expect him to offer anything to me.

The truck slows as we approach a ravine.

This could be it, where he finally gives in to that hatred for me that seeps from his pores.

I got a glimpse of that man last night.

He was rough, brutal, but I can also tell he wasn't as bad as he could've been. I have no idea why he held back, but I'm fucking determined to find out or die trying.

The latter may become a reality sooner than I anticipated as the truck rolls to a stop, his eyes pinned on the view past my head rather than on me.

I hate him for the lack of attention.

He almost grinned when he found out what I did back at the diner. It wasn't very noticeable, but I caught the slightest lip twitch. It felt like high praise coming from him, and my dark soul latched on to that for some fucked-up reason.

I didn't know I needed it or would even like it. I thought he gave me exactly what I needed last night, but I woke up sore, my face crusty with cum, and I needed more. More of the same, something different, it didn't really matter.

It bothers me that he isn't speaking to me. Even if he opened his mouth to make threats I know he's more than capable of following through with, my skin would feel like it's on fire. I wouldn't be fighting the urge to itch at it like an addict in need of a fix.

I huff a laugh at the thought. Street drugs have nothing on the drugs I use in the form of pain, abuse, and regret.

The danger makes me no less in need of what he may have to offer.

I feel like a child willing to get punished by acting out because being ignored is so much worse than abuse. I'm starving for it. I knew I would be tossed away, discarded like trash. It's what always happens, but I never wanted it to happen so fucking soon, not before I was used up and worthless. There are still so many cries of pain, so much begging for him to stop, left in me.

Why the hell can't he see that?

The desperation makes my stomach turn.

The ghosts in my head demand attention.

His silence and mine aren't the same.

"I'm glad we ran into each other. I'm not on a case right now, so I have nothing but time on my hands."

I grin when his fingers flex on the steering wheel, but instead of putting the truck in park and teaching me a lesson, he slowly pulls away from the ravine and back onto the road.

I have no idea why I'm taunting him. I like having the upper hand unless I'm working. It's the contrast in levels of stability that makes my heart sing.

I'm only allowed to be weak when captured, when in the pits of hell, some sick fuck's basement, and when it's sanctioned by the Bureau.

I've never done this before, tried to push someone into losing their shit so I can feed those dark parts of me outside of work.

Maybe I'm restless. My handler still hasn't gotten back with me, and I know that's his own damn choice. The man doesn't put his life in danger the way I do. He sits in his cushy ass office in DC. He goes home to his wife and two kids every night. There's no fucking reason for him to be avoiding me. When he takes a vacation, he forwards my calls and communications to someone else. He's punishing me because I took another break, because the last time I was in Costa Rica, there were too many close calls.

He knew this would happen. He knew I'd get the itch to get back to work. It's a power move, and I fucking hate him for it.

"I can just ride along with you for days," I say, instead of focusing on Alan and his lack of communication.

His jaw twitches, but he doesn't say a word.

Fuck him and this damn silent treatment.

Fuck wanting him to speak to me.

I hate that he's put me in this position.

Last night flashes in my mind, the pain, the pleasure, the way he did exactly what I needed. I swam in it last night as I lay crying myself to sleep. It was exactly what I needed and I hate myself for it. I hate him for it.

Most importantly, the thing I'm trying to keep from filtering in is why I went into his room to begin with.

I'm not working. I'm not on some mission to bring a dirtbag to justice.

I know it's the delay in assignment. I need to work, and since Alan is being a dick, I have to find that outlet somewhere.

Ignoring me is another form of punishment Angel is using, only this time, I hate it completely. I don't want the emotional punishment without the physical. The two go hand in hand, and he's depriving me of half of what I need.

I watch his face as he slowly drives the streets of Farmington. Maybe if I push him far enough, he'll flip that same switch he did last night.

Reaching for his thigh, I hide my grin when his leg muscle tenses.

He's not exactly immune to me. The tightness in his leg speaks of his hatred for me, but the beginning of a bulge in his jeans tells the other half of the story.

The man wants to fuck me. He enjoyed what happened last night even if he refuses to admit it. There's power in it, his ability to act a certain way while his body betrays his lies. I feel hungry for it, the lack of control he has on his cock when I touch him.

If he hates me for it, even better. It only means the punishment this time around might be enough to tide me over for longer than twelve hours.

I hate him, too. Down to the marrow of my bones, I despise this man.

He's a part of the problem I've worked my entire adult life to eradicate. He has no moral compass. The only thing leading him around is dollar signs, and fuck whoever he has to plow over to get paid. His only concern is himself, and that makes him more dangerous than some of the traffickers I've met along the way.

"You want me," I whisper as I inch my hand up further, brushing my fingers over his thickening length.

He doesn't make a sound as I trace the thick head of his cock with the tip of one finger.

I hate the way I have to swallow because of the desperation pooling in my mouth.

I hate the way my heart rate kicks up and the way my clit throbs just by touching him this way.

Hatred isn't new for me. I've become an expert on hating myself as much as I hate the men I bring to justice. They actually go hand in hand. Someone with an ounce of self-preservation wouldn't be able to do what I have in the past. It's what makes me such a commodity for the agency.

"Looks uncomfortable," I say, trying not to feel offended when he pulls his head back before I can plant my lips on his neck.

He doesn't slow the truck or shove me away when I pull his zipper down. He also doesn't help me at all to get his cock out of his jeans. There's no lift to his hips as I struggle with the denim.

There's no force, no begging, no threats or demands to please him.

It's another power play. He knows I want it, that I need him to give that shit to me, and he remains in control by not doing it.

I grin, my eyes cast down as I pull him free. Words mean absolutely nothing. He can't deny his own need. It's already leaking from the tip of him, glossy and slick... desperate.

He still hasn't said a word. There are no arguments for or against what I'm doing, but I know better than to assume I'm the one in the position of power right now. I know better. This man isn't the type to relinquish any form of control.

Teasing the head with my finger, I look back up to him, but nothing has changed. He isn't looking down at me. There's no challenge in his eyes. It's as if I'm not touching him at all.

My hatred for him grows once again.

He'll take what I have to offer and remain stoic the entire time. I'm not foolish enough to believe he'd grunt with pleasure and beg for more if I take him to the edge before backing off, but if I get him close enough, he may take charge and dominate me the way I need. Who cares if he's pissed when it happens? That's when I get the most relief from this constant itch under my skin.

Unclipping my seatbelt, I lean forward, my lips mere inches from the tip of him. He grows more in my hand as I sweep my tongue over the head, telling myself that I hate the taste of him, but knowing that I'm lying to myself. I circle my tongue, tracing the plush head before mouthing it.

Jesus, I despise him for how slick I am right now, hating myself more than I hate him for not begging me to strip naked and ride his cock while he drives around town.

I don't do shit like that. I don't willingly do anything sexual. It isn't what gets me off, and it doesn't feed the demons inside of me that keep me in a constant state of hunger for pain and humiliation.

That's what makes this man so fucking dangerous to me.

A smarter woman would've woken up and left town after what happened last night. My stupid ass sought him out, taunted him... wanted more from him.

Just as I open my mouth to take him deeper, his hand fists my hair.

I don't have a second to prepare before he uses much more force than necessary to shove me down onto his cock.

If I could manage a smile with a cock in my throat, I'd have one spread from ear to ear on my face.

Chapter 11

Angel

This bitch.

This bitch with her perfect fucking mouth, her perfect fucking lips.

Goddamn her and the way her throat opens to take me.

I tangle my fingers deeper in her hair, unconcerned about the gasps and gurgles.

I don't give a shit about the choking and coughing.

I don't pay attention to the tears leaking from her eyes or the redness in her cheeks.

She put herself in this fucking situation.

I know her game.

And fuck her twice for making me give in to it.

She wants this, the abuse, the power and control I have over her.

This is the shit she gets off on, and I played right into her damn hands.

It doesn't matter that my balls are tightening, that the warmth of her mouth is somehow better than any I can ever remember feeling. She forced me into this. She's getting exactly what she wants.

It makes me weak, malleable, easy to manipulate.

The urge to shove my cock so hard and so deep that she gasps her last breath on my cock is almost too strong to ignore, but I manage, barely.

I pull her off of me, my eyes pinned to the road in front of me, and when she doesn't say El Salvador, I push her back down, loving the tightness of her throat.

Her fingers dig into my thighs as she struggles to breathe, and I know she's trying to determine my rhythm, attempting to determine when I'll shove down, when I'll allow her a breath, so I keep changing it up as my eyes search for a place to park.

I don't know that I've ever been angrier while getting sucked off in my life, but I'm just as repulsed at the situation as I am in desperate need to see the end of it.

My truck tires skid on gravel as I pull over to the side of the road.

The area looks secluded, but that doesn't mean that it's completely deserted. Someone could drive past at any time and bear witness to what I'm about to do, but I also can't seem to stop myself.

After the shit she pulled in the diner earlier, I have no doubt she'd get some stranger involved in whatever this fucked-up side of her craves.

She could just as easily claim rape as come on my dick, and I hate that I can't seem to agree with the reasonable side of my brain right now as I slam the truck in park and climb out.

I drag her behind me, unconcerned about the center console or what kind of bruises are going to be left behind on her body once I'm done with her.

Seeing the bruises on her throat in the diner fucking turned me on. I know how they got there, how hard she creamed on my fucking dick last night when I was marking her up.

The bitch is fucking crazy, and maybe a man that was completely in his right mind would take pause, try to get to the bottom of what she does, try to figure out why she seeks this kind of attention, but that would mean caring. I don't give a shit about Lauren Vos other than wanting to hurt her, punish her for what I endured because of her inaction.

She must think of me as lower than the scum of the earth, no better than the men who she was going after in El Salvador. It's why it was so easy for her to step over me and leave me for dead. I have news for her, death was more desirable than what actually happened after she walked away.

"Don't fucking cry now," I hiss, locking her face in the grip of my hands as she struggles to stand.

I know pressing her to the front of my truck really isn't going to camouflage what's going on, but it puts my back to the barren field, providing me with the opportunity to see what's coming down the road, hopefully before a driver can spot us.

"You better fucking stand," I hiss in her ear as her knees grow weak. "I'll fuck you into the dirt if I have to."

I don't ask her to remove her clothes this time. I know she won't move fast enough for me. Instead, I reach around and force her zipper down, throwing the pull tab to the ground when it comes off in my hand.

"Please don't," she cries, her words coming out on sobs I ignore. "Angel, stop!"

There are only two words that mean a fucking thing to me right now, and even if she says those words, I don't think I'll be able to stop.

Threads snap, the sound somehow louder than her cries as I move her clothes out of the way enough to give me access to her cunt.

With my hand still tight in her hair, I press down on her back with my free hand. It leaves her in an awkward position that I know can't be comfortable, but I've never been concerned with her comfort. She's a hole to fuck and nothing more.

"This what you wanted?" I snap, pulling my jeans down enough that my zipper isn't resting uncomfortably under my sac.

She shakes her head as much as my grip will allow, her tears dripping from her eyes and flowing over the hood of the truck.

She screams in pain when my open palm meets the meat of her ass. She tries to get away, but I'm a fucking monster right now. I'd chase her through the fucking desert to get what I need. I don't care if anyone sees. I don't care who could drive up and try to put a stop to this. I'd likely slit anyone's throat that attempted to pull me away from her.

I'm feral, wild, downright uncontrollable, and I hate her for it.

I don't know if it's a moan of pleasure or a whimper of pain when I slam inside of her. I'm not in any fucking state to even attempt to decipher the sounds she's making. Not that I would bother at this point.

"You fucking whore," I pant, hating that I've let myself be forced into this situation as my hips snap forward and back.

She struggles. Of course she does. I'm a lot to handle on a good day. Any other time, I'd give the woman under me a second to acclimate, but this bitch doesn't deserve it. She earned this punishment, practically begged for it, and there's no way I'm not going to give her exactly what she thought she wanted. She can't change her mind after uncaging the fucking beast.

"Your fault," I remind her when she struggles enough that I have to re-tighten my grip on her hair.

If she doesn't have a headache already, she will by the time I'm done.

"You make me hurt you," I hiss. "Make me abuse you. Fuck, your cunt is so goddamned wet. Sick bitch."

"Angel, no." She whimpers her rejection, punctuated with a moan that threatens to make my balls seize in orgasm.

I fucking hate her for that, too.

"Stop!" She screams the word so loud, my hips falter, but then the rhythmic grip of her pussy tells me everything.

She's punishing herself as much as I am. She didn't want to come. That's part of the way she abuses herself.

I fuck her harder, drawing out her release as long as I can before I'm on the edge of losing myself.

With a grunt, I pull free from her, cum spurting on her ass, painting the handprint I left there before entering her.

She's literally making me insane, I realize as I release her and take a step back. My still-hard cock fights against me as I attempt to shove it back into my jeans.

I'm winded, my breath ragged as I look at her.

Her breaths are just as uneven, punctuated by sobs, but she doesn't look back at me, doesn't swipe at the tears staining her face as she tries to straighten her clothing.

I'm sick to my stomach as I walk around to climb back in the truck, breakfast threatening to make a reappearance. I hate myself for what I just did, and I hate her more than ever because I fucking loved it.

As she steps around to get back in with me, I hit the door lock. I can't bear another fucking second with this woman. I'm going to take things too fucking far, finally get the revenge I spent a very long time thinking of and even longer getting out of my head where she's concerned. I blame her for so many things, and that power makes me murderous. It's clear I haven't learned my lesson about Lauren Vos, but that's on me.

She glares at me from outside the passenger window, her eyes insisting I let her climb back inside.

I turn my eyes back to the road, put the truck in drive, and leave her standing on the side of the fucking road.

I tell myself not to look back, to simply drive away and finally have this woman out of my life for good, but I can't even manage that.

When I glance in my rearview mirror, I know I'm in serious fucking trouble.

Lauren is no longer glaring, and I realize just how fucking dangerous she is. The woman is smiling as if she anticipated my response and is—what, happy? Impressed?—that I left her there?

My truck carries me several miles down the road, but despite knowing how resourceful the woman is, I start to slow down. First, my foot comes off the gas, allowing me to coast awhile before I press the brake. I sit idle on the side of the road for long minutes before pounding my hand on the fucking dash.

I fucking hate her, despise everything that she is, but I also don't want someone else to get to her. I feel like I own her pain. I'm the only one who should be able to hurt her. Revenge on her is mine, and it would be a complete fucking waste if someone got to her for their own sick fucking fantasies.

I turn the truck around, heading back in her direction, and the miles stretch on and on. Lauren is nowhere to be seen.

My brows scrunch as I make it back to the spot in town when she first ran her hand up my thigh. I head back out of town, my truck inching along the road as my eyes scan the desert. No cars passed me when I started heading back to her, so this doesn't make any sense. I guess it's possible that someone picked her up and turned around to carry her back into town.

I should be relieved with the thought, but it sits heavy inside of me.

Cresting a small hill in the road, there she fucking is, her hair whipping around her, making her look like some fucking ghost that just appeared out of nowhere. As I slow down, the urge to drive right past her again hits me hard.

I don't understand it any more than I understand the effort she's been putting in to be near me. Maybe we're more alike than I want to admit because she seems very keen on being in my path despite what I've done to her so far.

I slow to a stop beside her, but she doesn't immediately reach for the passenger side door handle.

The woman glares at me from the side of the road, her eyes searching my face as if she can determine what will happen if she climbs inside.

I don't know what she sees, but eventually she pulls open the door and climbs inside.

This time she doesn't reach for the power button for the radio. She doesn't taunt me with words or try to touch me.

She's silent, something I should appreciate, but somehow her silence is unnerving.

I refuse to consider I took things too far.

Hell, I refuse to think at all.

The scent of sex fills the cab of the truck, but I don't lower the window. I revel in the scent of me still on her skin, riding back into town, the entire time wondering if she even made an effort to get my cum off her skin.

I don't ask and she doesn't offer that information.

Chapter 12

Lauren

My body is humming, the emotions so high that my hands are trembling when he pulls up to a gas station to refill his tank.

I want to stay with him. That's why when he goes inside to pay, I grab my bag and climb out.

I have no clue if he can see me walk away, but I get the distinct feeling that he doesn't care at all.

It thrills me, the way he ignored me before dragging me out of the truck.

I know it's fucked up. I know it's wrong to keep putting myself in these situations, but I can't seem to help it.

It feels like an addiction, like I've somehow managed to form a dependency on the man.

I love it as much as I hate it because I've prided myself on never needing anyone. I've lived my life alone, and despite having this itch to see how far he'll take things, I know I can't stick around. He's giving me exactly what I crave, feeding into my darkness, and, although punishing in his actions, it's exactly what I want. I can't keep it up. I can't keep seeking him out, hoping he'll give in to my demands.

I screamed and cried during what he was doing earlier. It's my mind and body's natural reaction to those types of situations, but I was also in heaven, enjoying the pleasure instead of getting off on the pain and brutality of it. The change is leaving me feeling off-kilter.

I watch as Angel leaves the gas station, pumps his gas, and drives off without so much as looking around for me. The indifference shouldn't make my blood pump faster, but I don't seem to be in control of such things these days.

We drove around for hours in silence after he picked me up on the side of the road, and as I walk down the street, I try not to wonder what it means that he came back and picked me up.

He doesn't fucking care about me, that's evident, but there has to be a reason.

Did he want to hurt me again, fuck me again?

If so, he made no overtures. He didn't look at me a certain way or suggest I suck his dick. He didn't pull up to a motel and demand I go inside and strip.

He watched the landscape, drove slowly past old buildings, and even drove through a trailer park without a word. When he drove down the same road where he took me against the hood of his truck, he didn't even bother looking at the side of the road where it happened.

But he picked me back up. It means something even if I refuse to listen to that part of my head.

The bikes parked outside of *Jake's*, the local bar, should make me turn around and leave. This is the Cerberus Club's hangout. If they're home from work, this is where the single men and Slick, the only single woman in the club, choose to hangout. They go trolling for company, although trolling isn't the best way to describe it. The women in town flock to this place once the guys show up. Women in town are either looking for a wild night or trying to figure out a way to have a permanent spot at the clubhouse.

Landing a Cerberus man means devotion, security, family. The women have declared themselves lucky to end up with an enduring man fawning over them are in search of such things. It all makes my skin crawl.

Someone building you up only to let you down later, a wolf in sheep's clothing, is worse than a man who shows you his dark side right from the beginning.

I nod at the bartender as I step inside, taking a spot at the bar.

As I guessed, the women in the bar are either chatting with the Cerberus men or are drooling from afar.

I've noticed many of the men looking at Slick like they want to approach but are too intimidated by her to make it happen. I've overheard some men trash talking her, expecting women to be weaker, less formidable.

These are the type of men that hurt women for fun. They like to overpower and dominate, but carry around so much little dick energy that they don't register but a blip on my radar. They're the ones pretending. They're nothing like Angel who has proven more than once in the last two days that he doesn't have to growl to have actual teeth.

I resist lifting my fingers to the bruise on my neck as Drake, the bartender, approaches.

"Good to see you again. What can I get you?"

I take a quick look around the bar, wondering if I'm up for putting myself in a dangerous situation tonight or not.

What would an attacker think if they pulled my jeans down and found another man's dried cum still marking my skin?

Would he wipe it away? The thought of that happening is unnerving.

"Just a Coke, please," I tell Drake with a quick smile.

He steps away to make my drink, grinning at me when he comes back.

"Not going to join your friends tonight?"

I don't have to look over my shoulder to know he's talking about the Cerberus guys.

I shake my head. "Looking for a different type of trouble tonight."

He chuckles as I wink at him before he walks away to help another customer.

The guys and Slick don't watch me the same way that the committed people at the clubhouse do. They're less judgmental, having their own kinks and ways to blow off steam. The ones in relationships are the ones I catch following me across the room. They can't believe the things I've done in my life and called it work. They can't wrap their heads around the situations I've put myself in, but I'm not theirs to judge.

"You've been gone for a few days."

I look over, giving Aro a genuine smile. The man flirts with everyone he deems available, and I'm no exception, but he never pushes. He legitimately thinks he's God's gift to women and if a woman doesn't throw themselves at him, they're not worth his time.

I'm not in the business of placating men or begging to be touched.

Force and aggression are my cup of tea, and this man couldn't offer me that. He's the type that will lie back on the bed with his hands clasped behind his head while a woman works hard to get him off. There would be no choking or harsh touching.

He's more of the *good girl, you're doing a great job* sort, whereas I need to be called filthy names and have my head pushed down on a dick.

I smile back at the man, doing my best not to let thoughts of Angel and what happened earlier seep in.

"I've been busy," I tell him, knowing he's as unlikely to ask what I've been up to as I am to ask what he does while working.

"We've been worried about you. Didn't know if that guy—"

"I haven't seen him since he dropped me off that night," I lie, instead of challenging him about his worry.

No one has called my cell phone or sent a text asking if I'm okay. He's placating me. Actions and words are two very different things.

He nods, his eyes searching mine for a long moment before Drake sets two pitchers of beer in front of him.

"You're more than welcome to join us," he says before walking away.

I don't have a real problem with the club. Honestly, if those people want to live in a dream world, let them. I'm not shocked that Thumper ended up there. He was never as dangerous as I tried to convince myself he was. He was always checking in, pulling his hands back before he could do much damage. He's the man that made me realize I had to seek out men that honestly did hate me instead of just pretending. I'm pretty sure that new woman of his wouldn't appreciate knowing he was paramount in my decision to go undercover in sex trafficking circles.

Two men sitting a little further down the bar draw my attention. I'm able to listen in on their conversation without them knowing, and it makes me want to laugh.

They're both trying to hype the other up to come speak to me, something they'd probably never have the courage to do if it weren't for the alcohol they've been drinking.

Maybe some women would be impressed, but that's the opposite way I feel when the teasing they're doing to each other turns sexual. I doubt either of them could even find the clit despite one's declaration to being able to *make me scream his name*.

This is exactly what I mean by little dick energy. A man who knows how to please a woman, even in the traditional sense—which is never something I'm looking for—doesn't have to convince himself that approaching a woman he's interested in is a good idea.

He walks up and takes his shot.

This is something I can give the men in Cerberus kudos for. They don't waver. They don't second-guess. They are the ultimate definition of big dick energy.

Instead of letting the guys beside me build anymore courage, I turn my head and glare at them, giving them a look that doesn't leave any room for discussion. Neither of them has a chance, and they'd be fools to even try. I'm not above hurting a guy's feelings. I'm not politically correct. I'm not going to giggle, sweep a lock of hair behind my ear and tell them thanks but no thanks. It's not my style. I don't have it in me.

One guy darts his eyes away as quickly as he can. The other lets his gaze linger before his throat works on a rough swallow. Suddenly, his beer becomes more interesting than me.

"Put your teeth away," Drake says as he approaches. "Do you need another Coke?"

I grin at him. He isn't intimidated by me, but as I look him up and down, I know he's also not capable of giving me what I need.

I have no doubt the man could please a woman, or a man, considering I've seen him flirt relentlessly with both, but he's not the kind of thrill I'm looking for.

Coming from pleasure and coming from force are two very different things. One I have no interest in and the other I seek out to my own detriment, which is kind of the entire point.

"I'm good," I tell him as I pull a five from my pocket and drop it on the bar.

I do my best to ignore the breeze on my lower belly from my busted zipper. Thinking of it makes me think of *him*, and as I walked away tonight, I told myself I'd leave that entire situation alone.

"Need me to call you a cab?"

I huff. "I had a Coke."

"It's dangerous out there," he counters. "Maybe one of the guys can give you a ride back to the clubhouse."

I narrow my eyes at him. I've hung out here with Cerberus before. I've arrived with them and left with them, but I've never had a conversation with Drake about any of it. He's either assuming I've been staying there, just going off what he has seen, or someone is talking about me. The hairs on my arms stand up with the thought. I fucking hate my name in other peoples' mouths.

"I'll be fine," I say as I stand.

I don't bother looking back at the table of Cerberus guys before walking back outside.

I don't know what bothers me more. Is it that he assumed I'd want to leave with Cerberus or that I can't handle myself in the damn dark alone?

I focus on those two things as I walk toward one of the motels in town because thinking of what my head wants to focus on isn't an option.

I'm done with Angel. He gave me what I needed... twice... and that's enough.

I shoot off another text to Alan, but at this point, I've gotten used to those going unread. I can't ask for another handler because it would bring up too many questions. Alan gives me a little more leeway than I imagine anyone else in the Bureau would. He knows the dangers I put myself in, but he also doesn't question me. He knows it would be pointless, so he no longer bothers to warn me. He gives me the facts about the case and lets me make my own choices on how to handle those situations. He's willing to leave certain things out of reports, and I'm grateful to him for it. I'd have to undergo another round of psychological testing if they knew what I really go through. Condoning the assault of an agent isn't something the FBI would ever want to be accused of, so going above Alan's head isn't going to happen, and he damn well knows it.

The guy behind the desk at the fleabag hotel leers at me like I'm fresh meat as I pay for my room. But when I stare back at him, he cowers and apologizes.

Since when did men become such pussies?

I'm agitated, irritated beyond measure, as I lock the door to my room behind me.

Despite knowing I'll be more exhausted in the morning than I am now, I force myself into the shower before climbing between the itchy sheets.

Maybe tomorrow I can head out of town. A trip back to Kansas may be in order. It's been a very long time since I visited my hometown. My skin starts to itch again with thinking of the pain that place causes me.

It may be exactly what I need to get back on an even keel.

Chapter 13

Angel

I haven't gone far from Farmington in the last week.

Tracking a ghost might seem impossible, but there are ways to get it done.

Without William Varon using credit cards, I've had to resort to old-fashioned hunting. It draws more attention to myself, and I'm not fond of that aspect of it, but you can't really wave a picture around town without people taking notice.

He's here, but for some reason he hasn't made a fucking move.

Something inside of me that was mastered a very long time ago tells me that tonight is the night he makes his move. I have that same feeling running down my spine that I got when my grandfather would look over at me displeased about something or the way the air felt in the house on certain mornings before I even got out of the bed.

I ignore the burn on my back, knowing it's phantom pain. The jagged mark was made over twenty years ago, a punishment by dear old grandaddy because I was unable to control my father's actions. If my father hadn't killed my mother, he'd be around instead of leaving my lessons up to an old man. My grandfather never let me forget what a fucking burden my presence was. Each day was a reminder. Each day marked with pain and a level of education I never asked for.

I parked my truck around the block, and just like it was difficult to stay hidden at Varon's house in Telluride, it's difficult now outside Sylvie Davis's house. Spade, the same Cerberus member that accompanied her to Colorado, is inside with her now. I don't know if they've just gotten complacent or if they've gotten intel about Varon's whereabouts that I'm not privileged to, but there is no longer a Cerberus SUV parked out front.

They're in there alone, and this would be the time that he'd strike. The man is egotistical enough to think he could take on one club member, but not dumb enough to think he could manage any more than that. I have no idea what Varon's mental state is these days, but knowing he's been lurking around town is a clear indication he's not thinking straight.

He's had more than enough time to leave the country, but he hasn't taken it. For some reason, he seems desperate to seek revenge. Sylvie Davis has nothing to do with his true self being discovered, but he's a narcissistic piece of shit and needs to blame someone other than the woman he killed before leaving Telluride.

A shadow moves across her lawn, but I hold tight in the darkness, having found a better vantage point behind a tree in her neighbor's yard.

My heart doesn't race. I don't wonder about different outcomes. I'm not concerned about Sylvie Davis or her male companion inside.

What I do work through my head is how I need to react. Killing this man could bring a storm of hell into my own life, but as easily as he could've disappeared, so could I.

I didn't have to stick around town after dropping that little girl off. I could've easily headed back to Texas or found a different job, but something about this man bothers me. The outcome of what he did doesn't seem settled.

It's not Greta. That stupid bitch had the chance to leave, and rather than hauling ass out of town, she walked right back into the lion's den. Look where it got her? Fucking dead.

As much as I don't want to think about it, I know it's the little girl.

I didn't get details about what happened to her, but I know she suffered. I doubt she was just beaten. Men like William Varon don't keep pretty little girls in captivity because they want daughters. They're there for horrible reasons.

Instead of breaking in like I expect, Varon rings the doorbell like he's an old friend or someone delivering a fucking pizza.

The balls on this man.

I hear yelling from inside the house just as the front door opens. It isn't Spade standing in the doorway but a frozen Sylvie Davis. She looks utterly terrified, as she should. It makes me wonder what Lauren would do in this situation. I have no doubt she'd pull a gun from thin air and put a bullet between Varon's eyes, but Sylvie isn't trained like Lauren is.

The porch light glints off the knife in the man's hand, and it seems to be his weapon of choice. I can give him credit for sticking to what he knows even though a gun would get his revenge much quicker.

"Hi, Sylvie," the man says, the sound of her name so sinister it makes me wonder how she never suspected him of being a monster.

"Will," she says, the tremble in her voice making her fear known.

I inch closer, making no noise as I approach. If she were to look over his shoulder, she'd see me, but her focus is on the weapon in his hand.

"I came to give you a gift." Varon has a necklace dangling from his free hand as I pull my gun from my waistband.

I don't know the significance of that stupid fucking piece of jewelry, but it has the power to nearly bring Sylvie to her knees.

Sentimental shit is dangerous. People will do anything to keep it close. It's why I don't own anything I can leave behind. It gives people power over you, and that's something I've avoided my entire life.

"No. Please no," she whispers, her voice taking on a broken note.

"You recognize it, don't you?" Varon taunts. The locket at the end sways back and forth, but the knife in his other hand remains steady.

"My dad was livid when my cousin brought her home. I was very young, but I can still hear them arguing about taking a woman so close to where we lived. Dad was certain that it would bring the cops to our door. She had the power to bring down the entire organization."

I have no idea why I'm still watching all of this go down. Maybe it's the tears on her cheeks, or the sureness in his voice despite Spade standing only a few feet behind Sylvie. The man has to know this isn't going to go well for him. He isn't just going to be able to walk away from Sylvie if he hurts her like he was able to do with Greta. There's a very real chance the man will die tonight, and maybe that's what he's seeking. Maybe he's ready for it all to be over for him.

"Lucky for us no one even filed a missing person report on her." Sylvie is shaking her head as if the man is telling the truth but she just can't believe it. "It was a gift, right? Something she always wore and never took off? My cousin told me she fought for it when it was pulled from her neck."

"Will," she says, the pleading in her tone making my skin crawl.

"Do you think she'd still love you today if she knew you gave up so easily on her?"

She begins to sob, her hand shaking as if she's willing to risk her life to reach out and grab the thing out of his hand.

I don't know this woman from one I'd walk past on the street, but her stupidity is about to get her killed. I know Spade would've already shot the man had he thought for a second he could do it and not hit his woman.

I step up on to the porch, pressing my gun to his head. "Give me a fucking reason."

Will doesn't spin around to face me, but he doesn't lower the knife either. It's clear he's fucking deranged, his mind only able to focus on Sylvie standing in front of him.

"Drop the fucking knife," I demand.

Varon smiles, the sight of it making me wonder just how fucked in the head he is, but then Sylvie is shoved to the side and Spade is plowing through the door.

The knife goes flying, and it's as if with Sylvie out of his direct line of sight, Varon can finally focus on what's actually going on.

He tries to run, tries to fight us off, but it's impossible. Spade is like an attack dog and won't even let the man take a breath as he's flung off the porch, breaking it.

As if the night comes alive, men with guns at the ready appear from the darkness. Before I can put a bullet in Varon's head, his hands are locked behind his back with zip ties and he's being led away. I feel no sense of closure as he's roughly shoved into the back of an SUV.

I want to argue with them, remind them that he's mine to deal with because I just can't seem to let this case go, but the sound of sirens quickly approaching make my decision for me.

"Hey," Spade snaps as I start to fade back into the shadows.

He watches my face for a moment before he holds his hand out. I look down at the thing, knowing what he wants but unwilling to just give it to him as he demands it.

"I appreciate your help," he says, not seeming to be bothered that I don't shake his hand.

I manage a nod.

"Say thanks by not bringing my name up in the report," I say before walking away.

The last thing I want is to be here when the cops show up.

As I climb back into my truck around the corner, I just don't feel right. Maybe it's the gratitude Spade showed but doing something good just for the sake of it isn't how I normally operate. Thinking of the pain that little girl suffered and letting it drive my actions is something the old Angel would've done. I haven't been that man in a very long time, and I don't like how it makes me feel.

As I crank the truck and drive away, I have this insistent urge to counter it by doing something terrible to level things out again.

Chapter 14

Lauren

It's been literally days since I climbed out of Angel's truck.

Days since I've seen another face.

I've been holed up in this motel room since I closed the door the night after leaving *Jake's*.

I have no fucking will to leave the room, and I hate when I get like this.

It's dangerous. To my mental health. To my body. To anyone who bothers me.

I'm like a caged animal, only I'm the one who holds the power to escape my capture.

Images flash in my head, memories I've tried for years to block out.

My life is a vicious fucking circle.

Need the pain, get the pain, regret the pain, need the pain again.

I fucking hate it, and I hate myself for it, but I guess that's sort of the point to my life.

Hating myself comes easy. I can live in it, dwell on the things I missed, the things I could've done. I can let it fester and hurt, infect every part of me. I roll it all inside and let it turn septic, eating away at me, but without work, I have no true outlet for it.

It'll kill me eventually. One of these days it will all become too much, and I long for those days. I crave the day I'm strong enough to do what I've been building toward for such a long time.

Today isn't that day, and a spark of hope sets my skin on fire when my phone rings.

CIRCUS MONKEY lights up the screen, but instead of answering it immediately, I debate whether or not I should. Letting it go to a voicemail that hasn't been set up is only punishing myself. Knowing Alan, if I don't answer, he'll refuse and do the same when I call him right back.

"Yes," I snap into the phone after the call connects.

"There's a problem."

My eyes squeeze closed as I pinch the bridge of my nose. With a federal agency with way too much oversight, there's always a problem, always red tape, always a lag in info and movement in my line of work. It's fucking dangerous, and the bigwigs in DC don't give a fuck that someone's life could be hanging in the balance. They need to make sure their bases are covered; their I's are dotted and their T's are crossed.

"What is it this time?" I mutter. "A Senator's daughter? A mistress of a congressman?"

Silence fills the line, and although it's not like Alan to leave me fucking hanging for nearly two weeks, I still can't stop the annoyance that's threatening to take over.

"I hate it when you waste my fucking time," I snap. "If you can't—"

"There's been an inquiry into Costa Rica."

My jaw snaps closed. "What did you tell them?"

"Nothing."

Of fucking course he didn't say anything. The man would never go to bat for someone on his team. If there's even a hint that his job is at risk, he'd throw his own mother under the bus.

"What kind of questions are they asking?"

"They're asking for everything. I've been evasive, but they're giving you two options."

My hand is shaking so badly that I have to press the speaker button on my cell phone and put it on the bed to continue.

"Which trip?"

"What do you mean?"

"Which trip to Costa Rica are they asking about?"

"Not this last one," he says, and it's all it takes.

This last trip to Costa Rica was bad, but that was because of the traffickers. The trip to Costa Rica, the one right after El Salvador, I was a different person. I didn't follow protocol, which is always hard for me because the captors are never operating under a code either, but I was even less concerned then. The pain and abuse I saw hit me differently. I knew I shouldn't have been back to work so soon after going to Cerberus for help with Thumper. I wasn't in the mood to play victim, to feed my demons. I was angry, livid that there were people in the world who thought they had every right to hurt those weaker than them.

It was a fucking blood bath. One Alan didn't even bat an eye at helping me cover up. Horrific things go on all the time in Central America. It didn't take much for it to look like a battle between cartels. No man in that house was left alive. I didn't take the time to sort out who was who. There was only one reason those men were there, and that was to take, to use up, to hurt.

The women who were set free thought I was their savior. No one knew I was an FBI agent. They thanked me and disbursed from that house.

I never thought it would creep back up and bite me in the ass, even after discovering that one of the men visiting just happened to be the son of a tech millionaire from California. He was just as guilty as the man who put a bag on my head and dragged me off the street two weeks prior. I saw what that man did to one of the younger girls there.

His father made it look like he was there for business, but I doubt his dad knew he was forcing a sixteen-year-old to suck his cock. I paid extra attention to that one. Sometimes when I close my eyes, I can still hear him begging for his life, offering me every penny of his father's wealth if I let him live.

"What do they know?"

"I haven't told them anything. I don't remember any details other than what was in the report. You know me. Too busy to focus on much."

Translation—I'm not putting my ass on the line for you.

"What are my options?"

"You can either come in for the inquiry or don't."

I clench my hands until my knuckles crackle.

"So what you're saying is to come in and end up going to jail because that's what will happen if I'm questioned. Or what? Run?"

He doesn't respond, and I know he's being very careful with his wording in case I'm recording this conversation.

"If I run and they catch me, I'll end up in prison too."

"As your handler, I have to urge you to come into the office. It's pertinent that you explain what happened."

I mull this over. I'm a good agent. I'm able to work well under pressure, handle myself in tough situations, but I can't beat an interrogation by the FBI. Just the technology they have will let them know I'm lying before the words even leave my mouth.

"I can't go to prison," I mutter.

Once again, he doesn't speak. His silence is telling.

He knows exactly what happened in Costa Rica. The man is just as vengeful as I am, only he'd never have the balls to go through with slitting a man's throat while he sleeps or gutting another man while he screams for mercy because he never showed any to the women he was fond of mutilating. Alan probably jacked off to the tales I've relayed about my time in third world countries, suffering through unmentionable shit while trying to cut the head off the fucking snake.

"Call me when you make your decision, but please make it soon. The longer you wait, the worse it will get. There's already been talk about considering you rogue and putting out alerts to find you."

The phone goes dead before I can remind him that I've been trying to get ahold of his ass for two weeks, not the other fucking way around. I just got burned by my fucking handler. I expect shit like this to happen with someone who didn't fully support what I was doing, but I guess I always knew that if heat was ever applied, he'd fucking jump ship.

I want to scream the walls down, throw shit, and set this fucking place on fire, but that's not the best way to stay off the radar. I have no doubt that Alan has already told them where I am, that he's been working with them to bring me in. Deep down, I know the alerts he warned me were coming soon are already out there.

It means I can't go back to Cerberus. Kincaid wants me gone, so he sure as hell isn't going to harbor me in his clubhouse. He'd never bring down heat on his family for me. I was never really considered part of that group. I'm not privileged to the same protections.

No one will fight for me, but that's nothing new.

Having no one is how I've spent my entire life.

I had the Bureau, the promise of work, the assurance that I could feed my demons while possibly saving others from the fate I craved.

Now I no longer have that.

I was being honest when I told him I couldn't go to prison.

Idleness kills me.

Silence drives me crazy.

This may be exactly what I need to conjure the strength I've been trying to find since my sister fought her own demons.

Chapter 15

Angel

I scrub at my face, holding my breath as the water rushes over it.

I'm fucking exhausted, bone fucking tired. Miserable.

I need to work, but I just don't have the strength to fucking care right now.

It's been nearly a month since I've been home, and despite needing to be there to rest, I had to stop.

Tomorrow, I'll make it back, but another shitty hotel on the outskirts of Lubbock, Texas is where I landed tonight.

I don't sleep well unless I'm at home, and even then it's hit or miss. I'm always at the mercy of my memories—either the ones I can't get out of my head long enough to go to sleep or the nightmares that haunt me when I finally do.

They've been worse recently. The familiar cries of my mother, the begging and pleading me for help, as if she thought I had the power to stop what my father was doing to her, have been quiet.

Instead, I've been vexed with the cries of children, the begging of faceless women I never hurt myself but also didn't lift a hand to save either. It's as if I'm being haunted by the choices I've made in life, and I'm realizing that I've never once made the right one.

I don't understand people not helping themselves. It's as if they're incapable even though they know what will eventually happen.

I know the psychology of it. I know my mother stayed after being abused. I know leaving was more than walking out of the house and getting in the car.

I know my father tortured her, threatened my life, and she didn't want that even though I never lifted a hand to help her. That forgiveness she always had in her eyes when she would catch me crying as a young boy for witnessing her abuse wasn't there that last day. There wasn't whispered I love yous. There was nothing. Cold, dead eyes in the morning sunshine. That's what I got that day.

"Fuck you!" I growl, slamming my fists against the dingy tile of the shower.

If there was a way I could keep all cognitive function but get rid of every fucking memory I've ever created, I'd take it in a heartbeat.

Give me my house and my money, and I'd be a happy man.

Instead I have thoughts of my mother, thoughts of Lauren, thoughts of that little girl I didn't help in time, bouncing around in my skull and threatening to make me fucking insane. I hate all three of them.

I hate the power they have to control my mood. I hate that I miss my mother, that I wonder if Lauren is safe. I hate that innocent little girl for just fucking existing.

The towel is abrasive on my skin as I scrub at it. The water on it at this point doesn't matter. I just need an escape, a way to get my damn mind off of everything that seems hell-bent on hitting me at once.

I don't like feeling. I never fucking have.

I need a decent night's sleep and my house. I need silence.

I need—

"Fuck you, too," Lauren says, her words heavy as she lifts a glass half filled with amber liquid when I step into the room.

I manage to hide my shock at her being in my hotel room, but the fact is that I never anticipated her being here. Lubbock is fucking over five hundred miles from where I saw her last.

"What the fuck are you doing here?" I snap, dropping my towel to the floor before grabbing a pair of sweats from my bag. "Haven't I hurt you enough?"

Her eyes drop to my legs as I pull my sweats on, but I'm too fucking riled from not hearing her come into the room to let it affect me the way I know she'd like it to. I'm also a little grateful to see she's safe. She walked away in Farmington when I went to pay for a tank of gas, and at the time, I figured she'd show up just like she has now, but she never did. I left town not knowing what the hell happened to her.

"Having a drink." She points to the nearly empty bottle of whiskey before lifting the glass to her lips and draining it.

"Getting drunk in the room with me isn't going to end well, Lauren."

A slow smile across her face. "Yeah? You gonna hurt me some more?"

My lip twitches at the challenge in her voice. "I like to cause pain in the moment. A drunk woman who only feels it in the morning isn't my thing."

"How often do you hurt women?"

"As often as I can," I lie, because honestly it's hard to find a woman who's willing to go through it and not threaten to call the cops. I've had the safe word called too many times for it to even be worthwhile looking for a woman who can withstand what I have to offer.

"How would you hurt me this time?"

"I'll fuck your ass until you bleed."

Her eyes narrow, but she gets distracted by the empty glass and promptly starts refilling it.

"The last guy who fucked my ass ended up with a slit throat."

"Sounds like a hell of a date," I say, but the information makes me seethe inside.

I can only imagine the situation she was in. Lauren is no fucking stranger to being at the whims of some of the evilest men I've ever set eyes on.

Housewives claim to be unvalued because their husbands don't take out the trash, or they don't feel valued because they caught the man they married looking at other women, or watching porn and jacking off after her fourth headache of the week.

Lauren purposely puts herself right in the middle of hell. She's been raped, sodomized, beaten, tortured, hurt in seriously bad ways in order to take out some of those men.

I think she's fucking crazy for it, but I also know there has to be an underlying reason.

I completely understand wanting a little rough sex. I can wrap my head around the hairpulling, the fast and quick invasion that burns in just the right way. Hell, I can get behind the smacking and bruises and the breath play, but what she does? It's fucked up. It's a way to punish herself, but the why will remain a mystery because it's not my fucking business. I have my own shit to deal with. I don't need her sad tales of childhood in my head.

"How are you even fucking here, Lauren?" I ask, my tone bored as I drop onto the bed.

I know better than to close my eyes with her around, but I'm a little too tired to keep standing.

She chuckles as if I told a joke, but it's once again interrupted by a long swig of her drink.

I know she's smart enough not to get intoxicated around people she can't trust, and thinking I'm someone who wouldn't just walk out of this room and leave her to fend for herself is a grave fucking mistake on her part.

"I put an AirTag in your truck." She smiles over her glass as if she's the most creative person in the world.

"Crazy bitch," I mutter, but I find myself smiling, too.

Modern technology is a fucking bitch these days. When I work, I have my older phone and drive my older truck. It doesn't make tracking impossible, but it makes it harder.

Lauren shrugs as if tracking someone's car is just an everyday practice, and maybe for her it is.

"Why here? Why not go back to Cerberus. You seemed cozy there."

She scoffs, her head shaking back and forth, making it very clear she doesn't have full control over her body. She lists to the side a little before catching herself and straightening back up.

"They already watch me and think I'm crazy for what I do for work." She shakes her head again, her eyes growing even glassier as she looks at the wall across the room. "I can only imagine what they would think if they found out that Liana was Daddy's favorite instead of me."

My heart skips a beat, and when it pumps the next time, my skin is cold, my eyes feeling like branding irons as I stare at her.

I said I didn't want this. I didn't want her to spill her secrets. I don't want to know why she continues to hurt herself in some of the vilest ways, but with her confession, I find I want to know more.

I don't speak. I won't open my mouth to ask, but I get the feeling I'm not going to have to. By sunrise tomorrow, I'm going to know all of her pain, her heartache, and the reasons she punishes herself.

"I found her, you know? The day she slit her wrists. I was the only one left alive in the house."

I swallow, refusing to think about those last couple of hours with my mother, the spread of red, the sunshine, the hammer.

"She was pregnant. At least that's what my grandmother said after the autopsy came back. That vindictive old lady died, thinking that my dad found out about the pregnancy and that's what started the fight. She always defended him. Always blamed Liana."

Tears, ones very similar to the ones she cried when I fucked her, slide down her cheeks. She doesn't bother to swipe them away. She remains confident even in her pain.

"I never told her the truth. She wouldn't have believed me. I don't imagine there are many that would believe that my father was the one to get her pregnant, that they fought because she wanted an abortion and he refused. No one would believe that he'd been hurting her for years. How could they?" she asks, looking in my direction. "I hid her diary before the cops got there."

I don't respond to her. I don't climb off the bed and wrap my arms around her. I don't promise her that things will get better. I'm a man of my own experiences, and I know time doesn't do shit to rid you of the fucking demons. Getting control of them is about hard work and dedication, about growing bitter and cold rather than feeding on them until they no longer have the power to hurt you. The monsters are ravenous, hungrier than you can ever satisfy.

I get the feeling that Lauren is very much aware of this, though.

"Years," she says, her eyes dropping to the liquid in her cup. "He was hurting her for years. I knew he was a violent man. I didn't always escape his wrath, but he never came to me for that. She was his pick. I didn't know until after I read her diary that he used that against her. It's how he controlled her. She took everything he forced on her to protect me. I fucking failed her."

She takes a deep shuddering breath before continuing.

"The day they argued, I was terrified. I'd never seen her stand up to him that way. He grabbed her by the hair while she was facing him, and from nowhere, she pulled a knife. I think she stabbed him four times before he let go of her hair. I could see the shock in his eyes as she stepped away from him.

"I thought we were finally free. We could run away and start a better life. I didn't think anything of it when she said she was going to shower, that she'd take care of him after she was done. She was covered in blood, and even at my young age, I thought it was weird. There was no way we'd be able to hide his body without getting more blood on us, but I just nodded, my eyes locked on my father as he bled out on the floor."

She shakes her head as if she's trying to throw away the memories, and I hate that I can sympathize with her and what she experienced.

"Her shower took so long, I went to get her. The longer the blood was on the carpet, the harder it would be to clean, but she wasn't showering. The water that was flowing under the door was tinged pink, and at the time, I thought dang, she had more blood on her than I realized."

I know where this is going, but I don't speak up. I don't stop her and tell her it's okay to keep the rest to herself.

This woman is just as fucking damaged as I am.

"She slit her wrists in that tub. My beautiful sister, my protector, my only friend, killed my father, something I found out later she'd been trying to build the courage to do for years. Years, Angel. That's how long he was hurting her."

I swallow, blinking slowly as I watch her face. She's positively gorgeous in her pain, and maybe if I hadn't witnessed so many terrible fucking things in my own life, I'd gasp and apologize for something I had no more fucking control over than she did at such a young age.

"I didn't want Liana to be in trouble, so I tried to clean up the floor around my father. It was an impossible task. I didn't call the police until the next day, and the detective who showed up couldn't understand that. Maybe in his world 9-1-1 is the very first thought after a tragedy, but in my house, it was never an option. The only reason I called was because I was terrified they were going to turn into ghosts." She chuckles, a humorless sound as she pours another drink. "I was terrified of facing my father even in death after what happened. I could literally imagine how angry he'd be about the stain his body left on the carpet."

She doesn't look back at me again as she drains her glass, only to refill it once again.

A friend would tell her to stop.

A friend would tell her that's enough, and she's going to regret her choice in the morning.

Only, I'm not her fucking friend. If anything I'm growing bitter by the moment with her confessions.

I don't want this shit in my head. I don't want to know what terrible things happened to make her the way she is.

I fully fucking understand her now. It's clear to draw a line from what she witnessed and the guilt she must've felt and how it led to her punishing herself in the way that she does.

Maybe if her father hurt her instead of her sister, then Liana would still be alive.

Maybe she feels like she should've been raped back then and since that wasn't her reality, she can go through the motions having that done to her now.

The mind is a fucked-up thing. Dealing with tragedy and trauma make us do even more fucked-up shit.

I shake my fucking head. There's no fucking chance I'm going to mentally withdraw and become goddamned Dr. Phil in my head.

"I hid her diary before calling the cops. I took her necklace off and hid it, too. Those are the only two things I have left of that part of my life. I keep them in a safe deposit box in my hometown of Dighton, Kansas."

She yawns without even bothering to cover her mouth, but she's still energetic enough to lift that fucking glass to her lips.

Her confessions shouldn't bother me, but they do.

Pieces, memories, regrets from my own childhood start to seep in.

I can take a step back and understand how fucked up my life was back then.

I know what my father did was wrong. My mother didn't deserve the way she was treated, the way she was murdered. I know I could've done more to help her. I also know that I was a child, looking through a lens, learning how to behave. Maybe it was selfish of me to sit back and let her take the brunt of every blow, to agree with my dad about her wrongdoings because it protected me. What could I have done? I couldn't square off with my father and come out victorious.

What took me so long to admit was that I didn't want to die like she did. It was intrinsic for me to survive.

The other side of that same coin was that I was taught from such a young age that women are less than men. They don't hold the same value as we do. That's a hard cycle to break and clearly something I struggle with even now.

But children?

They're to be protected, to be taught.

That's what makes me wish I was the one to put Lauren's father down like the sick, rabid dog that he was.

She never should've suffered that way. Her sister never should've had to deal with a man creeping into her bedroom at night.

I push away thoughts of blaming her mother. She didn't mention what happened to the woman, but that engrained part of me will always blame the woman first, to point a finger and say Liana suffered because her mother wasn't enough.

I scrape my hands over the top of my head, annoyed that I even fucking care to begin with.

I don't want to think about Lauren's life choices and how they probably all lead back to the way she was raised. It lends an element of culpability to something she couldn't control, and at the end of the day, choices have consequences.

She chose to step over me and leave me for dead, and there are consequences for that choice. She can't use her past and expect me to forgive.

It's not like she's asking for forgiveness anyway. The limited knowledge I have of the woman is she's always unremorseful, and I have no doubt this situation is no different.

"It should've been me," she mutters, her voice tired and distant. "Instead of Liana, it should've been me. Maybe things would be different. Maybe my life wouldn't be in fucking shambles."

She empties the dark liquid down her throat, and I hate the unblemished sight of it. My bruises should still be there. My mark should be painting her skin in blues and purples.

A soft, humorless chuckle erupts from her when she realizes she has drained the whiskey bottle.

"If you're going to kill me, do it while I'm awake not asleep." She gives me a weak smile, but it does nothing to detract from the darkness in her eyes. "I wouldn't want to miss it."

I don't respond, and from the blank look on her face, she doesn't expect me to. Most of the time we've spent together has been in silence, and there's no need to change things up now.

I don't tell her I won't take her life, but I know I couldn't. We're too alike. Ending her would be like ending my own reflection, an impossible task.

Hurting her, torturing her, fuck, making her come is just too much fun.

I wince from the sound, knowing she's going to have one hell of a headache tomorrow, when her forehead thumps on the table. Soft sounds escape her lips, making it evident she's finally passed out.

I should leave her just like she is, just like I left her on the floor the first time I fucked her, over a week ago, but there's just something a little too lifeless about the way her arms are hanging down, her neck at the wrong angle, that gets me to my feet.

I'm not careful with her. I don't squat low and gently lift her from the chair. I pick her up like I hate her because I do. Tossing her on the bed is lethargic, but I hate she isn't awake to experience it.

After stripping out of my sweats and making sure my gun is on my bedside table, I drop to the itchy sheets.

I can't fucking wait to be rid of this woman and back home.

Chapter 16

Lauren

"It's not like you're the only fucking person to live through tragedy."

His voice startles me, but even through the haze of alcohol, I'm able to stay completely still.

I can tell I'm in the bed, despite not knowing how I got here. There's only one way, but I refuse to think about him being kind enough to ensure some level of comfort for me.

He's not a kind or generous man, so it may mean he hurt me while I was passed out. I take quick stock of my body, but other than the throbbing headache, I can't perceive any other injuries.

Did he fuck me while I was asleep?

The thought of it makes my heart rate pick up. How fucked would that be? How utterly perfect?

But, no, I don't sense that it happened. There's no way of avoiding that burn his intrusion provides. It lasts for days, and I can't help but feel a little disappointed. I want to tell him not to start going soft on me just yet, but I keep my mouth and eyes closed.

"My father murdered my mother right before my eyes. I did nothing. Probably still wouldn't change what happened if I could go back to that day. You don't see me getting drunk and feeling sorry for myself."

I hate myself for my drunken confessions, but him doing the same in return doesn't ease me of any regret. I don't give a shit about this man. I don't care what he suffered. Most days, I don't care what I went through other than using it as the fuel for my self-destruction. I said those things because I couldn't stop myself, not because I wanted pity or sympathy.

He sure as fuck better not expect any of that from me. He's not going to get it.

I groan internally, knowing I spilled all of it. Liana killing my father before killing herself. Her being pregnant as a product of rape. My grandmother trash talking her because she'd never believe the truth.

Fuck, I told him about the diary and the necklace.

It makes me look weak for holding onto something as simple as a cheap necklace. I fucking hate weakness.

"My father is still alive, and I wouldn't doubt he's hurt another woman since killing my mother. It's not like he was the type of man that could fucking survive on his own. Make his own bed? Wash his own clothes? Cook his own meals? Not fucking likely."

His voice just does something to me that I can't explain, and more than listening to what he's actually saying, I'm just sinking into the bitter tone. He isn't making excuses, isn't saying he wished things were different like most people do. He isn't speaking of regret and wishing for forgiveness for the things he couldn't control as a child. He's accepted them as they are, things he could never change.

We're a lot alike in that sense I guess.

Both insanely fucked up and letting our pasts control who we are now rather than making any real effort to do differently.

"I think I'd kill him if I saw him today. Probably wouldn't hesitate. Bullet right between the eyes, and the fucked-up part is that it wouldn't be for killing my mother. She was weak and broken. I don't think she would've been able to survive without him either. He kept her so beaten down, she'd struggle in life without his constant direction. No, I'd kill him for what happened after, for leaving me with his father. That man was vile, evil, a sadist." His chuckle startles me, the unexpectant sound making the hair on my arms stand up with the menace it carries. "I hated him. Maybe just a fraction more than I hate you."

He continues to talk, but weariness takes over. Instead of being able to retain what he's saying, his words begin to feel like smoke on the breeze. I know they're there, but it's impossible to grab ahold of them. They're like tendrils of thoughts, mine mixing with his until I don't know what's real and what isn't.

What's evident with the way he continues is that he has no clue I'm awake and possibly taking any of this information and committing it to memory. As I start to drift once again, I realize it's probably intentional. He's very aware that even if I am awake, the bottle of whiskey I downed at a record pace will keep me from being able to use any of it against him.

Before long, darkness once again takes over, and it's no surprise when I wake up that he's gone.

Maybe I only dreamed of his perfection, his ability to give me what I need, his way of hurting me perfectly, all along.

Chapter 17

Angel

I don't like feeling lost, carrying around a sense of being adrift, but my chest felt nearly caved in when I woke this morning.

Lauren was still asleep beside me, but that was expected with how much she drank last night. I spent long moments looking over at her, contemplating slitting her throat, but it didn't take me long to decide that it wasn't her fault I was so quick to spill my fucking guts after waking only two hours after falling asleep.

There's nothing quid pro quo about this situation she seems determined to keep putting the two of us in. I don't owe her anything. I wasn't forced to make confessions just because she made her own.

I don't know why I started talking, why I would've risked speaking about the shit I went through. She didn't move, didn't budge at the sound of my voice, and rather than being relieved, I felt a little disappointed that she didn't hear me.

That was, of course, in the middle of the night when demons and things like regret seem just a little less dangerous. With the sunrise comes a new day and a way to shove all that shit back into the bottle. My secrets are safe. Her drunkenness assures it, but the sun also brought a disgusted sense of vulnerability.

I should've fucked her. That would've made me feel better. I woke up, my erection straining against the rough texture of the sheets, with her whiskey breath so close to my face I swear I could get secondhand drunk off of it.

And that just pissed me off even more. It's a level of power she has over me. Some minor control she has with the ability to make me hard just by fucking sleeping.

I went through every ounce of her things. I checked pockets, scrolled through her phone, dug into every corner of her bag.

I found and smashed the fucking AirTag she left in my truck, and I wanted to kick my own ass when I discovered it just sitting in the passenger side door. I bet it thrills the shit out of her that I've been so fucking sloppy that she was able to track me so easily, but I put an end to that.

I left her with her shit strewn all over the motel room. There's no point in hiding the fact that I went through her things. I want her to know what she did last night was incredibly stupid. It left her vulnerable, and she really needs to do better.

I manage to hide my shock when the bell rings above the diner door and she fucking walks in.

It doesn't take her eyes long to find me tucked in the back corner which gives me visibility to everything that's going on inside.

She looks miserable, her eyes tight and squinty, face free of any makeup. She's exhausted. It's clear in the slightly hunched set of shoulders, in the way each step looks like it's taking her more effort than she'd like to use.

She's fucking gorgeous.

She looks used and abused, and I let my gaze drift right back down to her neck, feeling bereft once again that my marks have faded away.

My cock threatens to thicken, a reminder that I could reapply those bruises in the bathroom here while fucking her, daring her to make enough noise for others to run to her rescue.

It won't happen though.

Hell, this shouldn't be happening.

I'm on the south side of Lubbock. I only stopped because I was in desperate need of coffee after getting little to no sleep last night.

She doesn't smile. It seems she doesn't have the energy to even fake it this morning.

I don't question how in the hell she found me because this is another mistake I've made where she's concerned. The visible AirTag was a decoy. I stopped looking when I found it, and it seems that was her plan all along. There has to be another one in my truck, or she's somehow managed to put tracking software on my cell phone.

If I were the type of man to issue earned praise, I might do it, but her being in front of me just pisses me off. I wanted to rid myself of her. I wanted the time it was going to take to stop thinking about this bitch, and that's impossible with her continuing to show up around every fucking turn.

I thought I taught her enough lessons, hurt her badly enough that she would leave, but she's like an abused fucking dog, crawling back on her stomach, too terrified to wiggle her tail but hopeful there will be kindness in my hands the next time I touch her.

But that's not true either, is it?

She craves the violence. She wants to be hurt, to be abused.

It's her penance, her punishment, for her sister being on the receiving end of all of it when they were kids.

It's how she says sorry to Liana. She lets others abuse her.

I should feel like an asshole for how I've treated her. I think most men after hearing her confessions last night would jump at the opportunity to tell her that he's sorry.

I'm not other men.

I'm not fucking sorry.

What I am is addicted.

I want to hurt her.

I want to taunt her about her pain while fucking her bloody.

Why?

Because it's giving her exactly what she wants, what she needs.

She comes so fucking hard on my cock when she's hurting the most.

It's not my place to worry about how she copes with her fucked-up past. Just like it's no one else's business how I cope with mine. We aren't special. There are more people than anyone could ever know that are struggling with battles. The level of fucked-upness doesn't even matter.

If she puts herself in a position to be abused, how is it my place to comment? I'm not exactly the fucking poster child for positive mental health.

What's fucked up is my demons like playing with her demons. We feed each other and that will become so fucking dangerous to both of us. Will I become her father, taking what I need when I want it? Will she become her sister, finally getting enough and plunging a knife in my chest?

My skin itches with the possibilities of finding out.

So am I the asshole for providing that to her or is the sensitive man, the one that feels bad, the asshole?

I choke down the growl at thinking of other men being inside of her.

That little hint of jealousy pisses me off. It's another sign of her control, of the claws she has in my skin.

I hate her even more for it.

I want to punish her more.

I want more cries, more begging, more tears.

I want to leave her drained and incapable of following me.

I want her fucking *gone*.

Only the chatter of other patrons float around us.

She orders a cup of coffee, and those are the only words that I hear from her for the better part of an hour.

When I stand, so does she.

When I climb into my truck, so does she.

I don't say a word.

Despite heading toward home, I know I'd never bring her there. I'm going to have to cut her loose eventually, but doing it right this very second isn't really a concern for me.

She doesn't attempt to turn on the radio. She doesn't complain when I roll down the window because the scent of her skin is driving me absolutely insane. She doesn't try to torture me with small talk like she did before. It's as if the woman is a shell of herself, as if getting drunk and laying all her bad shit at my feet left her completely empty and she's in no rush to get any of it back.

When I have to stop for gas, I find myself waiting to see if she's going to get back in the truck or wander off again.

As I near Mission, Texas, the place I've decided to call home for now, she's still with me, still silently riding in the passenger seat unexpectantly.

I don't head to my house. It's my sanctuary, and I know myself. I could bring her home, fuck her past her telling me to stop, but I'd never find the same peace there I have before. She'd ruin that for me.

Instead of telling her to get the fuck out of my truck, I end up at a local motel just as the sun is fading in the sky.

I don't ask her to join me or offer to let her stay with me, and when I climb out of the truck, she doesn't follow me. By the time I make it back out of the front office with my room key, she's gone.

Without bothering to search my truck for another AirTag, I head into my room, wondering just how long it'll take her to pop back up. I've thought before, more than once, that she was done with whatever sick game she's playing with me, only for her to reappear. I know better than to think we've said goodbye.

I'm anxious to get back home so I can use my computer software to find my next job. I purposely keep an older phone, one without all the bells and whistles in order to prevent people from tracking me, so that means I have to be home with my state-of-the-art firewalls to use facial recognition software that helps me match missing persons with women for sale online.

I learned my lesson about using physical infiltration in a sex trafficking cell to find my client's loved ones. Doing that landed me in El Salvador.

I guess I have Lauren to thank for forcing my hand toward more modern technology so I don't find myself once again strapped to a wall.

I'll never voice that, however. A punishment seems more fitting where she's concerned.

My shower is quick, and I do my best to ignore the swirl in my stomach when I walk out of the bathroom and she isn't taking up space in my motel room.

Dinner is up next, and because I refuse to use any form of credit, it means I have to leave the room to find something to eat. After being sequestered to the truck all day, I walk the handful of blocks to the nearest fast-food chain.

I keep my head down but eyes open. I may be in the city that I live, but it would be foolish to think I'm safe here. With the Mexican border less than twenty miles away, everyone in town has to be aware of their surroundings. I'm less likely to end up victimized by anyone than, say, a woman would be, but there are always idiots who want to press their luck.

It takes ten minutes longer than it should to get my food, but letting teenagers run businesses seem to be the norm these days.

I know she's back before I even step inside the motel room.

This woman left the door cracked, uncaring if someone other than me stepped inside with her.

I have no idea why I want to shake her until her brain gets back online when I step inside to discover she's not only inside, but in the shower and completely vulnerable to any person with the hint of evil inside of them.

Chapter 18

Lauren

I don't know what's real and what's just another way for my mind to fuck with me.

My memories have never been a fluid thing.

I don't know if my head made things up when I was younger to protect me from what was really going on around me, or if the things I "remember" actually happened.

It's a weird thing to not be able to trust your own mind.

As I shower, I have no fucking clue if he made confessions last night or if I dreamed of him doing so.

I can't ask. It opens the door for him to talk about my history, and that's the very last thing I want happening.

I have no idea why I came back to him. I could easily argue that using his motel room saves me money, but I've banked nearly every check I've ever gotten while working for the Bureau. You don't need much when you're always on assignment. I stopped leasing apartments because you can't exactly press the pause button while caged in South America because your lease is up.

Money isn't an issue, and even if it was, it would be less concerning than why I'm right back where I said I never wanted to be.

Angel scares me and not just in the physical sense. There's something about him that keeps drawing me in. No matter how much time I spend with him, no matter how many times he hurts me, I still want to be close to him.

He's not safe. There's not an ounce of security I feel around him. Yet, here I am, using the already opened bar of motel soap that he used before leaving the room like it's my fucking right to do so.

I feel his presence in the room as I rinse soap from my hair, closing my eyes when the suds drift into them.

I expect him to be angry, to tell me to get the fuck out of his room.

What I don't expect is for him to reach behind the flimsy shower curtain and drag me from under the stream by the hair.

If anyone with a lick of sense saw me right now, they'd question my insanity. They'd demand to know why, as my feet are flailing, trying to find purchase, there's a smile on my face and a laugh threatening to bubble out of my throat.

I used to be that person.

I was once an FBI agent that would cry when others were being hurt. Seeing women, honest to God, getting abused used to make me cringe.

It made me so angry.

Then it made me wish I were them. I didn't know their stories or how they ended up captured and sold into sexual slavery. There's no level of *you should've seen how she was dressed or she was begging for it* that could explain a man thinking he had the right to just snatch someone off the street and own her.

Deep inside of me, I knew I deserved it. I wanted to take that pain from them. I wanted to swim in it, wanted it to leave marks on my skin. The physical discomfort helped keep all the internal shit at bay. It made living just a little easier, and if those men should cross that line, then all the pain would be gone forever. It's good to have end goals. The aches and pains leading up to it are just a bonus as far as I'm concerned.

"I'd tell you you're a fucking lunatic, but I think you already know," he growls as he drags me toward the bed.

I fight him because that's my role in this, but my nails on his skin are ineffective, the water preventing me from gaining any real purchase.

"I just wanted a shower," I snap, trying to hit him in the face, but he's just too damn big.

"And you think you can get those things off of me?" He pulls me by the hair until his lips are right at my ear. "You think I fucking owe you something?"

I'm trembling, the ancient heater in the room unable to keep up with the winter weather outside.

I'm not shaking from fear, and that thought allows a level of disappointment to settle inside of me.

The first time he did this, I was terrified. The second time on the side of the road still managed to hold that level of what-if to it.

Right now? He's proven more than once that he has boundaries, but then I think maybe I haven't pushed him as far as he can go.

That thought makes unease swim inside of me.

Would pushing him work? Or would I regret it? Would he hurt me too badly?

Isn't that what I want?

Wasn't I shocked to even wake up this morning? It was too late to make a different decision when I realized the man has the ability to seriously hurt or kill me, but instead of even fucking me while unconscious, he put me in the fucking bed, so I could sleep more comfortably.

Just as I'm thinking he's nothing like I expected, nothing like I needed, he shakes my entire body with the force of his hand tangled in my hair.

I yell as my scalp screams like it's on fire, each tug and shake making me ache from head to toe.

"Answer me, Lauren."

"I'm-I-I just wanted to shower," I say, because I'm not capable of even recalling what he asked.

"Why do you keep coming back when all I do is hurt you?"

I still. I stop fighting him, looking up at his face to give him my answer. "I like it."

A slow, sinister smile spreads across his face.

"And if I take it too far?"

I swallow, wondering if my next confession will be taking it all too far. "I'll like that, too."

He watches my face for a brief second, and it's as if time stands still. He knows what I want, but he's struggling. Giving it to me is the very last thing he wants, despite the thickness of his cock, the proof that this turns him on just as much.

"I'm going to hurt you," he promises.

"Please," I beg, tears already welling in my eyes.

It's pain and relief and need.

"Suck my cock," he demands, releasing me so abruptly that I crash to the floor on my knees.

I don't just give in, however. That isn't part of the game.

He has to take it. That's his role in all of this. As he unzips his pants and pins me with his thighs against my shoulders to the bed, I realize this comes so natural to him.

He doesn't have to stop and think. He doesn't have to do calculations and wonder if what he plans is going to work.

With his fingers back to fisting my hair, he drags my head back until I can hardly breathe with the angle he has my neck at, then he presses forward.

There's no warning, no waiting a second to see if I'm ready, if my mouth is wet enough to take his dick. He wants it, so he takes it.

I keep my eyes open in challenge, the only thing I can control with the way he's manhandling me. His eyes are half-lidded, filled with so much hatred and anger that I feel like the victor in this situation.

He's not fucking my throat because he wants to, he's doing it because he has to.

He's unable to resist, but I don't know if it's me he can't seem to cut loose or what he's doing to me that he enjoys so much.

I feel nearly bereft in thinking that I'm just a series of holes for him to stick his dick in, that I'm interchangeable with any other woman he might encounter.

Anger roars through my blood, and along with digging my fingernails into his thighs, I clamp my mouth down on him. I'm not biting hard enough to draw blood because I know that's something I might not survive, but I can tell by the flare in his eyes that it's not comfortable either.

With a clenched jaw, Angel bends in the middle, that same evil smile on his face. He doesn't try to pull free, and surprisingly, he doesn't hit me across the face.

Instead, he wraps his hands around my throat until I have no other choice but to release him in an attempt to breathe.

Then the real fight begins because he doesn't release me as he drags me back to standing. My vision begins to tunnel, my temples throbbing as my body fights for air.

"You think teeth are a good idea?"

I can't formulate an answer before he sinks his own teeth into my shoulder, and I know he only releases my throat so he can hear me scream in pain.

In the next second, I'm thrown onto the bed, the thin blanket sticking to my still-wet skin.

He doesn't care that one leg is straight, and the other is bent in an effort to crawl away. He sinks his dick inside of me, chuckling villainously at finding me ready for him.

My body betrays me often, but nothing like I get when this man is around.

It feels dirty, his invasion, his fingers digging painfully into my hips, the brush of his chest hair on my back when he bends over to get more leverage.

"Get the fuck off of me!" I scream, uncaring if someone hears our interaction and calls the cops.

It would serve him right, getting arrested for what he does to my body.

He finds the end of me with every fucking stroke, the mix of pleasure and pain so close together I lose the ability to tell the difference.

"Scream and I won't let you breathe," he threatens, his hand coming back around and clasping my neck.

I can't control the way my body responds, and when I scream the next time, he presses my face so deep into the lumpy mattress, breathing actually becomes a challenge.

"Fucking hate you," he growls. "Hate every fucking thing about you. This tight cunt, the way your skin colors under my abuse, the way you tighten with pain. Fucking hate all of it. You stupid fucking addictive bitch. I'm going to kill you one day, and then I'll fuck your corpse, come into your lifeless eyes. Ah, fuck. The way you take a dick."

I want to moan, and at this second I'm glad he's stuffing my face into the bedspread. My body tells him everything he wants to know. I'll be damned if I want him to hear the truths with my sounds.

"Please," I beg when he goes back to gripping both hips instead of pinning my face to the bed.

I'm not able to fool him. His chuckle tells me he knows exactly what I'm begging for.

"Don't stop!" I roar when he slows down, his hips churning more than ramming.

I scramble away from him, knowing I won't be able to get far but needing to at least try.

Somehow this is more emotional than physical for me, and I fucking hate it.

He hates me? Well, same fucking goes, asshole.

I don't get far, but when he attempts to grab my throat again, I bite his fucking hand, the tanginess of iron hitting my tongue when he bleeds.

Once again he doesn't strike me. The psychotic motherfucker laughs, pulling me back to him by the grip of my teeth in his skin.

"So you do have teeth," he taunts as he licks at the blood on my lips when I release him.

The man is fucking brave, getting his face so close to mine, but the pure filthiness of him tasting his blood on my lips makes me whimper with a need I don't think I've ever felt before.

And maybe he feels exactly the same way because he forces me to my back, my body bent uncomfortably in half as he rams inside of me again.

His thick cockhead strikes at that perfect spot inside of me, and I know it's just luck, the man doesn't give a shit about my pleasure.

I lock eyes with him, my expression along with the way my body quickens confessing things I'd never admit out loud.

"You sick fucking whore. Come."

Jesus save me because I do. The orgasm is so strong I have to lock my eyes closed, lip pinned between my teeth because my first instinct as I come down is to thank him for the gift.

He reads me like an open book, laughing once again as he pulls out and sprays cum all over my skin.

Neither of us speak a fucking word as he crashes to the bed beside me.

It was painful, perfect, leaving me broken as I drift to sleep, but it was nothing compared to the pain I feel when he wakes me in the middle of the night.

* * *

I swat at the hand running up my thigh.

Sleeping well never happens, and the one fucking time I'm lost in a perfect dreamless sleep, I'm interrupted.

"Fucking quit," I snap, trying to issue a warning with my tone, but even to my own ears my voice is soft and pleading.

Warmth engulfs my back as that hand continues to wander.

I'm not delusional. I know who I'm in bed with, but his soft touches feel like a branding iron on my skin. It's another way for him to torture me.

The man is well aware by now what gets me off, and I know any time I push him, he's only going to push back harder, but I can't allow this.

Soft and easy, slow and sensual, feels disgusting to me. It was how Liana described what happened between her and our father. She called it love. In some entries she sounds like a smitten teen girl hooking up with a high school crush. She *loved* him.

Bile swims in my throat as I recall those entries.

I've been to so many trainings on trafficking and grooming to see it for anything less than what it actually was, but my sister killed him because she was embarrassed to be a pregnant teen, not because it was his baby. She killed herself because she was upset about losing him, not because she was in fear of getting into trouble. She was heartbroken at her loss.

"Quit," I hiss again, thinking I'm going to get my way when he grabs my wrist, but instead of forcing it over my head and pinning me there as he climbs between my legs, he runs his palm down my arm.

"Mmm," he moans as he settles over my body, his mouth in my neck.

He doesn't bite or pinch or growl. He doesn't threaten or try to hurt me in any way as he expertly finds the center of me.

He also doesn't find me ready for him, his head pulling back, confusion on his face as he looks down at me.

"I can fix that," he says, but instead of twisting my nipple until I scream out in pain, he simply slides down my body, locking his mouth on my clit.

And God does he fix it.

The change in behavior is so fucking strange, I can't even formulate a way to make it stop. It's like the man has somehow managed to make my brain go completely offline.

His mouth on me is perfection, the way he flicks his tongue before long, hot sucks. I like it fucking rough. I need it to even get close to coming, but I have no control over this. That part of me is built for stimulation. I don't care how uninterested I may be, attention there, soft hard, rough, tender, it doesn't fucking matter, my body is going to do what it's meant to do.

I slicken in record time, but he doesn't pull back. He moans my name as he drinks me down. His hips rock into the mattress as I come as if he just can't help himself.

"Jesus, Lauren," he mutters as he wipes his forearm against his mouth on his way back up my body.

I stare down at him, locked in place by the utter weirdness of this.

He covers me once again, one of his hands lifting my leg until my knee is high on his hip. He's successful when he enters me again, his eyes growing glassy in the light filtering in from the streetlamps outside.

I want him to stop.

I need him to stop.

It's absolute torture, the tender touches, and the way his face softens when he watches me take him this way.

I don't say a word as tears stream down my face, because it's painful. It hurts me for him to simulate any form of what may be considered lovemaking.

So I let it happen, and despite him shushing my sobs, telling me I'm perfect, I can't get a handle on my emotions.

It isn't cathartic. It isn't the break into my past that will finally let me heal.

It's distressing, horrendous. It's horrifying and traumatic.

It's fucking perfect.

When he grunts my name, his mouth on my skin, his cum filling me, I hate that it's over, but he allows me to turn over and sob without touching me again.

Chapter 19

Angel

Planning for something and having it turn out exactly the way you imagined it aren't the same thing.

I knew when I took Lauren last night that it would be more than she could handle.

I wanted to break her.

I wanted her pain, her tears.

She gave me exactly what I was looking for, and in turn, she acted exactly like I knew she would.

She allowed it, never told me to stop, despite it being harder to handle than when I had pulled her hair and hurt her after finding her in my shower.

She's into pain and degradation. I found out the pain doesn't have to be physical.

I wake up alone this morning, which I always knew I would.

The tangible pain is something she can manage. She can treat those wounds with antiseptic and bandages.

It's the psychological hurt, the emotions that live deep inside of her, that are impossible to cut out, that are the most distressing.

I thought pushing her to her limits would leave marks on her skin, but I found out differently.

Slow, passionate sex, giving her body what it wanted rather than ripping it from her with violence, was her breaking point.

I should feel happy that she's gone, and I do in a way, but at the same time, her absence in bed this morning also leaves me feeling a little empty myself.

The vacancy, the void inside of me, isn't a new thing. Noticing it, not liking the barrenness, is what alarms me the most.

I've lived my life this way, yearned for the desolation, the lack of anything.

Now it feels like I'm actually missing something.

There's a sense of loss.

I fucking hate it.

I don't waste time getting a shower. I dress and gather my limited belongings before scouring my truck for more AirTags. I find two hidden, one just under the driver's seat and the other crammed into the backseat. I wouldn't put it past her to have more in the truck, so after driving around town for a while, I drop that truck off at the storage facility I lease space at and grab one of my other vehicles.

I can't see her again. The ties need to stay severed. I can't risk the chance of her following me back to my house. It's not something she'd survive. Intruding at the motel isn't the same as showing up to her in my home.

I hit the shower not long after entering my house, and her distaste for how we ended our time together becomes evident under the heated spray on my back.

She had to have dug her fingernails there during the slower session because I never gave her the opportunity the first time I took her last night. I stay under the spray, torturing myself with the pain until it fades away. It's a goodbye of sorts I guess, or maybe it's a good riddance because the woman has taken up too much of my time, too many thoughts in my head lately to be healthy.

I'm honestly shocked not to find her in my home when I walk out of the bathroom, and it takes me checking the security system connected to my computer for alerts to actually believe she isn't here.

I ignore the disappointment as I check my phone. I have no notifications from her despite adding my number to her phone when I went through her shit as she slept off her drunkenness.

I have no idea why I did it. It's not like I'd go running to find her if she called me because she was in trouble.

Lauren Vos is the epitome of you get what you ask for.

She purposely puts herself in dangerous situations because it's fuel to feed the demons lurking inside of her. It's going to get her killed and we both know it.

Wanting or even expecting her to change doesn't count for shit.

The only thing that sets my skin on fire is knowing I won't be the one to teach her that final lesson.

Her behavior is going to get her killed. We both know it.

She's going to die a horrific death, and she seems to be getting closer to that ending with every day that passes. She seems almost relieved that it's going to happen. Her pain in living is greater than any death could possibly be.

After grabbing a granola bar from the kitchen and making a mental note to go grocery shopping after being gone for nearly a month, I head to my office.

I had software running the entire time I was gone, but nothing seems to catch my eye. I don't take jobs under a certain threshold, but even the higher paid jobs don't look interesting to me.

Images flash on the screen, matches from missing persons reports that coincide with dark web auctions for the same person, and it makes me wonder if Cerberus uses a program like this. I bet they could solve a lot of these cases if they did.

Not for the first time, I consider selling the program, knowing the price I'd charge would be enough to set me up for the rest of my life, but there's no thrill in having a bunch of money.

I have loads from working and it does nothing to ease that unsettled feeling inside of me that longs for even more.

As a child, I wanted to be wealthy because rich people make the rules. They don't get beaten for every little thing. They don't suffer violence at the hands of relatives because of a bad night's sleep.

As an adult, I know now that abuse doesn't have a price tag on it. With money comes stress, and those people have to find an outlet for that just as readily as a poor person does. Violence is second nature, and I argue with anyone who disagrees.

News articles fly across the screen of my computer. Murders are abundant as are missing persons and kidnappings. The area of Mexico right across the border is notorious for them. Criminals don't even hide it any longer. Anyone speaking out against it becomes a victim themselves, so they've learned to shut their mouths. The citizens never see a damn thing. Some other person getting hurt isn't worth them suffering the same. They've learned to look out for number one after the decades' old battles between cartels.

It's been really good business for me because those traffickers don't even bother to take their new products out of the city. If you're abducted in Tamaulipas, Mexico, there's a very good chance that you'll stay there until you're used up and murdered or sold. Those cases are typically easy to solve because no one even tries to hide what they're up to. The locals are much too scared to try and stop it. It's the perfect haven for nefarious business.

Those easier cases are also why I chose Mission, Texas for my home base. It often takes less than a day to go find someone and get paid. The overhead on those cases is very low. They make up for the shit like what happened with William Varon.

My skin is itchy with the loss of that money, but even as I look at the various cases available, I can't muster the motivation to pull the trigger on accepting a new case.

I know it has to do with Lauren being so close. The chances of her already being out of Mission are low, and I have to fight the urge to go look for her, despite knowing that, much like when I left her on the side of the road covered in cum, she won't be found unless she wants to.

The woman is trained to be a ghost, educated in how to blend in and remain unseen until she's ready to strike.

I block Henry Murphy after skimming his encrypted email blaming me for his loss of income after his wife was found murdered. I'm always upfront about how I operate. The satisfaction or money-back guaranteed is usually enough to get them on board, but sometimes I end up a day late and a dollar short. Greta Murphy was no exception to that. Henry Murphy didn't pay a cent toward my expenses this last month, and that irks me a little, considering he sold his fucking wife in the first place.

I crack my neck and pop a piece of nicotine gum into my mouth.

I need to wash my mind of Lauren and get back to status quo, working and making money.

I get the feeling as I look over several more jobs available, that it's going to take a lot longer than I'd like.

Chapter 20

Lauren

Unsurprisingly, my calls to my handler bounce back.

The decision is made by him blocking my number.

I know better than to call from another phone.

Hell, I should've dumped this phone before hitchhiking five hundred miles to catch up to Angel in Lubbock.

It's not like it's a lifeline. My contacts serve that purpose for me, but I no longer have a connection to the Bureau.

Alan blocking me tells me all I need to know. The Bureau is looking for me, not that I expect them to put much effort into it. What I know and the things I've been involved in hiding go much deeper than one dead man's perverted son. There probably isn't any push for me to be found. It wouldn't be until I started making waves that they'd worry. There's too much other shit going on in the world to get distracted by one agent who skipped the red tape and took matters into her own hands.

"You are a wet fucking dream."

I smile at the man, stopping to stand directly in front of him rather than shying away like a normal person would.

"You think so?" I ask, my teeth digging into my lower lip.

The move seems ridiculous, but men go crazy over shit like that.

Like the creep he is, the guy points to the front of his jeans. I know he's trying to showcase the start of an erection, but the guy just doesn't have what it takes to be considered impressive.

Bless his heart or whatever southerners say when someone is lacking something they're expected to have.

"All that for me?" I manage to say without laughing or sounding offensive.

"If you want it to be."

"I think," I say, dropping the tone of my voice as I step in closer to him, "that I'll need a drink before I ride that monster."

A slow grin spreads across his face, and I know I have him on the hook.

"Depends on if you're the adventurous type or not."

"I've been known to let loose."

"It's in Mexico."

I stop myself just shy of frowning. *It's not much of an adventure when all the details are explained beforehand, Chad.*

"I don't have a passport."

His grin grows wider, a little more sinister. It's exactly what I'm looking for. "You won't need one."

"I'm in," I tell him. "But I hear Mexico is dangerous. Will you keep me safe?"

His eyes scan me from top to bottom. "Of course. I'm parked right over there. Let's go."

I step in behind him, tossing my phone in a trashcan on the street before thanking him for opening the door for me.

"Doorhandle is broken on the inside," he says, and that sense of danger hits me once again.

"No problem," I tell him as I climb inside.

Most women would follow the instinct that tells them something is off about this guy, but this is the shit I live for.

The drive to the border isn't long, but I'm antsy as he parks the truck. I honestly thought he'd use the adventure excuse to get me into his truck before finding something, but I realize shortly after we each pay a guy to help get across the border without having to go through customs, that this guy is just a low-rent thrill seeker.

The adventure for him isn't what waits in Mexico. It's simply breaking the rules to get into a different country.

He's smiling ear to ear as the guy points to another truck. "The fun is in Tamaulipas. They take you."

We walk in that direction as the guy I just met takes my hand. We haven't exchanged names. He doesn't give a shit who I am any more than I care about him.

I can tell by the way he watches me that he wants to take something that doesn't belong to him, that there are thoughts swarming through his head about being capable of something like that, but he just doesn't have the balls.

Two guys waiting outside a van smile as we approach. Of course the ride to Tamaulipas costs more money that wasn't covered by our safe crossing into Mexico, but we gladly pay. The further from Texas I get, the closer to danger.

We ride in the backseat of the van in silence as the driver and his friend chat about mundane shit. It's clear the guy beside me doesn't speak much, if any, Spanish, but I became fluent in the language after joining the FBI.

The drive is long, close to three hours or longer. I have to guess because I threw my phone in the trash.

By the time we make our way into the city, the sun is setting.

"I didn't get your name," my companion says, looking like he's seconds away from falling asleep beside me. "I'm Ryder."

I highly doubt that's his real name, and if it is, his parents are assholes.

"Lola," I tell him, my agitation growing by the second.

The guy in the passenger seat looks over his shoulder at us, asking in Spanish where we'd like to go.

I look at Ryder, making him think I have no clue what's being said.

"A bar," Ryder answers.

Maybe he understands more than he lets on.

The passenger nods, relaying to the driver what we're looking for.

Three hours in a van with three strange men and I get fucking nothing. It feels like a waste of time, but I do know that we're currently driving through a city that is very much an epicenter for crimes against people. If I can't find my adventure with Ryder, then I know it won't take long for me to find it elsewhere.

Just the thrill of going out on my own, knowing I can't call Alan any longer when I get in trouble, makes my blood pump harder, my heart race faster.

Maybe this adventure will be my last. The idea of it makes me smile.

Ryder takes it as me being pleased with him as the van rolls to a stop near the sidewalk. The sun has gone down, and that means the smarter, more diligent civilians of Tamaulipas are safely tucked away at home. The people remaining are the ones looking for trouble. This is my kind of place.

As we step inside, the bar isn't too crowded, but it does take a while for the bartender to give us an ounce of his time. I glare at the man when he looks me up and down, his gaze locking on my chest before finding my eyes. Nice doesn't always get the job done. Sometimes you have to be mean, push a little, to get the desired results.

This bartender knows things, knows people and their business. I want to be on his radar.

Ryder? He's a fucking chump, but from the whispers going on around me, he may not be as safe as he's convinced himself he is. According to one man, he's in the way of getting me on my back. His friend agrees, but neither of them make any moves to rid me of Ryder.

With as much of an American accent as I can manage, I call the bartender an asshole in Spanish when he finally slides my drink over to me. The guy chuckles, shaking his head as he walks away.

I get nothing from him but bad service.

I'm not going to find what I need in this place, but at the same time, I also feel a little guilty at leaving Ryder to the wolves. American women are considered a profit around here, easily exchanged for goods or services. The feistier they are, the more money they bring. American men are looked at like the police, useless and in the way. They spell trouble and are sometimes taken care of quicker than the women. You chase ants with a magnifying glass. The game is torture. Snakes have their heads cut off because they pose the real danger.

Boredom sinks deep inside of me to the point I'm actually starting to regret coming along for this lackluster adventure.

I could be trying to find Angel and killing him for the shit he put me through last night.

Making love?

The man really is a fucking psycho, unlike all the idiots in this fucking place.

"I've got to go to the restroom," I tell Ryder, leaving my glass on the bar.

He nods at me, his eyes on the television above the bar, showing replays of a soccer game.

I won't be coming back, and that's a shame because there's a real chance someone, not likely Ryder's dull ass, will drug my drink. I just can't stomach the lackluster way my day has gone.

The women's bathroom is just as disgusting as I would've predicted. The floors are sticky and it reeks of piss. It's clear the men use this one as well. There's no toilet paper in the doorless stall, nor any paper towels at the discolored sink.

This place is a shithole, exactly what I was hoping for when Ryder suggested a bar in Mexico, but I'm growing increasingly underwhelmed.

Of course there's no latch on the window, meaning anyone can come and go as they please.

Cold, night air hits my face as I climb out.

I wonder how long Ryder will wait for me to come back or if the guys in the bar will even give him a chance before they drag him out back and beat the shit out of him.

I stumble, the tip of my shoe catching on a rock in the uneven sidewalk, as I make my way to the end of the alley.

I hear a couple catcalls, but the words translated in my head don't seem like they will offer me what I'm looking for.

The street is crowded on either side, with buildings that practically share walls with each other. They could either be homes or businesses, or a combination of both. Concrete locks in the warmth of the sun from earlier and lacks any breeze that tries to get past.

It's a weird vibe of quiet but not silence at the same time.

I swallow thickly as I sense someone approaching in a rush and feel just as relieved as I do disappointed when a man rides past me on a bike without so much as acknowledging that I'm there.

My heart is pumping as I wander, avoiding small groups of men who look dangerous, but give me that rape-and-kill vibe. The whole point of getting abducted is working toward taking down the men that run the organizations. Getting killed in the middle of Tamaulipas without hurting some of those men who think they can do whatever the fuck they want is never the goal. It serves no purpose. It doesn't matter that I'm no longer with the FBI, I still want to help as much as I want to give my demons the nourishment they deserve.

I know if I do get lucky enough to end up trafficked, it's going to be even more lackluster than the time I spent with Ryder at the bar.

There's just no way around it.

After spending several nights under Angel's calloused hands, I know nothing else will compare. I'm going to end up hurt without the normal thrill and sense of satisfaction to go along with it.

Doing this was a mistake. I should've headed north, back to Kansas, instead of walking the streets of Mission, looking for trouble.

Footsteps creep up on me, and for added flare, I fake another stumble. It wouldn't be uncommon for a woman to get drunk and try to make it to safety by walking down these streets. It makes me an easier target, not that I would fight them too hard. I don't want to actually get away from them. I need to be in their den. I need to help the other women they may have.

I smile the second I feel weight pressed to my back, and despite the tears running down my face when I feel the pinch of the needle in my neck a second before a black bag is shoved over my head, I'm actually happy that my wait is over.

Maybe they'll manage to hurt me enough that Angel will be a long-forgotten memory.

Chapter 21

Angel

I'm always at peace when I'm home.

Well, I used to be.

That restless feeling I've had for the last couple of weeks didn't drop away once I opened my front door.

It lingers, haunts, keeps me from sleeping well, and is like a constant dripping faucet, annoying and beyond frustrating.

It's her fault.

She did this.

My life was perfectly fucking fine. I didn't have to worry about anyone. I didn't have to wonder what they were up to.

It was me, alone, secluded.

I wasn't checking out the windows without an alert to my security system, wondering if she was going to show up.

My blood didn't pump harder every time I got out of the shower with what? Hope? That she was going to be sitting on my bed.

I'm disappointed in the way I feel.

And admittedly, disappointed she hasn't shown her damn face.

I growl at the kitchen counter when I cut it too close and bang my hip into it.

I'm not the type of man to let every little thing bother him.

Well, I wasn't.

I spent the last two days traveling, needing to get out of this damn house, and even in returning things it still feels off, a little out of place. There's something I can't put my finger on, and it's bugging the shit out of me.

I'm restless, annoyed, wishing she was here just so I could take my frustrations out on her.

"I swear to fucking God," I mutter when I sit in my office chair and coffee spills on my jeans.

One deep breath in. One long breath out.

I'm not one for using any type of calming techniques. Spilling blood normally does that to me, but there's no fucking blood to spill right now, and it's making me antsy.

With a clenched jaw and heavy hands, I pull up my computer program for work. I've spent way too long hanging around here, thinking she'll find me. It's time to get back to work.

Lauren Vos isn't a part of my life. She never was. She never will be.

I scroll, finding myself looking at faces more than price tags, and that irritates the hell out of me too.

Who these people are shouldn't matter. The amount I'd be able to put into my account is all I should care about.

The thrill I normally get when searching for a job is dulled somehow. It doesn't carry the same rush I'm accustomed to.

The girls being sold on the dark web all look the same—beaten, broken, abused. If I had a heart, it would probably make me sad.

My fingers freeze on an image, my throat threatening to seize, and my earlier declaration of not having a heart is betrayed by the damn thing beginning to pound in my chest.

She's there. Lauren. Glassy, barely opened eyes looking at the camera.

She looks worse than I've ever left her.

I no longer see that same fire, the defiance in her eyes.

It's only been three days since I got back home.

Three days since she left me sleeping in the motel room across town.

Did she leave to go get coffee or something and get swiped from the street?

I've been agitated by the memories of her, and yet she's been going through horrific things.

My anger grows as I take further stock of her.

There are bruises on her skin that I didn't leave behind, and the sight of them enrages me. The fact that someone other than me thinks they can hurt her makes me fucking murderous.

Instinct tells me to throw my computer across the room, but logically that won't help anyone.

I set about buying her, keying in my information, and waiting to be directed to a secure account.

I won't make a payment for her past the deposit required, but as I make that transfer, my fingers ache for the feel of her throat under my hand.

If she thought I was rough when I hate fucked her before, it's going to have nothing on what's coming.

She had to have done this to herself. She's too smart, too wily, to get abducted without letting it happen.

As I wait, I pace the room.

Other men touching her, tasting her, *taking* her.

I roar into the room, my fist striking the fucking wall.

Who the fuck do they think they are, touching what's mine?

The thought should stop me in my tracks, but the adrenaline, the need to feel their blood on my hands, won't allow it.

Mine.

I normally hate the word unless it has to do with money or the serenity I usually find at home.

Pacing isn't helping. If anything, it's only making me more annoyed, but there's literally nothing I can fucking do until the sellers get back to me.

I have no fucking clue where she's at. She could be a few miles from here or she could be in South America already.

I leave my office because the real chance of destroying my computer equipment is growing with each pass I make across the room.

I grab everything I'll need for a longer trip, but I also get together a bag for a short trip, pulling out different forms of identification, weapons I'll need, and the cash required for travel and her purchase.

If I spend this hard-earned fucking money on her, she'll never leave my sight again.

The thought of actually owning her fucking thrills me, but it does nothing to make the anger I'm feeling dissipate.

I'm mad at the world at this fucking point. At her, at them, at anyone who threatens to get in my fucking way on my path to retrieve her.

I try to focus on thoughts of how I'll punish her for putting herself in this situation. Thinking of what she could've possibly gone through since I saw her last has the power to turn me into a fucking maniac and knowing that makes me feel like I have bugs under my skin. It leaves me itchy and uncomfortable because she somehow has that level of power over me.

I know I shouldn't care, but there's no fucking denying it now.

Heading back to the office, I notice the notification I've been waiting for.

God have mercy on their souls because I sure as fuck will not.

Chapter 22

Lauren

Time has stopped mattering.

I'm unconcerned of the hours that have ticked by.

One day? A hundred?

I don't have a clue.

The needle to the neck was only the very first time they drugged me.

I lost count of how many times they repeated it after the fourth.

They don't like it when I fight back once the drugs start wearing off.

It doesn't mean that they don't hurt me. I know they have.

I feel the burn on my skin, the burn between my thighs.

I'm mindful enough to know they're hurting me, but the drugs prevent me from doing anything about it.

I can't fight or help others like this.

I can only hope that they sell me, that they hand me over to someone who likes the women they buy to have all their faculties. If they don't, I could actually be living the last days of my life.

The worst part about this entire thing isn't the drugs, or the repeated assaults.

It isn't that I've seen Liana more than once, watching from across the room with a frown on her face.

If I close my eyes, I can hear her.

The things I endured for your safety, and this is how you spend your life?

Only that isn't real. She isn't real. The ghost of her, the memory I wanted to maintain of her for so long, is shattered by her truth, by the words written in her diary.

A woman's scream from another room reaches me on the lumpy mattress I was discarded on. I want to help her, but I can't even lift my arm to reach for her. Once again, I try to speak, but that is fruitless as well, my words coming out so garbled, I don't even understand myself.

I weigh a million pounds, but the sounds around me are somehow amplified, the begging, the crying, the pain. It's as if they're broadcasting their torture through the entire house. It sickens me, but instead of having a solution, all I can do is lie here with tears running from my temples into my ears.

All of it sucks. It always does, but this time is the worst.

This time my head fills with thoughts of him.

The rainbow at the end of the storm doesn't look as bright this time around.

The thrill of accepting the punishment I've always put my body through isn't there.

It all feels wrong, like I've made the biggest mistake of my damned life.

It's regret, something I rarely feel where work is concerned.

I accepted how I serve my penance a very long time ago. This no longer feels like that.

He did this to me. Somehow, with his rough angry hands, he made me feel worthy of more, worthy of consideration.

I hate him now more than ever for making this harder to endure, for making me feel like I've done something wrong.

As a shadow crosses in front of the single light in the room, I pray the drugs help me forget him as well.

Angel Guerra doesn't matter. He can't. Things that matter make you weak.

"Ready for more, whore?"

I try to crawl away, but I'm unable to move.

I felt like a complete idiot when I woke up the first time and saw him standing in the room. I knew I failed. Something about my radar was way off.

"Ryder," I try to mutter but no sound comes out.

His smile is sinister, not even close to the shy, unassuming one he first met me with on the streets in Mission.

For the first time in my life, I feel utterly defeated.

I fucking hate it here.

Chapter 23

Angel

The meeting is scheduled for tomorrow at an undisclosed location, but when I found out she was being held in Tamaulipas, I couldn't just sit around at home and wait.

If I were working, if this wasn't personal, if they hadn't taken what was mine, I would've kept that scheduled time, but I need the element of surprise. This isn't a normal case, one where I no longer give a shit about anything but collecting the thing that gets me paid.

I used to care. Getting paid had always been number one for me, but I always took pleasure in eliminating a few pieces of shit along the way. That changed in El Salvador, but I don't question why I'm sitting in my truck, waiting for a guy to walk out of an internet café. I know Lauren is to blame for that, but she's mine to punish.

I tracked the communication with the sellers to this location, and a response came so quickly when I asked for newer pictures of my purchase, I was already sitting outside the building. It's not uncommon for traffickers to use public internet to make their transactions, and knowing this, I know exactly who I need to keep an eye on.

The man emerges, a cocky swagger to his walk, a wide smile on his face. He's already counting the money he expects me to be bringing for Lauren. Little does he know he'll never see the light of day again.

He has to be known around town as being dangerous because I watch as several people move out of his way as he follows the sidewalk to a house closer to the end of the street. He's conducting business in a public place less than three hundred yards from where he's keeping his products. It's not very smart, but there's so much crime in Tamaulipas, the police just can't keep up. There's always the chance the police are taking their cut from these guys as well. If so, that just means that the not-so-honest men and women of law enforcement here are about to take an unexpected pay cut. Instead of collecting their hush money, they're going to be collecting bodies.

As I climb out of my truck after waiting fifteen minutes after the guy enters his house, I feel less prepared than I ever have making entry on a location. I normally spend days scoping out a place, making sure that I'm protected. I can't get paid if I'm dead, and although dangerous more often than not, no job is worth dying over.

Until now.

The shadows swallow me up, the people milling around either not seeing me or minding their business, which is common around here. No one is willing to invite trouble into their already hard lives, especially where these trafficking rings are concerned. They seek vengeance for fun. They don't keep their business further away to avoid suspicion like William Varon and his family were known to do. They flaunt their captures. They want the women around them to be scared. It gives them a sense of power.

It's brazen, but the guys don't even have the windows boarded up like I'm used to. You can't see anything from the street, but it's easy for me, peeking through the slats in the blinds to count the people inside. The open floor plan is more industrial, one vast space that includes only a kitchen, and a single door that leads to what I have to assume is a bathroom. The rest of the space is wide open, several filthy mattresses strewn about, each one with a woman on it.

I search the beds for Lauren, my eyes barely glancing over one of the women being hurt in the far corner. The man hurting her will pay, but he's not my primary focus.

My eyes land on her naked form.

I guess I should be happy at the sight of the used condoms littering the floor around each of the beds, but it makes fire ignite in my veins. The fact that they're being safe comes secondary to the hatred I feel for any of them thinking they could touch her in the first fucking place.

I count two other men in addition to the fucker that just arrived back here.

A sinister grin spreads across my face at the possibilities, but this isn't about vengeance. This isn't an opportunity to let my blood-thirsty demons out to play. My goal is to get Lauren away from here as fast as humanly possible. Drawing as little attention to what's going on is key. I'm going to need to pay attention to her on the drive back to my house, not spending my time looking over my shoulder, wondering if I've been followed.

I twist the silencer on the tip of my weapon, checking and rechecking to make sure I'm locked and loaded.

Three men, meaning three bullets, but it won't hurt to use a couple extra on these guys.

There's no tremble in my hand as I make my way around back. These guys aren't even smart enough to have a dog in the fenced yard to alert them. Either it's inexperience or cockiness. Either way, it's going to make killing them that much easier.

The climb through the open bathroom window isn't a graceful scene, but it's a silent one. I consider waiting for one of them to come in here, but a woman's scream draws me out.

The room is brighter than it looked from outside. It's as if these guys want spotlights on the damage they're causing.

I shoot the man standing over Lauren's bed first, wanting to believe that right now is the first time he's pulled out his dick in front of her, because that would be less painful than the truth. Next is the guy who I followed back here. The bowl of cereal he made while I was climbing through the window sprays the room in milk after falling to the floor.

If he was the last one I needed to take down, I'd spend a few quiet moments watching the milk mix with the blood draining from his body. The swirl of red always intrigues me.

The guy raping the other woman in the corner dies last because he's the one that posed the least amount of threat to me. His distraction only allows for a few seconds longer in this world.

She screams when he falls forward, pinning her to the bed with more force than he was using to hurt her.

A decent guy would help her, but that woman isn't my focus.

Lauren's eyes flutter as I inch closer to her, and I can immediately tell she has no life-threatening injuries, but she's not herself either.

The used needles discarded on the floor near her bed mean either some form of paralytic or possibly heroine.

But it doesn't matter right now.

A lot of things shouldn't matter right now, but the way I want to grip her fucking neck and warn her of what's coming from me is trying to beat all other emotions out.

The urge to fuck her right into this dirty mattress hits me pretty hard.

It's beyond fucked up, absolutely fucking terrible to think of something like that, but that doesn't stop my eyes from drifting over her battered body. Doesn't keep my mouth from watering at the need to reclaim her as mine.

When she sees my face, she tries to speak, but it comes out a mess of syllables that make no sense.

A thump across the room draws my attention, but my weapon trains on the woman in the corner who finally managed to get the dead man off of her. She stares at me in terror, and I'm not shocked by it. It's not unheard of for one group of traffickers to raid another's location to steal their product. Sometimes it's easier because collection is usually the hardest part. It's what brings the most heat, depending on where they're abducting women.

She knows not to be relieved because she has no idea which camp I'm in right now.

I turn my attention back to Lauren. I really need to grab her and get the fuck out of here, but she's fucking filthy, covered in spit and cum. My stomach rolls at the sight of her.

For good measure, I walk around the room, putting two more bullets in each of the dead men. It's fruitless. It makes no difference. Each of my first shots were true, ending them quickly, showing a mercy they didn't deserve.

When I drop low beside Lauren, she tries to lift her arm. I know what she wants. She's pointing at one of the other beds, but those women aren't my focus.

She's relentless, however, managing to wiggle and growl as I reach down to lift her up.

I glare at her eyes, and even in her drugged state she manages to glare back. I'm ready to refuse, but it's the sight of a single tear rolling down her temple that forces me into action.

With frustrated steps, I make my way across the room, pulling a knife from my pocket. I make quick work of cutting through the ropes tying two women down. Each of them shies away from me, terrified of what I might be capable of.

I don't open my mouth to assure them they're fine. I don't urge them to get away. They have to make those decisions on their own. I'm not their fucking savior. I'm making a mental list of what Lauren will owe me for forcing me to waste my time.

The woman in the corner, the one who was actively getting raped isn't tied up at all. She's curled up in a ball in the corner. It seems these guys liked their women in different states of captivity.

When she looks up at me, I just point at the fucking door before heading back to Lauren.

"I'm not fucking carrying all of them out of here. They can unlock the goddamned door and leave if they want."

She nods, her throat working on what looks like an incredibly painful swallow. It hits me in the chest, making me pity her for a second before I can shove it down. There will be time to express my disappointment in her later. Now is not the fucking time.

She whimpers when I stand and head back to the bathroom, but I ignore her. It's another way for me to punish her, and I hate that it doesn't feel right.

It takes forever for the water to warm, but I'm not exactly concerned about her comfort. What I do know is that I'm not taking her into my truck covered in another man's cum.

She's dead weight in my arms as I lift her from the mattress. Although I'm not exactly gentle as I place her in the tub, I do go as far as making sure she doesn't drown despite wanting to shove her head under the water for a few seconds.

I don't want her to be grateful I showed up. I want her fucking terrified. I want her to beg to be left, to be mad I killed the other men because she knows what she's going to get from me is going to be worse than they ever could've imagined.

But then I use gentle hands to run soap over her body, my heart racing as more tears leak down her face.

Everything I do is contradictory.

I hiss angry words at her, blame her for this entire situation, all the while cradling her head against my chest as I wash her gently between her legs.

In order to get better control over myself, I leave her in the draining tub while I head back to my truck to grab a blanket I brought with me. It's not for her comfort, but peace of mind for the guy that will help me get back across the border into Texas. I don't need his conscience rearing its fucking head at the sight of a naked, battered woman beside me in the truck.

She's shivering when I reenter, the open window letting the cool winter air into the room.

I'm in no rush to wrap her up, to ensure that she's warm and comfortable. The agitation the cold causes will help her body fight the drugs flowing through her veins, and I need her completely aware when we get back to my place. I need her to know who she's with and that I'm so fucking mad at her.

Two of the three women in the room are gone by the time I carry Lauren out of the house. The one in the corner remains, but I pay her no mind as I make my way to the truck.

Getting across the border goes smoothly despite my mind racing with all of my plans for this woman.

She only thought she was experiencing hell in that fucking house.

Chapter 24

Lauren

Hangovers have nothing on what it feels like to wake up from a drug-induced stupor. The headache is different, more intense.

I have no idea why they let the drugs wear off, but it can't mean anything positive for me. These types of men don't change overnight. They don't get a rush of conscience. Maybe they were tired of my lethargy and are in need of more of a fight, more struggle.

I do my best to paint a smile on my face. Nothing riles them up more than a different response than they're expecting. It may mean more pain for me, but it also opens the door for mistakes on their part.

My arms are heavy, but it doesn't take me long to realize I'm tied up, arms splayed out to the sides. It's not ideal, but I've gotten out of such restrictions before.

Normally, my first considerations would be helping those around me. I've never focused on my own needs because that's not the reasoning I use in situations like this, but I can't keep those ideas away—the need to escape, the self-recrimination for being here in the first place.

This time is different, and it has nothing to do with how I'm being treated. There's only so many ways an evil man can hurt a woman. As sinister as some of them can be, their means of torture and pain have easily become rather run of the mill, common, uncreative.

Right now, I just want to be someplace safe, someplace where I can relax and recover, reevaluate what the fuck I've been doing.

It's so dangerous to want those things, to think even for a second that I deserve it.

My dreams have been the most brutal of all—thoughts of Angel being my white knight and rescuing me. I'd laugh if my throat wasn't so fucking dry.

He'll never be someone to go out of his way and help someone he loved to hurt so much.

I squeeze my eyes closed, hating the burn of tears behind them. I blame the drugs in my system for my lack of controlling my emotions.

With a deep breath, I let that pain sink inside of me. This is what I deserve. This is how I honor my sister. I asked for this, and wishing things were different have never benefitted me in the past. Why change things now?

I roll my body, taking care to feel the soreness in my muscles. It's an inventory of sorts, allowing me to determine where my injuries are and if my body would be capable of fighting back if given the chance.

I ache from the top of my head to the balls of my feet. Everything hurts, but I'm no stranger to pain.

What's new is the desperate urge to cry, to beg for mercy, to ask my captors to set me free.

I don't want to help others. I only want to help myself at this point.

I make a plan in my head to seek my revenge, and it's not on those that have me bound to the bed. No, that energy is focused on Angel. He made me weak. He made me want things I have no right to consider. He made me lose sight of what I need to do and how I need to spend what little life I may have left.

If I ever escape this time, I'm going after him.

Darkness swirls around me, very little light filling the room as the bed dips.

I sneer, turning my head toward the intruder. He's just another man who wants to hurt me, to take things from me.

Maybe he'll be surprised when he discovers I have nothing left to fucking give. I'm drained of it.

I flinch when a finger presses into a bruise on my arm, and I hate myself for it.

I'm all big talk in my head.

I have so much to lose, and pretending in front of one more person doesn't seem possible right now.

I attempt to jerk away from the man, but my restraints are tied tighter than I initially realized. I fight down the urge to sob at knowing it might actually be impossible to get away.

I've never let defeat sink inside of me. I've always had a plan and then another plan if that one didn't pan out.

I have nothing right now, and for as long as I thought I'd be relieved to die, I find myself wanting to fight those thoughts.

I have nothing to live for, but it doesn't stop that intrinsic need to live from bubbling up and taking over.

I open my mouth to speak, but it makes my throat hurt, makes the corners of my mouth tear because of their dryness.

When a cold cup is placed to my lips, I want to jerk away, refusing to take anything that's offered to me because it's never done in kindness. A slick throat is easily fucked, and I learned my lesson long ago about biting. It left me with a concussion, forcing me to spend several more weeks in captivity, whereas just letting it happen would've meant I could've helped other women quicker.

My body's responses aren't my own, and I drink greedily, grateful that it's actual water and not a cup full of vodka or whiskey. The cup is pulled away when I start to cough and choke. I lift my head as high as I can manage to get another sip, but it doesn't come.

Teasing with food and drink is a common tactic by these guys, so I'm not at all surprised, but it doesn't stop me from begging for more.

The shadow lifts the cup to my lips once again, and I don't waste the opportunity I'm provided. Taking any form of kindness from them seems counterproductive, but I can't do much when I'm starving and dehydrated.

Without a word, the man leaves. He doesn't hurt me again or say a word.

It doesn't take long before darkness takes over again.

The second time I wake up, the evaluation of my body doesn't take as long. I'm still tied to the bed, naked and starfished on a mattress.

With the bedroom door open, more light is cast into the room.

I cringe at the sight of the IV bag hanging near the bed, and I'm not surprised to follow the plastic tubing to the back of my hand.

I must've been sold without realizing it, but experience tells me that just because I'm being nursed back to health doesn't mean I'm safe.

There isn't a single person in the world that buys someone out of the goodness of their hearts. If that were the case, I would be covered instead of freezing with the ceiling fan blowing cold air on my body. I wouldn't be tied down and alone.

Hell, I would be in a hospital, surrounded by helpful staff, not in someone's dark room.

I do count the good things. The mattress I'm on is soft. I'm not surrounded by putrid scents of an area that hasn't seen disinfectant and a scrub brush in a decade. I hear no screams or begging from other women. All in all, I can say that this place is much better than some of the others I've been, but I don't allow false hope to settle in. Some of the most sinister people I've come across are capable of some of the evilest ways to hurt people. Class and sophistication just mean they have the money to hurt someone differently, more creatively.

I focus on the backlit body of a man as he nears the bed, and I run through the ways I can react to his presence. Some men want a woman that will obey, someone they can manipulate and groom to be who they think they need. These are the best kinds because freedoms are earned which means the ability to kill them or escape.

"How are you feeling?"

Every muscle in my tired, exhausted body locks up.

The voice is familiar, and I just know it has to be another fucking dream.

I try to reach for him, but the ropes on my wrists prevent it. The thought of him is painful, but the need, the desire for this to be real, hurts the most.

Hope that I realize is false washes over me before I can even consider how to shove it back down. Sadness leaks from my eyes as I turn my head away from him. Mistaking him for someone he isn't is so fucking dangerous.

"Lauren? I asked you a fucking question."

I shake my head, sobs bubbling out of my throat. Hope is such a cruel fucking thing.

"Look at me when I speak to you." A rough hand grabs me by the jaw, forcing my face in his direction.

I know I should keep my eyes closed, but instinct has me facing my attacker.

He doesn't fade away. Angel doesn't disappear, doesn't transform into a monster.

"Angel?" I swallow down another sob. "How?"

I try to shake my head, but his punishing grip on my chin prevents it. He's forcing me to see that it's him.

Anger swarms around me before settling so deep inside those hidden parts of me, I'm not sure I'll ever be able to dig them out.

"Fucking untie me," I demand. "Right fucking now."

His laughter is somehow both welcome and the cruelest thing I've ever heard.

I struggle against my restraints, the burn of the ropes on my skin, sweeping down my arms like wildfire.

He doesn't speak, doesn't reach for the ropes.

I expect him to walk out when he releases my face, but he doesn't budge from the edge of the bed.

"Why am I hooked up to an IV?"

His focus is on the skin on my shoulder, not my face, when he speaks.

"I've kept you sedated."

My breaths are ragged as I try to understand exactly what he's explaining, but it's difficult. Whatever is in my system isn't allowing me to think in a straight line.

"How long?"

"Ten days," he replies, like it's not a big deal to keep a woman tied down for a week and a half.

He's given me more information than I think he realizes, but I've been in this situation before. I know exactly what it means.

The IV ensures hydration, meaning I've been pissing this bed the entire time. I can only hope my fucking bowels have shut down due to the narcotics those other fuckers were pumping into me, but it won't stay that way forever.

He's been taking care of me because I can easily tell I'm not lying here in my own fucking filth.

This enrages me more than anything else.

I don't want to be fucking cared for.

"The other women?" I ask, because focusing on myself might invite in those pesky fucking emotions I haven't been able to control recently.

I never want this man to see me as weak.

I watch his shoulders lift. "I gave them every opportunity to get away. No clue if they took it or not."

Rage boils inside of me, but I shouldn't be surprised he doesn't give a shit about others. He's no FBI. The man is a hired fucking gun. Green is the only damn language he speaks. The other women there aren't his concern. I'm left wondering why he cares about me at all, but maybe that's a mistake as well, because being naked and tied to his bed for ten fucking days doesn't exactly spell affection.

"Don't fucking touch me," I snap when his finger trails over my shoulder and down my left breast.

I'm not surprised by the laughter that rumbles out of him, but I am worried about the way my body threatens to delight in the actual sound.

I don't know that I've heard him laugh and the gravel of it affects me in a way I refuse to focus on.

I hiss in pain when he twists the tip of my breast between two punishing fingers.

"You seem confused, so let me explain it to you." His face drops lower, mere inches from mine. "I fucking own you. I bought you with the deaths of three men."

I'm only now realizing the depth of my depravity because a thrill at his words races up my spine.

"I was working," I say on a gasp of relief as he releases my nipple, only to trail his finger further down my stomach.

He presses a rough finger into a sore spot on my hip, smiling when I try to fight the discomfort by not moving or complaining.

"I think you're mistaken. Paperwork has been filed with the Bureau. Lauren Vos is not only no longer employed by the FBI, but she's also actively being sought for crimes against the government."

Knowing it was a possibility and actually hearing that those things have come to pass are two very different things.

"That means you either got yourself abducted on purpose without the backup of your agency or you were so distracted that someone grabbed you by surprise. Which is it, Lauren?"

I clamp my lips closed. He has no right to any explanation from me.

His eyes sparkle with mirth in the limited light as he watches my face. "There she is. I thought those men beat and fucked that spark out of you."

"Untie me," I demand again, but it falls on deaf ears.

Angel stands, running his eyes down the length of me one last time before walking away.

"You can't keep me tied up forever," I yell to his back.

This makes him stop in his tracks as he turns back to face me once again.

"I'm willing to test the theory."

"Why are you fucking doing this to me?"

He's silent for a long moment. "You seem to need it. So I'm going to give it to you."

"Does this mean you aren't going to hurt me?"

That same sinister laugh flows over me once again. "Oh, no, baby. I'm going to hurt you more than anyone ever has."

The door closes behind him, and I try not to think of the way his statement makes me feel.

I'm so beyond fucked up, doctors could spend their entire careers, working through all the shit that's wrong with me.

I jolt at the sound of a crackle coming from the bedside table.

"In today's podcast, we're going to discuss how to overcome childhood trauma."

My eyes widen. For a man that likes to live in virtual silence, he sure as fuck doesn't seem averse to using psychological warfare as a means of torture.

"I'll fucking kill you!" I scream as the speaker starts to list the ways to overcome the horrors someone has experienced.

Louder than ever, that same laughter echoes from the other room.

Chapter 25

Angel

I reconsider pain being the best way to hurt someone as I watch Lauren struggle against her restraints as the podcast plays in its entirety.

My skin is itchy, and I know it has everything to do with her being in my home. The noise she's making along with the recording only acerbates it.

I didn't stop to think about my own suffering, my own consequences for letting her invade my space.

It makes me want to go in there and find my equilibrium between her thighs.

My cock jerks at the thought, but that's what she expects to happen. I have no doubt she's already made her predictions about how this is going to go, and I need to keep her guessing, keep her off-kilter for as long as possible.

I'd take things too far if I went to her now. I want my toy to last as long as possible.

In addition to the meds to keep her sedated, I've also pumped her full of antibiotics, not only for whatever sexually transmitted infections she might have contracted while captured but also to help her body heal.

She was covered in bruises, cuts, and scrapes, and it disgusted me to see those marks on her skin. I want to be the one to hurt her, to make her bleed.

I want to hit the intercom button and remind her that she's only hurting herself, making the wounds at her wrists worse by struggling against them, but I resist. I'll allow injury to herself while she's in my care.

My hatred for her has only grown since she got here, and it has nothing to do with being responsible for her bathroom needs or the four-day period she had right after I got her here.

I hated that I wanted so badly to paint her skin with that blood but couldn't. My desires lean toward her pain, and doing shit while she's unconscious serves no purpose to me.

I know it's crazy to be mad that she's passed out because I'm the one drugging her. That's why her IV now only has saline. I decided no more drugs. I want her awake. I want her to know who she's with. I want her worrying about what my plans are for her.

I want her to regret ever getting into my fucking truck outside the Cerberus clubhouse. Her need for adventure and putting herself in harm's way ends in this house. I'll put an end to that desire inside of her one way or another.

The thrilling part is that it may be the death of both of us.

She settles against the mattress—my fucking mattress—as the podcast ends.

I don't believe in any of the shit I just played in the bedroom, and I know she doesn't either. That's the fun part of torturing her with it.

I've spent the last week and a half watching her sleep, and I'm tired of it.

I make my way back into the bedroom, watching her as I cross the room to the bathroom. Luckily, this house came with a bathtub or there wouldn't be one. I'm not the type of man who's going to sit in a pool of water. My showers are quick and economical. The only time I'll spend any length of time in there is when I get hurt and need the water pressure and heat to ease the soreness in my muscles.

Honestly, I need it now because my couch is shit for sleeping, and I've been out there since she's been in here.

Physically, I could easily fall asleep beside her. The IV drugs ensured she'd stay sedated all damn night, but mentally, I found it impossible the very first night I brought her back here. Nearness made me want things I had to wait for. The distance is the only thing that kept me from punishing her long before she woke up.

I turn on the taps, making sure that the water is warmer than what would be comfortable for her. Each action of mine has purpose, and the thought of her skin turning pink from the heat makes me hard.

"I need to piss, and before you tell me to just do it in the bed, keep your fucking mouth closed."

"That's a lot of spitfire coming from such a weak person," I tell her as I untie her legs.

She proves my point by trying to kick out at me and is barely able to lift her leg. After removing her IV, her arms are next, but they fall to the bed. She does manage to wring her fingers around the sore spots she created on her skin.

"You're a dick," she spits when I help her sit up.

She's been inactive for two weeks now, and it's astonishing how fast the body loses its ability to function after short periods of no movement.

"I'm being nice," I say as I make sure to keep all parts of me away from her mouth. I wouldn't put it past her to take a chunk out of me.

"Nice." She scoffs. "What the fuck are you doing?"

I don't answer her rhetorical question as I continue to tie her arms behind her back.

"You said you needed to piss."

I walk her slowly across the room instead of carrying her. At some point in the near future, I'm going to need this woman to fight back, and I'm not doing either of us any favors by coddling her.

"You're fucking kidding, right?" She glares at me as I sit her down on the toilet.

Silently, I stare at her, standing my ground.

Stubbornly, and very true to her character, she just glares back.

It isn't until I step away to turn off the water in the tub that the sound of urine hitting the inside of the bowl can be heard.

Of all the things this woman has experienced and suffered through and she gets shy about peeing?

"What now?" she snaps.

With the water off, steam billowing up from it, I turn back to give her all of my attention.

I eye the toilet paper before looking back at her face.

"Untie me," she growls.

"Kick me and instead of bathing you in that tub, I'll fucking drown you," I warn as I step forward.

"Don't touch me," she hisses as I grab some tissue and bend lower.

I know how she feels. She probably sees me cleaning her up after using the restroom as more degrading than anything I've ever done to her, so I take my time.

"You know how many times I've washed this cunt over the last ten days?"

Her chin trembles as I push her legs farther apart. I watch her face the entire time as I wipe, celebrating the tears welling in her eyes as she points her face toward the ceiling.

"I gave you antibiotics," I tell her as I stand.

Her eyes find mine then, and there's something about the gratitude in her eyes that hits me differently.

"Thank you," she whispers, and I know that was so fucking hard for her to say.

I'm a very good judge of character, and I can easily tell she means it. I'm sure part of her aftercare while with the FBI included all sorts of medical checkups and testing.

Instead of focusing on how she's able to control my emotions with her gratitude, I decide to keep as much footing with her as possible.

"Your period lasted four days, so it seems you aren't pregnant either."

Her eyes narrow. She knows the game. She knows exactly what I'm doing.

"Was never a worry," she says as I lift her to standing from the toilet. "I have a birth control implant in my arm. Plus, I'm pretty sure they used condoms. Sick fucks for thinking we're the ones with diseases when they're the ones abducting and raping women."

Three bullets each weren't enough for those pieces of shit, but I don't tell her that. It honestly makes me hate her just a little more because she's bringing back pieces of me that I was proud of before we met in El Salvador. Those were the things that made me weak, looking out for others instead of only being concerned for myself.

"I can bathe myself if you just untie me," she says as I walk her toward the tub.

"Good to know," I say, lifting her over the edge without making a move to remove her restraints.

She hisses as she sinks into the water, but she doesn't complain.

She doesn't say a word or try to inch away when I run a bar of soap over her skin.

"Two in one?" she mutters as I pour shampoo into my hands. "Fuck, I don't even have dandruff."

"Neither do I," I tell her as I rub the product into her wet hair. "Because I use this fucking shampoo."

Without thinking, I swipe away a pile of bubbles rolling down her forehead. I hate myself for protecting her even in the smallest ways.

She narrows her eyes at me as I grumble to myself, but she remains silent.

Stupidly, she starts to struggle when I drain the tub and pull her out, but if she falls to the floor, that's going to be on her.

I manage to dry her with her hands still tied behind her back. I know if given the chance, she'd claw my fucking eyes out.

I don't think she's playing a part any longer. She isn't looking for ways to upset me so I overpower her the way she likes.

I want to ask her what happened in Tamaulipas to change things for her, but that would show concern, and I've been doing my best to fight that desire in me.

Instead of showing comfort, I toss her on the bed and pull her ass to the edge.

When she tries to scurry away, I flip her to her back. I know her arms are digging into her back. I know from experience how fucking painful it is to lay that way.

I enjoy the wince on her face as I tug her closer to me.

"What the fuck are you doing?" she snaps.

"Anything I fucking please. Spread your fucking legs."

She doesn't oblige, but I never really expected her to. That's not part of how she operates, and as I spread them against her will, I realize she isn't playing a game like she has before.

"Angel, don't."

"Beg me to stop," I taunt as I rip down the front of my sweats and smack her pussy with the tip of my cock.

Her jaw clamps closed. She'd rather me take her any way that I want than beg.

"Have it your way." I groan as I enter her, my fingers digging into the flesh of her thighs.

It feels so fucking good, I hate her for it.

"Don't close your fucking eyes," I hiss, grabbing ahold of her jaw and pointing her face at mine. "I want you to fucking watch."

It doesn't take long, a simple five snaps of my hips, before my balls grow tight.

My hand slides from her face to her throat as she stares at me defiantly.

"Fucking bitch. If you come, I'll hurt you."

I have no idea which way this is going to go. She could let herself experience that pleasure in defiance or she could refuse. As I watch her face, I know she's struggling with the decision.

I don't give her body the chance to decide as I jerk free of her and paint her bruised and mottled flesh with cum.

Her breathing is ragged, and it tells me she might have been close and is thoroughly pissed that I was done using her before she got hers.

A single tear rolls down her cheek, and I fucking hate everything about the way it makes my heart clench. She doesn't deserve sympathy or guilt.

Knowing that and accepting it aren't the same thing.

I lean forward to kiss her. Maybe it's an apology of sorts, but I find I've met her threshold of tolerance when she bites my lip so fucking hard I taste blood.

Chapter 26

Lauren

If he comes back at me with soft shit like he did when he brought me to Mission, I'll lose my fucking mind.

I'm barely holding on to my sanity right now as it is.

Instead of striking me, a slow smile spreads across his face, his teeth marked with his blood from where I bit him.

I can't determine which guy he is.

Is he the man he was in El Salvador, the one that whimpered when I stuck my hand in his jeans and stroked him?

Or is he the man that just fucked me while tied up with no regard to what I went through recently?

Is he a combination of both?

Does he want to kiss me or does he think that's what I need? Is it a way to show his own remorse?

I don't want any of it. I don't want his compassion or guilt. I don't want to be responsible for his feelings on any level.

I have to look away from him, and for some reason, this time, he allows it.

I hate myself almost as much as I hate him right now.

Despite my pain, despite the ache in all of my muscles, despite knowing I was drugged and abused, he knows just how to fuck me.

Maybe I should feel my own form of guilt over that, but I can't seem to muster it right now.

Long ago, I stopped worrying about how I go about getting what I want. It doesn't matter to anyone else how I punish or pleasure myself, nor how those two things most often go hand in hand.

I accepted my fucked-upness long ago, and concerning myself for how others perceive me isn't part of who I am.

"Let me go," I tell him in a flat tone when he pulls back and slips his cock back into his pants.

He doesn't listen to me. Rather, he situates me back on the bed, taking his time and chuckling again when I fight him, as he ties my hands back to the bed. I have almost no strength in my arms or legs, and it makes me wonder how high the doses of the sedatives were that he gave me.

The IV bag, still hanging by the bed, is plain with nothing written on it so it doesn't provide any clues as to what those drugs were. I don't ask because I know he won't tell me. He likes to torture me with the unknown.

I hiss when his fingers pinch at my nipple, just barely managing not to clamp my legs together. I don't want him to know he left me needy. I nearly died of embarrassment when he cleaned me on the toilet. It gives him too much power, too much control. Not that I think he really cares how I'm left—wanting, hurting, begging. So long as he gets his pleasure from my body, the other shit doesn't matter.

He bought me with the lives of the three men who were holding me captive. He owns me. At least that's how he sees it.

I want him to go into detail about their deaths and how in the hell he even found me, but I doubt he'd give me that information.

Then I remember him telling me about my termination from the FBI.

"Did you tell them where I was?" I ask, more fearful that they'll come and take me away than wanting them to find and rescue me.

It says a lot about who I feel is the real villain in my world, but I can't focus on that right now.

He scoffs. "They're dead."

"Not the men who took me. The FBI. Do they know where I am?"

His eyes search mine, and I have no fucking clue what the man is looking for. "I didn't tell them shit."

"Where the fuck are you going?" I ask when he stands from the bed and leaves the room.

I scream out a million frustrations, to the point my throat is on fire by the time the door opens again a short while later.

"I won't fight you if you just let me go," I barter when he walks back into the room.

"I like when you fight," he says, the wickedness in his eyes sparking something inside of me.

I should be freaking out. I should be begging, pleading, asking for him to release me, but I just can't bring myself to do it.

Deep down, I don't know if that's what I even want.

The man terrifies me, but there's a certain thrill, a sense of excitement in trying to figure out what he'll do next.

Before he showed up in Tamaulipas, I was ready to die. The fight had left me, and only when I decided I would seek my vengeance on this man was that spark relit. I can't satisfy those goals tied to his fucking bed.

I struggle against the ropes, re-aggravating the rope burns on my wrists.

"Stop," he says, but there's no urgency in his voice.

It's as if he really doesn't care but saying the word is expected of him.

"Don't," I whisper when he looks up at me, his face full of sadness and concern.

I'd rather be hurt all day, every day than face whatever this man feels the need to get off his chest.

His split fucking personalities, the one wanting the soft kiss after fucking me without permission, is making my damn head spin.

"Don't get soft on me now," I taunt. "Don't turn into a pussy."

His eyes drop to his hands, and I pray this is just another one of his games, a way to throw me off by preventing me from getting a real read on him.

"I'll let you go."

Instead of joy, I feel disappointed.

"On one condition." He lifts his eyes to mine. "You have to promise you'll stop putting yourself in danger."

I think most people would rush to agree even if it was a lie, but I keep my mouth closed, my eyes narrowed on him, my brain struggling to figure out what his endgame is going to be.

"You no longer have a job with the FBI, so there's no point in doing it."

I know I made confessions to him. I know I explained as best I could while drunk why I do what I do. He has to know that until I take my last breath, I can't stop. The punishment and pain are deserved. I've earned it by not seeing what was happening with Liana sooner. I earned it with not following her to the bathroom when she said she was going to shower. I earned it for not being enough for our father to split the punishments so that maybe we would both be just a little fucked up rather than her being dead and me being a complete lunatic.

But I don't get to change the past. Just like I can't alter the path of my future.

I don't know how to tell him I don't want to leave, and there's no way I can tell him how this last time was different, that I regretted what I did.

I also know that despite the pain it caused, both mentally and physically, I'll never do it again.

There's something about him and the memories of him that made what I was doing wrong. I've always known it was a bad plan, but knowing and being able to stop myself are two different things.

I know that when there's any amount of distance and time between the two of us, I'm going to go right back to old habits.

I have no idea how to tell him that I feel like I need him, that I feel like our fucked-up souls need each other.

Needing is a weakness, one I've shoved down my entire life. I have no idea why I'm clinging to it now.

"I can still get work done without the support of the FBI," I say, instead of agreeing to his terms. "I can help women. There are not enough people helping. What I do is important."

"You're going to get yourself killed," he says with very little emotion, as if he's just stating a fact rather than actually caring.

The man makes my fucking head spin.

"I might be able to save more women and kids before that happens."

"You sound resigned to it, like you have no control over what happens to you."

I have to look away from him. I've always known how things would end for me, and honestly, it's taking a lot longer than I had originally planned for.

"Why do you even care?"

"I don't," he answers quickly, and I'm unable to hide the wince from his truth.

He doesn't look pleased at my reaction to his insult.

Hell, I don't even know why it has the power to hurt me. People not caring for me hasn't been a problem in the past.

The FBI didn't give a shit if I completed a mission, past them worrying that getting myself killed would've been a waste of federal resources, since a lot of money and time has gone into training me.

Maybe that's his game, making me wish for things, want things even subconsciously, only to remind me that I'm worthless.

It's the type of pain I feed on, the shit I need more of.

I'm worthless, useless, undeserving.

It's why I like to be dominated, controlled, degraded, insulted. If it's a bad thing, I love it. If it physically hurts, even better.

"The next captor is likely to kill you."

He's said this already, and despite his declaration, it proves that he does in fact care.

My heart sings with it, all the while also hating him a little for it.

"Maybe the next guy will be the one to finally put me out of my misery," I mutter.

"The misery you feel because you couldn't save your sister, or the regret that Daddy didn't love you enough to fuck you like he did her?"

I fucking lose it, fighting against my restraints and screaming at him to eat shit and die.

All I get from him is a smile as he backs out of the room.

Chapter 27

Angel

Lauren's head jerks, her eyes opening wide when I reenter the room a few hours later.

Her eyes follow me, and for a second, it makes me feel more like prey than the predator I claim to be.

I've never met another woman like her.

Where most would expect the bravado to fade, to turn into begging, Lauren is standing her ground.

She could've easily agreed to my terms, but maybe she realized I was lying, that I'd never let her go. I spilled blood for her. There's nothing she can do to pay that back in full, and that means she'll owe me... forever.

"Are you fucking kidding me?" she growls when she sees the plate of food in my hand. "You made me a sandwich?"

"Presumptuous little bitch aren't you," I say as I get closer, picking up the sandwich and taking a huge bite.

Hatred fills her eyes as she watches me chew.

I grin when her tongue sneaks out to wet her lips. I know she's fucking starving. The IV has been giving her just what she needs to survive, but it's nothing compared to actual food.

"You don't want it?"

She looks away from me as if she doesn't have the strength to verbalize her rejection.

"If you don't eat, I'm going to hurt you," I threaten, delighting in the way she turns her head back in my direction, a defiant uptick of her chin.

Reading people is practically required in my line of work when you don't have a long amount of time to determine if someone has nefarious plans for you.

It doesn't take but a split second for me to understand she wants what I'm threatening.

I could leave it at that, pull her hair back and shove the fucking sandwich down her throat. I could force her to do anything I want. People always bend. Regardless of her declaration about being put out of her misery, there's a reason she hasn't done it herself.

I'm not foolish enough to think it's because she honestly wants to live, but it takes a certain level of courage, an insanely determined person, to commit suicide. A lot of people see it as being weak, but it takes so much courage to look at one's life and decide that the unknown—or the absolute known if they're religious—is better than what they're facing.

Her sister wasn't a coward. She was probably the bravest person she ever met.

I don't have the strength to do what Liana did, and I doubt Lauren does either, or she would've done it already. She needs to force someone else's hand to doing that for her.

She glances back down at the sandwich, her mouth practically watering at the sight even though it's nothing but two pieces of bread with a thin layer of turkey. It's dry as fuck because I'm not one to keep condiments in the house, but that's also intentional. I need her to eat, to gain her strength for what I have planned, but I'm not going to give her gourmet food. I need it a little dry and tasteless. I want her begging for more or for a sip of water. Her discomfort is my joy, and I'll seek it out at every fucking turn.

"How about I'll hurt you if you do eat it," I counter.

Her eyes widen before narrowing as if she can't believe I'm calling her out on her desires.

She doesn't speak, and I can't just leave the sandwich on her lap with my warning and walk out of the room. Her arms are still tied.

Instead of trying to force the sandwich into her mouth, I sweep a soft, gentle finger over her arm before bending to press a kiss to the bruise on her shoulder.

She shudders, but not out of disgust because I'm pressing my lips to her flesh. She hates the soft, and after her drunken confessions, I have a better understanding why that is.

"Feed me the fucking sandwich," she snarls, and I know that she's asking more for me to stop the soft shit than her need for food.

She glares at me the entire time I lift the sandwich to her lips and as she chews.

She starving, but she's also aware of her limitations. It makes my blood boil that she's taking her time, evaluating how the sandwich is settling in her stomach before taking the next bite. She knows it doesn't matter how hungry she is, if she eats too fast, she's going to get sick.

It means she's done this a time or two.

She's put herself through a lot. I knew that when I met her in El Salvador.

The problem right now is that knowledge bugs me more now than it did back then, and I fucking cared a lot before. So much so, that I put myself between her and the men coming to hurt her.

I earned two bullets that day. It was the day I stopped caring about her safety and started dreaming of my revenge.

Yet, here I fucking am, hand feeding her a fucking sandwich.

It takes longer than I really have the patience for until the sandwich is gone.

She doesn't thank me, but I would never expect that from her.

"Where the fuck are you going?" she snaps when I get up to walk out of the room.

I turn back to her with a raised eyebrow, and my cock thickens at the irritation on her face. I stand there, wondering if she's even going to speak again.

"You fucking promised," she finally manages.

She twitches, antsy, as I approach her and place the empty plate on the bedside table.

I know what she wants, and I did promise, but we seem to be in the business of lying to each other.

She's more annoyed than anything when I brush a lock of hair from her face, letting my fingers trail down her cheek.

She catches herself before she can lean too far into it, but I catch her reaction.

"Stop," she hisses, jerking her hand away. "You said you'd hurt me."

"Aren't I?"

She nips at my fingers, and I have no doubt if my reaction time wasn't faster than hers, she'd bite the shit out of me.

"You know what I want."

I know my cock wants it too.

"Does your unmarred skin hurt?" I whisper, my soft fingers brushing the tip of her breast. "Do you need more bruises?"

She doesn't answer me, but I don't expect her to. She's the type to push someone to hurt her rather than ask for it. One is a win, the other is defeat.

"Your food needs to settle. I'm into a lot of shit but getting puked on while getting sucked off isn't one of them."

I grab the plate and leave the room. She doesn't stop screaming at me for half an hour.

I wait three hours before I go back into the room, once again waking her up.

I don't hesitate to climb on the bed and shove my cock into her mouth. She doesn't bite me the way she did my lip when I kissed her earlier, and that speaks volumes. As quick as she is to admit to wanting things to end, she isn't putting herself in a position to force my hand and make it happen.

I may have thought of killing her more than once in the past. I needed to focus on it so I didn't lose my damn mind in El Salvador, but she'd be no use to me dead.

Not when she has so many holes to fill and fuck.

"Deeper," I growl, fisting her hair until those little lines pop up beside her eyes.

I don't really give her the chance to wrap her lips around me. I'm literally using her throat again like I did in the motel room.

As my balls tighten, my orgasm imminent, I reach down and tease her clit.

She's fucking slicker than she ever has been. Maybe it's the way her arms are tied, but I fucking love it.

She can fight and argue, beg me to stop as much as she fucking wants, but this greedy cunt of hers never lies.

My cock kicks, convulsing rhythmically as I orgasm, and the second it's over, I pull from her mouth, pleased with the way my wet dick slides down her chin.

She growls when I pull my hand from her body, but I know she won't ask for an orgasm. I know she sees it as beneath her. She'll take them if she's forced but asking would be too much.

She wants the pleasure. God, does she fucking want it, but she's unwilling to cross the line she drew for herself.

I almost want to give it to her, to reward her stubbornness, but that would give her the upper hand and I'm not ready for that just yet.

I doubt I ever will be.

Chapter 28

Lauren

Maybe it was the sandwich or the water he's been giving me, but I still feel drugged.

I'm exhausted. Every muscle aches. I have a headache that just won't go away.

I refuse to think of the possibility that I was hurt more than I thought while in captivity.

Maybe there's something seriously wrong?

I've never been one to imagine things as being worse than they are. I'm a critical thinker, someone who takes shit at face value.

But thoughts of disease and cancer have somehow seeped into my head.

When I wake, not only are my arms still tied, the strain in them causing enough pain to make me consider begging for mercy, but now my legs are tied.

I roll my eyes over my body as best I can. I do this every time I wake up, assessing for more damage.

I've come up empty since I've found myself here with him, but then my eyes land on a small incision on the inside of my bicep. I immediately know what it means, and my blood fucking boils.

I'm once again starfished and naked on this huge bed, and Angel is nowhere to be seen.

I don't even hear the man in another part of the house.

Tears seep from my eyes, my mind thinking of all possible catastrophes. Did he leave me here to wither away and die? Is he cruel enough for something like that?

I try to convince myself that he isn't, but I know better. The man is vindictive, just as broken as I am. The only difference is that I've tried to use my own pain to help others. Angel will only ever be about himself. I'm tied to this bed because I'm a toy to him, one he will eventually get tired of. I'll be discarded, and even though I'd like to deny it, I know I'll never be the same.

I hate change, hate that I'll once again have to adapt the way I do things.

As I struggle against my restraints, I hate Angel more than ever.

"Let me go!" I scream, my eyes locking on the camera in the corner.

He's watching me. I fucking know he is. The man didn't even try to hide it. He doesn't disguise the camera at all.

It feels more invasive than what he does to my body.

I want to cry and stew in my pity, but I refuse, knowing now that he can see me. It's a spotlight on my vulnerability, and I've always tried to keep that to myself.

It doesn't take long for my screaming to transition into begging for relief.

The longer I stay tied to this bed, the longer it's going to take to bounce back. I could tell when he helped me to the bathroom that my muscles had already lost so much power. I could hardly stand on my own. It's another reason to hate him.

"Did you need something?" he asks after opening the bedroom door.

He's chill, his demeanor bored as if he's unimpressed at seeing me struggle so fruitlessly against the ropes.

"Let me go," I hiss, trying to hide my wince when I pull the rope too hard and it cuts through my skin. "I'm going to have permanent fucking scars from this shit."

His eyes run over my body, locking on the blood dripping down my arm.

"You don't want a lifelong reminder of the time we spent together?"

I freeze, my body responding to that statement in a way that would surely get me locked in a padded cell if I were to ever describe it out loud, but then I notice the way his eyes drift to my lower belly.

A slow smile spreads across his face as he inches forward. My pulse kicks up and my nipples harden. My anger is real, but so is my arousal.

"You cut out my fucking birth control?" I hiss.

He shrugs. "You're mine to do with as I please."

His words are a reminder that the last time he was in here, he made promises he didn't keep, taunted me for wanting what I know he's capable of giving.

I didn't respond the way he wanted me to, and this is his way of punishing me for it. I'm a fan of being punished, but he's torturing with denial.

Denial of pain, denial of orgasm.

"I fucking hate you," I growl, but it only makes him smile wider.

The man is fucking disarming, so goddamned handsome that I have to look away from him.

He's not classically good looking. He's the man women cross the street to get away from. They would read his dark eyes as soulless, and they'd be right.

They see him as a monster. To me? He's utter fucking perfection.

And I hate him for it.

"I hate you, too," he responds, but that sinister smile never leaves his lips as he trails a finger up my hip to my ribcage.

I do my best not to wiggle away from his touch, but it proves to be too much. My nerves are fried, and my control over my body isn't what it normally is.

"You know how to get released."

"I'm not agreeing to anything you want. I'm going to live my life how I want."

His eyes lift to mine, and he spends a minute just staring at me. It's unnerving, as if he can see right through me without even trying.

"Your life is mine to dictate."

His fingers start to move over my flesh again, tracing my collarbone, teasing my nipples.

He chuckles when I try to close my tied legs as he inches down my stomach.

"There's another way to get loose."

I bite my lip to keep myself from speaking.

El Salvador.

He's reminding me that four simple syllables will have me untied and freed.

If I do, I lose.

If I do, I'll be expected to leave.

I never want to be defeated, so I'll never say the words.

He wants to break me. I know it in every cell in my body.

Like I know he won't give up until it eventually happens.

The idea of that doesn't bother me as much as it should.

What makes me want to scream is if I survive it, he'll be done. No one wants a broken toy.

I try not to concentrate on it, but I know I don't want to leave. I don't like the realization, but that's the truth.

There's something about this man, the fact that he can give me every single thing my dark heart desires, that makes me want to stick around.

His procession, whatever it is that's driving him to keep me around, won't last forever, and that's what causes the real pain.

For the very first time in my life, I want to be wanted. I want to be cared for in the way I require. And maybe that's his goal. He wants me to need him because cutting me loose is how he will issue the final blow, the one that really hurts me.

"Never," I hiss as his thumb circles my clit.

"Good," he whispers, sounding a little distracted as his eyes follow his fingers down my thigh. "I'm thinking about keeping you. There's nothing better than owning a hot, slippery cunt that's always begging to be abused."

I can't deny it. I can feel the cool air in the room on the slickness forming below.

There's no sense in using words to deny what he can see with his own eyes.

Then he walks away.

Rage boils inside of me.

I hate being alone. I hate silence.

He fucking knows it. It's one more way for him to get inside my psyche, one more way to control me.

Before long, he's back with a plate of food and I remain calm, although I'm close to begging for a bite as he slowly places the plate on the bedside table before untying my legs. He helps me sit up, the warmth of his body against mine as he lifts me under the arms. I resist the urge to take a bite out of his neck because I'm fucking starving.

His fingers wander between bites, and the softness of his gentle touch is enough to drive me insane.

I make a plan in my head as he offers me the last bite, but it's like he has access to my thoughts, because he moves quickly out of the way before I can kick him.

He chuckles as he stands, and that laughter carries him out of the room.

The first chance I get, I may kill that motherfucker.

Chapter 29

Angel

Lies come easy to me.

I'd even consider myself a professional at them.

But when I told Lauren I was thinking about keeping her, it didn't sound like the lie I intended it to be.

It left me on edge, feeling a little out of control.

The woman is tied to my bed, yet is still somehow driving me insane.

I can cut her loose, set her free, but then she'll run.

I don't know why that thought bothers me so much.

Isn't her leaving what I want?

I grip the steering wheel harder.

I had to get away. If she weren't in my house, I never would've considered what I'm doing now.

The email requesting me to meet up has gone unanswered for weeks.

Liam Jones—I seriously doubt that's his real name—wants to work with me.

He had the balls to reach out like I was running some sort of fucking business and thought it would be a good idea to contact me directly.

I have no idea how he heard of me or how he found me, but I had to get out of the house, away from that bitch I'm forming an addiction to.

South Padre is less than two hours from my house, so I decided this morning to meet with him.

I could be walking into a trap. He could very easily be employed by some federal agency. I could've just driven away from my house for the last time. I might be waking up in a cell in the morning.

You'd think that knowing all of this, understanding that Lauren may be tied to my bed until she dies, would stop me.

It doesn't. I only drive faster.

I see Lauren Vos as no different from cancer. She has somehow sneaked inside of me, eating away at parts of me. Even though I know now what she's done, she took over so thoroughly, I know she's going to be the death of me.

I don't want to go to prison, although anyone who knew all my secrets would think I belong there. By legal standards, I guess I do. I'm a criminal. There's no other way to look at it. I know Lauren has committed crimes, done things she'd never get away with if they were committed on US soil, but her actions were for the greater good.

I just kill people when working because it's the easiest way to get paid and get back home.

So, yeah, prison would suck, but I realized her being at my house is just another form of prison, one I openly welcomed by pulling her from Mexico.

I put myself in this situation, and I need to learn from my mistakes.

The thought of getting incarcerated and leaving her to rot on my bed makes my stomach turn. She dies, she needs to be just as beautiful as she is while living, my marks painting her skin rather than shriveling up from lack of nourishment.

It also makes me take a moment's pause after parking my truck at the beach.

Even though it's winter here in Texas, there are still a handful of people walking close to the water. It wouldn't be impossible to kill the man I'm meeting, but those people pose a risk.

Seagulls cry out overhead as I climb out of my truck and make my way to the sand.

I'm honestly surprised to see Liam sitting on the beach ahead of schedule.

He emailed about being in Chicago, but didn't complain when I scheduled this meeting this morning for the same day.

It either means he's very eager, or he was already closer to me than he claims.

My suspicions immediately go up, despite him sitting in the speedo I suggested he wear.

The noise of the water and the ever-circling gulls will prevent anyone nearby from overhearing us, and the lack of clothes makes it harder to hide any type of surveillance equipment.

I sit down beside him without a word, and to his credit, he doesn't look over at me as I scan him. No jewelry, watch, or sunglasses despite the bright afternoon sun. He isn't even wearing shoes.

Brilliant blue eyes stare out at the water, sandy blond hair whipping around in the breeze. The stubble on his jaw adds a little mystery, but overall, he's a very unassuming person. He looks like one of those bro-dudes that would wear boat shoes and is always holding some sort of frozen, fruity drink.

People look at him and see him as either trustworthy or uncaring. Either way, it works in his favor.

"Are you a fed?" I ask directly.

A slow smile spreads across his face as he turns to look at me. "Do I need to pull this speedo off?"

My jaw clenches. I'm already annoyed to be here, and ready to get back to Lauren. Knowing it keeps my feet planted on the damp sand.

"I didn't ask if you were wired. I asked if you were a fed."

"You probably wouldn't believe me if I said no."

"You're correct."

His smile only grows wider. "What can I do to prove that I'm just a guy with a certain set of skills in need of a job?"

"Nothing," I answer quickly.

He nods, his attention going back to the water, and eventually I turn my eyes that direction as well.

We sit in silence. He doesn't complain about me wasting his time or the goosebumps that pop up on his skin when the air turns colder.

"How did you find me?"

I hate to be the one to break the silence, but he doesn't taunt me for losing the game.

"We ran into each other a few months back."

I nod. "I don't remember you."

"Kind of the point, isn't it?"

Sand filters from his fingertips. He's composed but diligent, I realize, as I catch him clocking every person walking around.

"It was in Guadalajara on the Pinkett case."

"How does a white boy go unnoticed in Mexico?"

His face is serious when he looks back at me.

"People see what they want to see. You have to know that some of the fastest growing trafficking rings are being led by white guys."

He isn't telling me anything I don't know. The man that was standing in front of Lauren when I found her at the house weeks ago was as Caucasian as they come.

What does surprise me is that this guy just said all of that in perfect fucking Spanish.

His grin tells me I must not have hidden my shock as well as I would've hoped.

"Besides," he says, going back to English. "Aren't horny white men the ones buying all the abducted women?"

"For the most part," I agree. "You were in Guadalajara for the Pinkett job?"

He shakes his head. "I was there to watch you work."

I take stock of who is around me, and what my chances would be of slicing his throat and getting out of here before anyone noticed.

"How did you know I was going to be there?" He's looking more and more like a fed to me.

"A friend told me."

"I don't have any friends."

He doesn't look flustered. He doesn't start jabbering like most do when caught in a lie, and the man is lying. I can tell.

"Want to tell me the truth?" I challenge.

"I searched for you on the dark web." He turns to look at me. "Actually, I just bumped into you in Farmington a few weeks back."

My skin feels like it's on fire despite the cool ocean breeze.

"Okay. I saw you a couple of weeks ago in Kansas."

This motherfucker is following me, and I didn't even know it. I realize I've been distracted since the second I walked into the Cerberus clubhouse and saw Lauren standing there, but he's been keeping an eye on me for much longer than that. He's gone unnoticed, undetected by me, and that's cause for concern.

"Which one of those is true?"

All humor leaves his face when he looks at me again.

"All of them."

"What are you not telling me?"

His eyes search mine for a long moment. "I'm number three-fifty-two."

I swallow, my hands growing clammy. That burned patch of skin on the back of my neck feels as fresh of a wound as it did years ago when I had the tattoo burned off.

I don't say a word as I stand and walk away, the number three-fifty-eight on repeat in my mind.

Chapter 30

Lauren

No matter how hard I wring my hands together, the trembling just won't stop. It travels up my arms and settles in my chest before making its way through my torso and legs.

It's as if I'm standing in a frozen wasteland, frigid, frozen to the bone instead of the living room.

"Don't touch him," Liana insists when I reach toward my father's face.

"What did you do?" My voice is broken, sobs making my question come out in syllables rather than words.

"I had to," she whispers, her hand strong and steady on my back when she offers a comforting touch.

"You didn't," I argue.

"You don't understand."

I look up at her, trying to see her through my tears but finding it impossible. She swims in my vision until I swipe at my eyes. "He's dead."

"He had to die." She glances away from me, her eyes locking on our father.

"Because of a couple bruises?" I point to the handprint he left behind when he grabbed her.

They'd been arguing all morning. I hid in my room, curled in as small of a ball as I could manage in my closet.

"What did he want you to keep?" That's the only part of the argument I can recall, and now with the knife sticking out of his neck, blood pooling around his body, those memories are already fading.

"Nothing," she says, and it angers me as much as it always does.

My older sister is the queen of secrets. She never answers my questions, responding instead with don't worry about it, or you're too young to understand.

"I'm not a fucking baby!" I scream, the bad words foreign in my mouth.

I look back at my father, wondering if breaking one of his rules will bring him back to life just so he can punish me.

"It's none of your business," she spits back, just another familiar response when I demand answers.

"We have to call the cops." My voice is pleading. "You're going to be in so much trouble."

"We'll be in trouble," she clarifies. "You watched it happen and didn't try to stop it."

I shake my head, immediately rejecting her words. "I didn't do this!"

She frowns at me like I'm the disappointment here when she's the one that stabbed our father. She's the one that stood back while he gasped for breath, blood spilling from his neck as he begged for help.

She stood back, arms crossed over her chest, much the way she is now. She let him die, and it was nothing like I've seen in the movies where someone is stabbed and they fall dead to the ground. He rattled, his hands clawing at his throat. He twitched after falling to the floor.

I squeeze my eyes closed, wanting this day to have never happened.

"They'll take me away. Do you want that? Do you want to go live with our grandmother?"

Just the thought of living with that woman makes me look at my sister for alternatives as I shake my head.

"We'll leave. We can make it on our own."

I want to believe her, but my sister can't even make curfew. How will she ever make a living at fifteen to support us?

She brought her consequences on herself. I don't know how many nights I heard her begging him to stop the punishment she earned only to go out and do it all over again the next night.

She begged the therapist he brought to the house to help her.

She begged the man next door he enlisted for help even though we were always warned to never be caught alone with him. It's the same man that looked at me when he was here last week and asked when Dad expected that I'd need his help. My father telling him soon has kept me on my best behavior.

Nothing has helped her. She's determined to break any rule set in front of her.

"I have to shower," she says, the blood on the front of her shirt drawing my attention.

"Don't leave me down here," I beg, but she shakes me off when I reach for her.

"I'll deal with it when I'm out of the shower." Her voice is flat, emotionless, just like the many times it has been after Dad brought a visitor home.

I can't be fooled into thinking she's sorry for what she's done because she never is.

Her shower goes on forever and ever, and she's only making things worse. The longer she takes, the more we're going to have to clean up.

Pain shoots through my head, and I know it's probably because I haven't had the chance to eat, but it isn't the first time I skipped a meal to avoid the risk of being seen by my dad while arguing with my sister.

I don't want to be called a disappointment the way he calls her.

I close my eyes, wishing it all away, but when I open them again, I'm no longer on the couch.

I feel weightless as I try to blink away the steam filling the bathroom.

Liana is there, her hand running over her lower belly, and I don't understand. She's probably sick to her stomach from what she did, or maybe it has to do with the red welts on her back and bottom. They look like they hurt.

I keep quiet because she'd be so upset with me if she knew I was in here with her. She's always complaining about having no privacy to both Dad and me.

After plugging the bathtub, something I find very weird because she has the shower running, she climbs into the tub, letting all of it pour over her.

My first thought when I see the knife in her hand is that Dad is going to be pissed. We aren't allowed to take any dishes out of the kitchen, but then I remember that he's dead. She won't get punished for it.

I gasp when she drags it from her wrist to the inside of her elbow, but she doesn't hear me. It's as if she's transfixed on the rush of red that blooms on a wave.

She doesn't stop there. She's not content with one arm. I scream when she does the same to other, noticing how she's already growing weak from the injuries as the knife doesn't cut as far the second time.

I'm locked in place, unable to go to her, unable to help her the way I did Dad earlier today.

The knife falls from her hand, not making a sound as it sinks to the bottom of the rapidly filling bathtub.

"Pitiful, isn't it?"

I jerk my head toward the voice, but it doesn't make sense. Liana is somehow in the tub but also standing beside me.

"What have you done?" I scream.

She doesn't wince or tell me to keep my voice down.

She smiles, her eyes locked on her body in the tub. She's started to turn that weird gray color that Dad turned after he stopped twitching.

Tears burn my eyes. I know what's happening. I know this means I'll be left all alone.

"Why did you do this?" I sob.

"I had to." It's the same answer she gave when I asked about Dad's death. "You'll be fine."

Liana turns me to face her, but I can't look. The girl close to me is the same putrid green color as the one in the tub.

"You'll be fine. I promise."

"I won't."

I expect her to argue, to attempt to assure me that everything will be okay, but instead, I get a sinister laugh.

It bubbles out of her, somehow sounding exactly like Dad did when he was dying.

The tears don't stop. I don't know if they ever will.

"You did this," she says, her voice vile and filled with hatred. "You're the reason I did this."

I shake my head.

"You hid. You let him hurt me, let those other men hurt me. My death is your fault."

I want to deny it, but I can't. I was a coward, always staying hidden, always trying to be the best daughter I could be because I saw what misbehaving included.

"I'm sorry," I whisper, my head hung low.

Once again, warmth covers my cheek, and I'm almost tempted to lean into it, but she's being so mean to me.

"You can end your pain, too," she urges.

I shake my head. I could never do what she just did. It would hurt too much.

"I'm not brave enough," I confess.

"You are," she urges. "We can be together again. You're older. You have access to ways that will be quicker, less painful."

"Older?" I look up at her, once again confused.

But she's gone. The bathroom is gone. Even the sound of running water has disappeared. I'm standing in blackness with nothing but silence. I scream into the pitch black, but only my voice echoes back at me.

I'm too scared to move, too scared to run.

It's in this darkness that I realize that the pain is gone. My heart is no longer racing. My skin isn't clammy. My mind is blank. I don't know what I'm missing, but even that sense of isolation fades away until calmness takes over.

Did I do it? Did I manage to finally slay my own demon?

"Lauren?"

The voice is like a bomb going off. It bounces around me until I have to cover my ears.

"Lauren?"

My eyes flutter open, the warmth on my face from Angel's hand on my skin.

I feel so out of place and disoriented. I know it was a dream. I've had it many times. I know I never witnessed my sister's suicide, never had a conversation with her ghost. She never opened her mouth to blame me. That finger pointing was read in her diary, her only outlet for the pain she'd been suffering for years. Her diary was a mix of rants about my father and the abuse, about the way he brought other men into the house to hurt her the same way he was. The other half were hearts and flowers, and how much she loved him and hated that he claimed the world wouldn't understand the way they loved each other. She was tired of the secrets.

I feel sick just thinking about it, my body hot and shaking from the dream that just gets more real every time I suffer through it.

Angel watches my face silently, but the sinister man is gone. All I'm looking at is pity. He feels sorry for me, and that is a cut I can't survive.

"Let me go," I whisper.

He shakes his head. "I can't."

I watch his face. He looks as exhausted as I feel, and I know what I have to do to help us both.

"El Salvador," I whisper as I close my eyes.

* * *

This time I dream of cool breezes on my skin, but it feels off. The freedom in it feels short-lived, and when I open my eyes, I understand.

I'm no longer tied to the bed. My body is covered with a blanket, and I know without even having to leave the room that I'm alone in the house.

I no longer sense him near.

He's freed me.

I knew it would happen when I spoke the safe word, and I can't really take it back now.

I'm weaker than I've ever been as I climb out of the bed and make my way to the shower.

Bathing takes forever, but despite being more tired than I've ever been in my life, I force myself to dry off before digging through his closet for something to wear.

I have no plans, no direction, no safety net, as I scrounge around in the kitchen and pack some food and water into a bag I found in his bedroom closet.

I don't leave a note.

This isn't a goodbye, see you later.

This is forever.

El Salvador ensures it.

His truck is gone when I step out onto the porch, fighting the urge to call Cerberus. I don't know that they'd even help if I begged. I wore out that welcome long ago, but I also don't want to risk any chance of them going after Angel.

I shouldn't feel the urge to protect him, but somehow I do.

I can't stay even though deep down I know that's what I want. I'm not allowed a reprieve from my pain. My dreams remind me of that constantly.

If only I were as brave as Liana.

Chapter 31

Angel

There's only so many times you can watch the same thing before your mind alters the outcome. Or maybe it's hope that switches things around.

I've seen Lauren leave my house a million times in the last several days.

I've watched her stumble on the last step of the front porch and walk off the property without looking back.

But as I rewind the video again, I see her look back, watch her eyes as if she's standing in front of me, begging me to stop her.

Then the glitch and she's walking away again.

Over and over, I watch to find that one time she pauses, and I never find it.

My mind made it up. My head is trying to convince me to go after her, to find her, to catch her and tell her I was joking and that untying her was all part of my game.

It wasn't at the time. She said the words I never thought I'd hear, and I had to hold up my end of the bargain. I gave her that out the first night, and I would've bet everything I own that she'd never speak it. Not that she didn't want to but because she was too damned stubborn for her own good.

I never imagined a fucking nightmare would make her end things, that it would be something in her head rather than the violence in mine that would be the final straw.

I underestimated the pain she's lived with since childhood.

It's so fucking stupid of me because I know the power that shit carries.

I scour the video feed for her return. I look into every alert. Even the half second movement ones, knowing it's going to be a fucking bug or a bird because the alert would've been longer if it were her.

Each search is fruitless.

I left the house after cutting her loose because I knew I wouldn't be able to watch her leave in person. She has no cell phone. I couldn't follow her any further than the edge of my property.

She's gone.

I think of the scars she'll have, a constant reminder of our time together.

I think of her empty belly because I didn't get the chance to fuck her after cutting her birth control implant from under her skin.

I don't fucking know how I feel about it.

Knowing Lauren, she'd never go through with a pregnancy anyway. She wouldn't want anything slowing down her destruction. Having to care for anyone else would contradict just how fucking selfish she is. It would never happen.

The thought of her killing my hypothetical baby makes me see red. It makes me want to track her down, which only makes me feel completely impotent, because I purposely let her leave without being able to find her.

If she wants to be here, she would've had to stay or will have to come back on her own.

I grin as I look over at my safe. I have insurance of course. I don't trust that she won't get herself killed before coming back, but I know she will.

Waiting for it to happen sucks. That's why I scheduled a purchase in Tamaulipas for later this evening. I'll go, get paid, and be back before midnight. With any luck, she'll be waiting here for me when I return.

***

People don't change overnight.

It's very damn seldom that something happens and people see some light that makes them change their ways.

Habits are incredibly hard to break.

Someone on the outside looking in would probably be disgusted to see me sitting in my truck, waiting for the man to show up with my latest purchase.

After finding Lauren beaten and covered in cum, many would want to burn down the world and rid it of every evil person walking the planet.

I know myself enough to not even try.

Besides, dead people don't pay. I found that out many times before El Salvador changed the way I looked at the world.

The goal is to step on people before they have the chance to step on you—or *over* you as my life experiences have dictated.

I'm not raiding a trafficking house. I'm not going to kill the man who delivers this woman to me. I'll take her back to her boyfriend and the trafficker will go back to work.

Lauren would be so ashamed of me.

It's a low-paying job, but I needed something to fill my time while I wait for my girl to come crawling back to me.

I ensure that the bundle of cash is in the inside pocket of my jacket as I see the car approach, and I scan the area to make sure I'm not about to get jumped. Getting robbed while buying this girl is just as probable as any other outcome. Sometimes this happens by other people in the same crew as the sellers, but this park is known for criminal activity and some fuckers are just opportunists.

No one approaches me as I stand by the decrepit picnic table I was instructed to stand by, but I keep my eyes moving from the car to the surrounding areas.

The client told me his girlfriend had been kidnapped just a few days ago, but I can tell she's already been broken. She doesn't fight as she's pulled from the backseat of the car. She walks as fast as the man urges her to despite the black bag over her head.

The transaction is smooth. I hand over the money, and he hands over the woman.

I don't remove her eye cover as I guide her back to my truck, and I don't do it even after we're back on the road heading toward the Texas border. I don't speak a word to her or try to calm her fears as she sniffles from the passenger seat.

She doesn't beg for help when the man near the wall helps us across without going through customs.

When I make it to the rendezvous point with the client, I park my truck in front of his car and flash my lights.

I don't cut the rope on her hands until my phone dings with his payment.

I reach past her and shove open the passenger side door.

"Get out," I say, and she moves quickly.

She has no fucking clue what's happening, but she still obeys.

Lauren would never fucking act this way. She probably would've tried to claw my face off the second I cut the rope on her hands. That's why I did it while she was asleep.

I drive off with the woman standing in the middle of a secluded parking lot, not bothering to look in the rearview mirror to see if her boyfriend rushes to her because I don't give a shit.

Compassion and apathy were beaten out of me long ago.

Chapter 32

Lauren

Liana haunts me.

Thoughts of Angel haunt me.

I don't know how to deal with it.

It took me over a week to make my way back to Kansas.

Once an FBI agent, I've broken a handful of laws to eat, clothe myself, and find a means to travel.

The most awful part of it is that I don't feel bad about any of it.

I think that has more to do with the horrific things I've been through and using reasoning to not feel guilty about taking clothes from a money-hungry chain store or slipping the money meant to pay for lunch off a table as I walk by unnoticed.

I feel like I deserve it, and the only thing that does make my skin crawl is the fact that I'm meeting my own needs out of a sense of entitlement rather than suffering through the hand I've been dealt, which is how I normally go about things.

I don't know on which leg of my journey I made the decision to finally exorcise my demons, but as I step in front of the bank in my old hometown, I know I no longer want to be the woman who punishes herself for the things I can't control.

It'll be hard, but I want to be fucking normal.

Just the thought makes my skin crawl, but I also know it's about little steps rather than thinking I can just wake up one morning and be different.

After dealing with this first issue today, I can settle in at the local motel and make a plan. That will be the very first difference because I've been taught that writing shit down can be dangerous. It's why as agents, we're trained to memorize shit.

I smile at the woman at the front counter as I approach. It feels fake because it is, but she smiles back, either uncaring or fooled. Either way, it doesn't matter to me.

"I'd like to close out my safe deposit box please."

She asks for the information along with my ID, and I have to pause for a second.

If the FBI is looking for me, this is going to flag in their system.

Knowing how far the nearest office is, I quickly hand over the identification, confident I can get out of here before they arrive.

She frowns as her eyes scan the computer screen.

"Box two-thirty-one?"

"Yes. Is there a problem?"

"That box has already been closed."

My hands start to shake immediately. I wanted closure. The new direction I want to take my life demands it. Without the necklace and diary destroyed, I'll never be able to move on. I'm certain of it.

"Closed? That's not possible."

"Just a few weeks ago," she says, pointing at her screen as if I can see it from this side of the high counter.

"By whom?" I snap, my palms sweaty.

"Your husband. Angel Guerra."

My heart fucking stops. I swear it. Not beating, no sound around me, nothing.

The rush of it all coming back nearly takes me to my knees.

The teller watches my face, and I'm able to see hers go from business to concern.

"Is everything okay, ma'am?"

I shake my head, but it's more rejecting this entire situation than answering her questions.

"Are you unsafe? Now that I think about it, I remember the man that came in. Has he hurt you? I can call the police if you're under duress."

I back away from the counter.

She'd never understand my position, that Angel hurt me many times but I also liked it.

There's no way a woman in a bright pink dress and lovely blonde curls haloing her face wouldn't gasp at the bruises that man has put on my body or understand that I hate that the last ones are already fading.

"Did you say weeks ago?"

She nods, giving me the exact date. It's the day after I climbed into the truck with Ryder, the guy I thought was boring, who also ended up being the ringleader of the group that abducted me.

"My mistake," I tell her before turning around and hauling ass out of the damn bank.

Angel has my things.

I shouldn't be surprised. I know I confessed about the stuff when I was drunk. I didn't tell him that my hometown was in Dighton, but the man has to be skilled enough to track down that information with my legal name.

I practically handed it to him.

Emotions swirl inside of me, leaving me confused, wanting answers to questions I have no business even thinking.

Is this part of his game?

Did he do it to hurt me?

Does he want me back?

Can I survive not destroying them?

Can I just walk away and let it go? Let him go?

He took the things before he discovered that I was abducted. Does that mean he wanted me back then?

If that's the case, then why did he cut me loose?

Nothing makes fucking sense.

I've always followed my gut instinct, and it's kept me alive more than once, but my stomach is turning right now and I can't translate what it means at all.

I duck down an alleyway, hoping I fly under the radar from the FBI long enough to get out of town.

I have no family here. My grandmother was my last living relative, and she died years ago.

No friends.

No family.

I could die today, and no one would notice.

The thought doesn't bring the same relief that it normally does, and that's one more reason to hate Angel.

I want him to miss me. I don't want him to just be able to steal my stuff, cut me loose, and forget about me like I never existed.

As I walk, that hatred thickens inside of me. It makes my skin hot and feverish. It makes me vengeful.

That's exactly what I need.

In order for me to move on from this, I have to end Angel Guerra once and for all.

Chapter 33

Angel

I believed Alan Moore, Lauren's handler, when he told me the FBI had cut ties with her, but that hasn't stopped me from tracking him. As far as I can tell, she hasn't made contact.

He's just one more dead end.

I fucking hate waiting. I'm a man of action.

These long days without her agitate me, and I have every intention of taking it out on her when she finally comes slinking back.

I'll tie her to the bed for months if I have to. I'll give her body enough of a workout that she won't have to worry about atrophy.

I decided weeks ago that the woman was mine. My miscalculation was thinking that she wanted to stay. I know she likes my brand of attention. I know she craves it. I love giving it to her. I love abusing her body, taking out my own retaliation, and when she comes?

"Fuck," I grumble, swiping a hand over the top of my head.

My balls ache for release. My fingertips itch to pinch and rip and shred.

I hate her for making me *need* her, but I'll have my revenge soon enough.

I don't know how long it will take her to realize that I've taken her most prized possessions, and I know she'll never just walk away from them.

When she gets here, she's going to be pissed, with thoughts of killing me.

I have news for her. I'm just as pissed at her for staying gone so fucking long. Hell, I'm livid she walked away in the first place.

I plan to spend the rest of my life teaching Lauren all the lessons she'll ever need.

Maybe she didn't have people in her life growing up that wanted her to succeed. She wasn't educated the right way, and I'm going to enjoy hurting her until she gets it right.

She may not want me, may not plan on being mine, but that doesn't mean it won't happen. If Lauren Vos steps foot on my property, I'll never let her leave. I can't risk feeling the way I do now, again.

My skin hums every time I step into the shower, my body fighting my mind to end it quicker so I can find her in my bedroom, and yet she's never there.

The days get longer with no one to focus my attention on. The nights are nearly impossible to bear without her strapped to my bed.

I feel like I'm going insane, and I have no one to blame but myself for untying her. I took a chance, thinking she'd climb out of my bed and be waiting in the kitchen when I came back home. Making the same mistake twice won't happen.

I looked for her everywhere when I left the house earlier. She wasn't at the grocery store nor the coffee shop. The trip away from the house was a distraction, another opportunity to try and sneak in and catch me off guard, but the house was just as empty as I left it. There were no alerts on my security system when I returned.

I fight the anger I'm feeling as time slips by without her showing up. I do want to hurt her. I always will, but I don't want to damage her to the point that she stops begging for the pain. Her enjoying what I do makes me harder than I've ever been in my life. Sex with her is fucking phenomenal.

Clenching my jaw, I pull up my encrypted email. On a whim, I shoot a job over to Liam as a test.

I still don't trust the motherfucker. He's just too damn pretty for that to ever happen.

I open a notification from him and have to smile. He completed the job, a recovery in Monterey, not far from where my home base is.

He was quick and efficient, but time will tell if he just got lucky because he didn't spend half the time I would've preparing.

I required fifty percent of the profit but was nice enough to cover expenses. Liam didn't argue with the terms. He'd be a fool to open his mouth.

I verify the eleven-thousand-dollar deposit from his work before looking for another job to send him on. Liam claims he has the skills to work but isn't capable of finding the jobs. The ones posted on the regular internet go very quickly, and he reports missing opportunities. I have the skills and programs to be one of the first to have access to new online sales.

I still haven't determined if he's working with a policing agency, but I'm also not breaking any laws where he's concerned. If the man does something illegal or worthy of criminal charges, he'll be responsible for it. I'm merely a temp agency finding the man work.

My computer program finds another job, this one with a higher payout because of how dangerous it is. I send Liam the information, wondering how far I can push him before he folds, telling me he won't do it or he gets killed. Either way, I don't really give a shit. I'll just sit back and collect the money I make from him until he's no longer viable for me.

It's nice getting paid while sitting at my computer, but I also know it won't last forever. I'll get that itch, the one that will lead me back into the field, but I have to stay home right now. The last thing I want is for Lauren to show up while I'm on a job. I wouldn't want her to get lonely.

I narrow my eyes at an email from a new person, and it pisses me off enough to redirect Liam to my house so I can slit his fucking throat.

I take a deep breath as I read the email from one of Liam's friends who's also looking for work, but as much as it pisses me off that Liam had the balls to send someone else my way, I can also see the benefit in it.

I shove down the irritation of feeling like a fucking office manager scheduling mercenaries for a job and send this new asshole a link. The job is so fucking dangerous, right in the middle of cartel territory in South America, that I would skip over it. But if the guy takes it and succeeds, I'll be thirty thousand dollars richer.

I pause with my fingers hovering over the keyboard rather than typing out a message to Liam with the equivalent of *eat shit and die, you're fired.*

I can see the benefit of having others do the rough and dangerous shit for me, but this was never part of my plan. I never wanted to be a goddamned administrator.

With a deep breath, I close down all programs on my computer but my security. I scan through the video from last night slowly, treating it like I haven't already watched this footage three times already.

Just like the times before, there are no shadows, no lurking forms, no reflections in the distance off of binoculars.

Nothing.

It makes me feel empty, desperate, ready to burn down the world to find her.

Picking up my phone, I stare at the damn thing like it's done something to personally offend me.

I've been avoiding this call. I never ask for help, but the way I feel is ten times greater than how I'll feel for placing the call.

"Thumper," the man says, caution already in his voice from the call showing up as *UNAVAILABLE* on his screen.

"It's Angel."

Silence fills the line. He may have been surprised and maybe a little relieved to see I was alive when I showed up at the clubhouse, but I'd never mistake that for us being friends.

We aren't the same, and I know he probably feels about me the way the other members weren't shy to express. What I do for a living is disdainful, wrong. They see it as me taking advantage of people when they're at their lowest points in life.

"I'm looking for Lauren."

"Okay."

I huff, half in irritation and the other half because good for him, not just offering up any information. I don't know that she knows she has that level of protection from them.

"I have some information to give her. She must've lost or had to get rid of her phone. My calls aren't going through."

The truth is, she dumped her phone before she ended up in Tamaulipas because I tracked the motherfucker to a trash can on the other side of town near the hotel we stayed at.

"If we're able to get in contact with her, we'll give her the message."

I clench my teeth until my jaw hurts.

"It's like that?"

"How else do you expect it to be, Angel?"

On one hand, I'm glad he's not just handing over her information, on the other, I want to strangle him for making this more difficult for me.

Instead of arguing with a man capable of sending the entire Cerberus MC after me, I simply hang up the phone. It's very possible that Lauren is standing right beside him, just like it's possible they haven't seen her since she rode away with me after dropping that little girl off.

I've considered her going back to the clubhouse but shoved it away. Lauren doesn't like to look needy. She's as much of a lone wolf as I am. But as I stand from my computer and stretch out my back, I just can't stop thinking about the possibilities.

Planning not to leave any stone unturned, I decide I'll fly out tomorrow to check. When I do find her, it's only going to make me hurt her more, make her beg for more, because Kincaid was very clear about not being welcome on their property.

Chapter 34

Lauren

Darkness has always been my friend. It's a shield, a way to hide not only physically but also emotionally. Tears can run down my cheeks in darkness and stay a secret. I can clench my hands against pain unseen in order to not appear weak.

The darkness tonight, half a mile from Angel's house, is different. It comes alive around me, and not in the living creature sense.

It's fucking cold, most animals having enough sense this time of year to find warmth until the sun rises.

It's the thrill of what I'm doing, of the unknown, that is animating the air around me, the ground under my feet.

My body vibrates with all the possibilities.

I refuse to think of what comes next. I have no plans past tonight because making them would be fruitless. There's a real chance that I'll never see sunrise.

Angel wanted me gone, couldn't even be bothered to stick around after untying me from his bed.

He was disgusted, just done with the idea of me.

I have no illusions that I can sneak up on him, that I can fully surprise him.

He had to know after clearing out my safe deposit box that I'd seek vengeance. I can only hope to hurt him before he renders me incapable of further revenge.

My stomach rolls with thoughts of being able to overpower him. I know I have to, but deep down, I don't want to be the one to come out victorious. I've fought all my life to put myself in situations that will finally end my pain, but there's always that part of me that pops up, needing to fight.

The same will happen tonight. I can only hope that he's relentless.

As I creep closer to the house, I attempt to shake off the memories of his skills in playing my body, of giving me exactly what I needed. I don't need that shit in my head, in my body, but I'm also incapable of clearing my mind.

My pulse races, my body quickening with the possibilities.

I can guess what will happen tonight. I know he'll use me before he discards me. That's his own weakness, his own inability to have me in front of him and not take what he wants.

I know I'm just as much an addiction to him as he is to me, and he hates me for it. I see the animosity in his eyes every time he looks at me.

Well, not every time.

I freeze, my feet planted firmly on the ground when I think about the soft touches, the light brushes of his fingertips.

I hate myself for wanting that side of him as well, even though he was only using it to disarm me. It was another manipulation, not his own need to comfort me. I can't let myself imagine any differently. Getting delusional, hopeful, will only make things end too quickly.

I want the pain long and drawn out. I need to feel alive, even in my death.

The sight of my breath leaving my lips on the chilly night air grounds me once again. It's as if experiencing everything for the very last time is almost cathartic. Before long, I'll no longer hurt or feel cold. I'll no longer ache or need. It's a thrilling experience as I silently step onto the front porch.

For a flash of a second, I consider just knocking on the door. He'd never expect that, and maybe the sight of me standing in front of him will startle him enough that I could get the upper hand just a little. I want to hurt him, want to draw blood, even though I know how this ends.

I know I have to beg him to destroy the necklace and diary before I draw my last breath. I know I'll spend the rest of my eternity haunted by them if he doesn't. I pray he'll grant this one final wish, but I doubt he will. Torturing, even after I leave this earth, would be more his style, and it makes me pause once again.

My heart is racing, the sound of it so loud in my ears that I can't determine if the front door makes a noise as I work to open the lock. As I tuck the lock kit back into my pocket, I listen for noise, try to sense any movement, and come up empty.

He could easily sneak up on me. The man has the same if not more skill level than I do at this sort of thing.

I toss away the idea of searching his house for my possessions. I have no idea where to look, and if my returning for his final justice is his plan, he'd never leave them out where I can find them. He'd never risk avoiding the confrontation.

I know he's here. I watched from a distance as his house went dark, each light turning off.

From spending time in bed with him, I also know he's as much a restless sleeper as I am. It's difficult to experience and do the things we do and just fall into a peaceful sleep at night. It means I only have a short time to catch him fully resting.

A zing of excitement at what's coming rushes up my spine, the thrill of apprehension chasing right after it as I make my way silently toward his bedroom.

When I woke up untied, I didn't spend much time in his bedroom. The urge to crawl back on the mattress and wait for him was too strong. I said the words that ended whatever it was we had, and for some reason, he kept his end of the bargain.

I'm slow and cautious as I make my way through the house, determined not to alert him by making the mistake of running into a piece of furniture. Thankfully, his house is sparsely furnished, making it easy to get to his bedroom door silently.

The door is cracked, and I hold my breath, as if it makes a difference, with a prayer in my head the door doesn't squeak.

It moves, silently and efficiently, and I pause, staring at the form on the bed.

A wave of emotions hits me right in the chest, making my breathing ragged, unlike the soft breaths coming from the bed.

Endings are always tough whether it be by death or just closing the door on a certain chapter in life.

He took my ending. I was meant to destroy my sister's items and move on, try to open another chapter in life. I let myself dream of being normal or finding a regular job and gaining as much happiness as I could manage.

With what he's done, he has prevented me from doing it.

My knife makes the slightest noise as I pull it from the sheath.

Coming in and killing him first thing was never my plan, but my anger boils over as I watch him sleep.

I've been torn up, flayed to the fucking bone, since walking out of this house, and this motherfucker has the ability to sleep soundly as if he has no fucking cares in the world.

I wanted to find him miserable, heartbroken on some level that his toy was gone.

I focus on the anger, the flash of maybe in my head.

Maybe I'll get closure with his death. Maybe I'll find Liana's things and destroy them like I planned. Maybe I can still have that next chapter in life, no matter how unreachable it seems right now.

This is the fight I was thinking of earlier. Accepting death is impossible for me. It's why I could never do what Liana did.

Decision made, I spring into action.

The second I jump on the bed, I realize my mistake.

I meet nothing but softness instead of Angel's muscled frame.

He knew I was here all along.

My body sings with all the possibilities.

Chapter 35

Angel

I know she isn't this careless. She had to have known that I'd be watching from the shadows of the room, but as I watch her stare at the lumps in the bed, I have to question her skill level. If she's this blasé about her life, I'm honestly surprised she's been through as much as she has and survived.

The sound of her pulling her knife raises goosebumps on my arms, the absolute thrill of surprising her making it hard not to move too soon.

The scent of her fear swarms around me, making my cock thicken.

She took her fucking time getting here, but I'll get vengeance for that soon enough.

The wait, the planning, is all part of the exhilaration.

She doesn't make a sound as she jumps on the bed, knife held high.

In the darkness, I can't tell if she's really willing to kill me over a necklace and the fucked-up ramblings of her dead sister.

I read every word—the hatred she had for her father mixed with the fucked-up love of a young girl being groomed from an early age to think what was happening was right, despite the sickness with it all that threatened to take over many times before she finally got the courage to end it.

I know Lauren has read it too. The pages were flimsy with wear. I know she's terrorized by what her sister went through, and I almost let myself feel sorry for the things I said to her before and after finding out what her father had been doing to Liana.

Almost.

I don't want to lose sight of my own plans for Lauren. Hurting her has always been a part of my vision. Those fantasies have kept me awake at night as much as the promise of her return.

I spotted her on my security cameras over an hour ago, and I have to give her kudos for her patience, but she has to know my skills are much better than hers. The FBI can't train you to know the things inherent to me and my demons.

She gave a good try, however.

Her gasp of realization is music to my fucking ears as I rush her. Like a cobra strike, I'm fast and efficient, covering her back with my body in an instant.

I allow the struggle. Overpowering her immediately isn't as much fun as making her think she has a chance.

The sweet burn of her knife as it cuts into my arm makes me smile, as does the snarl on her lips when I flip her to her back.

"Hey there," I whisper, pinning her arms over her head.

She struggles, moving her body in an attempt to dislodge me, but I have over a hundred pounds of muscle on her thin frame.

"I'll fucking kill you," she snaps, but her body starts to settle.

I know better than to think she's already admitting defeat. This is as much of a head game for us as it is a physical one.

"Crazy. I had the same plans for you."

Her eyes widen with surprise before they narrow to slits.

I hate that I didn't turn on the fucking lights, that I'm forced to proceed with only the moonlight coming in through the window.

"Did you miss me, baby?" I nuzzle her neck, knowing it will fire her up more than anything else I can do.

She hates me for it, doubling her attempt to get away.

I hate that I like it so fucking much, hate that I want to just hold her like this, that I'm having thoughts of spending time in bed with her curled into my body.

I used to think of Lauren as a virus, something to eradicate like mice in the attic or invasive weeds in the yard.

It wasn't until I accepted that I liked her brand of crazy that I was able to set my mind at ease.

She isn't something to rid myself of. She's my other half. She's a requirement, a necessity, and as much as I hate it, I also love it. We'll never be equals, but even knowing that, I'm well aware of the fact that without her, I can't be me.

"I fucking hate you," she rasps, her breathing becoming more difficult as I press more of my weight onto her.

She can't even fool herself at this point when her legs fall open as I settle on her, my thick cock pressing against that needy cunt of hers.

When she turns her head, refusing to look at me, I know she wants to beg for it. If I weren't so needy for her myself, I might make an effort to force her to do that, but I've been waiting too long for her return. I no longer have the restraint to make it last, but I mentally add it to my list of things to do later tonight or tomorrow morning.

"How wet are you, you sick twisted bitch?"

"Dry as a fucking bone," she snaps, even knowing I'm going to prove her wrong.

I can feel the heat of her against me, the wetness that has to be pooling between her thighs.

The fucking jeans she's wearing are going to be a problem, but I've overcome bigger hurdles in my life.

"I want my shit!"

"I'm going to give you everything you want and more," I promise.

Her body jolts with the declaration, and I know it's half thrill and half apprehension.

"You could've made this easier for me," I complain as I reposition my hand so I can keep holding her down while I reach for her zipper.

"Never," she hisses, once again struggling to get away from me.

"That's my girl."

Her head snaps up, her teeth locking on my shoulder.

I live in the pain for a few seconds, nearly blowing my load on her stomach when she moans at the taste of my blood on her tongue.

"So fucking dirty," I praise when she pulls her head back. "My turn."

I don't go for her shoulder or pain, rather I lock my lips over her nipple through her shirt.

She whimpers, needy and ready for what I have to give her.

It's enough of a distraction for her to drop the knife she still had clenched in her fist.

"You're making this a little too easy for me, baby. Does that mean you want it?" I ask as I use my free hand to pick up the knife.

Her eyes track the movement of the knife, and I want to slap the shit out of her when she angles her neck, giving me more access when I trail it down her cheek.

"Is that what you really want?" I lean in close, my lips brushing hers as I speak.

It's a dangerous move for me with her penchant for using her mouth to cause pain.

She blinks up at me, and even in the dim light I can see the battle in her eyes.

"You deserve the pain I give you."

She shakes her head, denying it, but I drop the knife and clench her face roughly in my hands.

She isn't rejecting the fact that she disagrees with the pain. She feels as if she's earned it. It's the fact that she's getting something she wants, something that feels so fucking right on her skin that she can't accept.

Being worthy of something isn't in her vocabulary because she's been torturing herself for as long as she can probably remember. She doesn't know anything else.

"Hurt me," she begs, and I know what it takes for her to do it.

"I'm going to take you nice and slow, baby. Be patient."

She doubles her efforts to get away just like I knew she would.

I find myself wanting both sides of her—the woman who needs the pain but also the one who desires the soft touches and gentle words, because they make her feel loved not because she's using them as another form of punishment.

It may take years, but I'm willing to put in the work to achieve both sides of that woman.

She ended things once, muttering the two words I gave her, and I don't know why she doesn't whisper them now. Maybe she thinks they won't make a difference since I just caught her trying to kill me.

She'd be right of course.

That safe word may stop what I'm directly doing, but it will never again be a full release. I need her, and as long as I do, this woman is mine. I'd prefer to only have her tied to the bed when we're playing, but I'm flexible on the idea of hand feeding her and walking her to the bathroom when she needs it for the rest of her life.

"Angel," she whispers, tears streaming from her eyes and rolling down her temples.

Her plea encompasses so much, and it has so many confessions right on the tip of my tongue.

"I'm going to hurt you."

She nods.

"I'm going to fuck you raw."

She nods again.

"I'm going to keep you when I'm done."

Her eyes lock onto mine.

"I can't do that," she finally whispers.

"I'm not giving you a choice."

More tears flow down her face as she swallows.

"Promise?" she asks on a sob.

"Yeah, baby. I promise."

A serenity I've never seen from her before settles over her features, but it only lasts for a second before she's back to struggling.

I chuckle as I pick the knife up and cut into her jeans. I don't make the mistake of releasing her hands because I know she'll try to claw my eyes out.

"Don't fucking touch me!" she screams when I cut a hole big enough for my hand to slip through.

I'm met with slickness, her desire as hot and as prevalent as I suspected.

"You run and I'll chase you to the ends of the fucking earth," I warn as I release the hand pinning hers above her head. "Now get my tits out."

I pinch her clit until she winces when she doesn't obey, and as her hands move to pull up her shirt, I'm met with another rush of wetness on my fingers in her panties.

"Stupid bitch," I spit, smacking her trembling hands out of the way so I can get the task done faster.

She glares at me, brows drawn, forming a crease between her eyes.

"Keep looking at me like that and I'm going to fuck you nice and slow," I warn.

The threat has her trying to scramble away, which is fucking perfect because she's now on her stomach.

I rip at her clothes, leaving them in scraps hanging loose off her body. I don't need her completely naked. I only need access to that amazing cunt of hers.

"Tell me I'm the only one that can hurt you," I demand as I smack the tip of my glistening cock on her ass.

"Angel!" she hisses as I spread her cheeks, letting the tip of me skim that forbidden spot of hers.

I'll fuck her ass at some point, but there's no reason for her to think I won't do it right now.

"Tell me," I growl. "Or I won't even use lube."

I press my thumb in, wondering if I need to change my plans when she moans with pleasure.

I may be going about this all wrong. Giving her what she wants, the pain, the degradation, may not be the way to operate when dealing with Lauren. There's definitely a learning curve where Lauren Vos is concerned, but thankfully I have a lifetime to figure out all the nuances that make her tick.

"Only you can hurt me," she pants. "So fucking hurt me!"

I slide home, nearly losing my mind when her pussy grips onto me like it has missed me as much I've missed her.

My thrusts are hard, as deep as I can manage them. My grip on her ass is punishing, but that's all I can manage.

My brain has gone offline with the pleasure of being inside her again.

I no longer have to do everything in fear of never experiencing it again. This cunt will be mine to fuck again tomorrow and the next day.

"My pussy," I growl as I lean over her, taking her throat in my hand as I lean in close to her ear. "Right?"

She chokes from my grip, but even when I loosen my grip, she doesn't agree.

"You have a lot to learn," I hiss, my hips jerking forward.

I'm no longer in control of my own body. It's going to do what it wants.

I can barely manage words or thoughts at this point.

She feels that fucking good.

"It's fucking mine, Lauren. Tell me."

She doesn't.

I fuck her harder, choke her more, pinch her nipples and clit, and the stubborn fucking woman never agrees to the ownership.

She tells me she hates me after she comes and threatens to end my life when I spill inside of her.

"You took out my birth control implant," she screams. "You're going to get me pregnant, you piece of shit!"

I lean in closer, my breaths erratic as I bite the tip of her ear just enough to remind her who is in control.

"Didn't know I had a breeding kink until you just said that."

My cock thickens again as I roll my hips.

"You can't," she argues.

"I'll do anything with my pussy that I want. It'll serve you well to just accept it now. It'll save you a lot of pain."

Her head rolls, the pillow bunching up under her cheek. "Never."

Chapter 36

Lauren

I woke up minutes ago, but I refuse to open my eyes.

I don't want to risk that last night was a nightmare.

What happened was the nightmare. I fucking loved it. I can feel his abuse all over my body. I throb from head to toe.

But what if none of it is real?

I know it physically happened, but the thought of what he said being another manipulation? I don't know if I can handle it.

I shove down those familiar thoughts I always get when things go my way or I get things I want.

He used the word deserve last night. He said you deserve the pain you get.

He didn't say it in a way to hurt me. It was him saying that it's okay to want what I want. That I shouldn't feel ashamed for needing the things so few are capable of providing.

It wasn't a threat. It was a promise.

And even as I lie here, refusing to open my eyes, I want to believe him.

I'm a fan of being manipulated, of being surprised. Disappointment is sort of a kink for me as well, but I don't think I'd survive if I discovered he didn't mean it, that it was one more sick way to cause me pain.

Those are heart matters, the promise of keeping me. They have the power to fucking destroy me more than anything physical ever could.

Knowing I can't put the truth off any longer, I let my eyes flutter open.

The room is different than it was when I was here before. Rather than the curtains being drawn, they're open, along with the blinds, allowing sunlight to flow into the room.

The furniture is nothing spectacular—a bed, a dresser, a side table, but none of the shadows that were lurking around remain.

My throat threatens to close at the sight of the cold Diet Mt. Dew sitting beside a couple pain killers on the bedside table. I don't recall ever telling him I loved the drink, but I'm also not surprised to see it sitting there.

I groan with discomfort as I swing my legs over the edge of the bed before reaching for the drink.

The cap is sealed which is a little disappointing because it means he's not going to drug me.

It also means I'm going to have to face him with all my faculties. For a flash, I think I'd rather chew broken glass, but I know we have to face each other.

But then I swallow, wondering if he's going to be gone again.

He swore he'd chase me to the ends of the earth, but I imagine he'd say anything when he was eight inches deep inside of me.

I pop the pills, taking a long swig of the soda before noise somewhere else in the house grabs my attention.

I'm torn between wanting to avoid him and wanting to run to him and beg him to tell me that what he said was true.

With a sigh, I stand and slowly peel away the ripped clothes from my body. In an effort to annoy him because his room is pristine, I leave them in a pile on the floor. If he thinks I'm going to obey him or do what he wants, he's sadly mistaken.

The threat of him correcting my sloppiness sets my skin on fire as I open the bedroom door.

The scent of maple bacon wraps around me as I creep toward the kitchen. He doesn't have music playing or the television on like any other normal person would. He doesn't stiffen or show any other indication that he knows I'm close, but I'm not convinced that he isn't well aware of my presence.

"I was wondering if you were going to get your sweet ass out of bed or if I was going to have to eat it all myself."

I try to hide the smile sweeping across my face, but it's impossible.

"I didn't realize you were such a pussy."

He turns a little, looking at me over his shoulder. His eyes sweep the naked length of me, and it takes a lot of power not to preen at his perusal. There's no denying the need that flashes in his eyes, and it's almost strong enough to make me clench my thighs together.

I point to his boxer briefs when he doesn't say anything. "Afraid of getting a little bacon grease on your dick?"

His grin is quick, a little sinister, as he looks from the pan and back to me.

I have a sudden urge to run as tears burn behind my eyes.

He fucking notices because the man is an expert at reading people. He turns off the burner, moving the pan to the back of the stove before prowling toward me.

His hand is behind my head before I can decide on my next course of action.

"I'm going to hurt you, Lauren. I'm going to fuck you so hard some days, so long that even your begging won't make me stop because that's what I'm going to need from you."

I nod, my throat thick with emotions.

"I would never cause you that kind of pain."

I shake my head, refusing to believe him.

"I will bite you, whip you, draw blood on your skin. I'm a sinister motherfucker, but I'd never pour hot fucking grease on you."

I'm shaking at this point, the fear from thinking he could do something like that mixing with the realization that the man can practically read my mind. It's exactly what I thought, and as much as I've been hurt, burns are the worst.

"Understand?"

I open my eyes to find him watching me. He has to shake me by the grip he has on the back of my neck before I answer.

"Yes."

He leans in closer.

"If you fucking kiss me, I'm going to kick you in the balls."

A wide grin curls his lips up. "There's my girl. Now, how do you like your eggs?"

"Fried," I answer before thinking, as if I'm being asked for my order in a restaurant.

His grin grows wider. "Scrambled it is."

I watch his gorgeous ass as he walks back to the stove, his back muscles rippling under his tan skin.

"I'm going to sit you in my lap while we eat. Just telling you so you can decide if you're going to let it happen or if I need to tie you up."

His eyes are dark and promising when he looks back at me again.

I still haven't made up my mind as he puts all the food on one plate before walking across the room and patting his lap after sitting in the only chair at the very small kitchenette.

"Is this because you only have one chair?" I ask as I cross the room.

Other than when he's fucking me, I think this is possibly the most we've really spoken, and I'm feeding off this attention from him.

"And I don't plan to get another one," he confirms, pulling me back further against his chest when I try to sit on one knee.

I wiggle on his lap, the only way I can think to rile him up.

He grunts, and I try to hide my smile and fail.

"Maybe I should get naked for this," he says, but instead of shoving his underwear down, he picks up his fork and stabs at the less than fluffy eggs on the plate.

He holds the fork to my lips, but when I open my mouth to tell him I'm not a baby, he shoves the fork inside before I can get the words out. I turn my head and stare at him as I chew.

"I don't have many hard limits, Lauren, but if you spit food in my face, you will not like the results, and that's not a promise of giving you what you say you don't want but actually do. Don't fucking test me on this."

"I'll never ask you for anything," I say after swallowing.

He smiles around his own bite of food, smacking my hand when I reach for a piece of bacon.

I have to wait for him to put the fork down and lift the meat to my mouth, and I hate it as much as it thrills me.

I'm actually paying attention to him, something I couldn't do when he fed me before when I was tied up because I was starving.

His eyes flash with his version of happiness which is a mere step under irritation as I chew.

"Does that mean you'll never beg me again?"

"I won't," I vow just as another piece of bacon meets my lips.

He swipes his thumb roughly on the grease left behind, and I squirm in his lap when he moans as he sucks it clean.

His hand drops to my thigh.

"I know I can make you beg."

"Maybe I'll just take what I want instead of asking?"

A slow smile spreads across his face, and goddamn this man is just too fucking good looking.

"Yeah?"

I nod.

"You think you're powerful enough?"

I shrug. I know better than to challenge him.

I slip my hand between my legs, grazing my clit as I reach further down. His cock is right there. It's been pressing against me since the second he pulled me onto his lap.

"Still hungry?" he asks as I grip his length. I think he may have been right about doing this while we were both naked.

I think sitting on his cock while he feeds me might make the way he's watching my face a little more bearable. I hate feeling so open and exposed, and I know it has absolutely nothing to do with my lack of clothing.

He reads me too easily. I've always prided myself in being able to lie so convincingly.

Maybe that's his appeal, the fact that he's nothing like anyone I've ever met.

"You think you can just take that?"

I bite my lip, looking down to watch my hand work him over between my thighs.

I squeal when he lifts me, forcing me to straddle him as if I weigh nothing.

"We aren't the same, Lauren," he says, his fingers pinching my nipple hard enough for me to cry out in pain before he wraps those perfect fingers around my throat. "This isn't tit for tat. What I do to you does not on any level give you the right to do them in return."

With his free hand, he pulls down the front of his boxers, and my body fucking sings, my head getting a little light from his grip on me.

"Roll up then sit," he commands.

I want to argue, to draw this out, but my body obeys before I can convince it otherwise.

I groan as he slips inside me, taking a little pride in the way his mouth falls open an inch.

He feels it. Without even having to voice his truth, I know he can sense this fucking connection between the two of us.

It's fucking electric.

"This isn't the perfect position for knocking you up, but I'll just keep my cock in you for an hour."

I try to scramble away. Joking about breeding me is hot. Actually getting pregnant would be catastrophic. There's no chance I could ever be anyone's mother. I'm too fucked up. Hell, he's too fucked up.

I know with him giving me exactly what I need, I don't think I'm going to go out and find trouble, but that doesn't mean he's going to stick around.

Everything ends, and I can't let myself think that isn't going to come crashing down as well. A kid is fucking permanent, and my past is way too fucked up to think I'd be any good at it. I've got no interest in continuing that vicious fucking cycle.

"Stand up," he demands but grips my hip the second my feet hit the floor. He pins me there, holding me in place by his grip on my throat as he fucks upward, spearing me.

Jesus, it feels so good.

I refuse to think of the limited pain, and it's almost impossible to reconcile enjoying this as much as I enjoy when he fucks me with his teeth imbedded in my skin.

"Fucking perfection," he pants, his eyes locked on his pistoning cock.

I try to pull away, still unable to accept that I bring him pleasure, that what he does to me is more than a power play.

The man left me my favorite soda on the bedside table, a very sweet gesture, but I can't imagine him actually enjoying what he does to me outside of the pain he inflicts.

It's clear I have a long way to go.

"I'm hoping for a boy. I'm going to teach him everything I know."

I claw at him then, my fingernails digging into the skin on his arms.

That familiar sinister smile is in place when he looks up at me again.

We lock eyes just as his cock kicks inside of me, and before I can pull away, he sits me back on his lap, impaled on his cock.

I struggle for fifteen minutes before he finally lets me get away.

Chapter 37

Angel

I feel like we're hanging on to a fraying thread.

The last six nights, Lauren has been in my bed, and I haven't hesitated to sleep right beside her.

I wake with a start every day, long before the sun rises, terrified that I'm going to find the spot beside me empty.

It hasn't happened yet, but I know it's coming.

She fights me just as much as she did the first time when I take her.

My marks are back where they belong on her neck, her arms, that fattest part of her perfect ass.

Yet, I can't let myself believe that I own her, that she's mine.

I try to force that promise from her lips, but no matter how many tears flow down her face, she just won't give in to it.

I'm almost at the end of my rope with it, wondering if I'd be able to force her hand if I tie her back to my bed, but making her stay and her choosing to herself are two very different things.

And fuck do I want her to choose me, to choose this life I've promised her.

I send the emails to Liam, Hollis, and a third guy that has reached out to me by the name of Nash. I haven't met the last two guys, and we've only communicated through emails, but they're kicking ass and taking names while I stay in the house, fuck my woman, and rake in the cash.

It's quiet today, something I used to relish, but Lauren is a fucking tornado. She talks just for the sake of hearing her own voice, and as much as I thought it would drive me crazy, I've grown somewhat used to the chatter.

Today feels different. It feels heavy in its quietness, and I know things are going to change.

She has had more than one opportunity to take off. I've tested her, leaving cash and my truck keys lying around, but she's never attempted it. I know better than to get complacent, and that's what has me moving from my office to the living room.

It's empty, as is the bedroom and bathroom.

I find her standing on the front porch, my truck keys dangling from her fingers as she stares out over the barren land surrounding my property.

I don't know what she's looking for, what she may be missing, but I know she'll never express her needs without them being forced from her lips.

Getting her to open up has been more difficult than I originally thought it would be, and she refuses alcohol every time I offer. We both know it's like a truth serum to her, and although I've thought about pouring it down her throat just to get a little fucking insight, I haven't crossed that bridge yet.

I watch from inside the house as she works through whatever has her head fucked up today, wondering if I'll be strong enough to let her leave if that's what she decides.

She may not have opened up to me about what she's struggling with but I know her enough to know she never pictured her life like this. She was going to push the limits, push the boundaries in captivity until one of those sick fucks pushed back too hard.

I swear every time I close my eyes, I see her shifting her head to the side as I dragged the knife down her neck. She wanted it to end, wanted the pain inside of her that she couldn't control to stop. I could read it in every tear that dripped down her skin.

It haunts me, just like I know the thoughts of her sister and her childhood haunt her.

She hasn't asked for the diary or necklace. She hasn't gone digging through the house in search of them either.

If she isn't chattering about absolutely nothing of importance or getting fucked, she's quiet and reflective. She's like two different people, and sometimes all it takes is the sun setting and rising again for the transition to happen.

One day, she's all smiles, teasing me until I fuck her hard against the wall, and other days, her pretty eyes are filled with so much pain, she's hateful and taunting until I end up fucking her.

We always end up fucking, but it's not like I'm fucking the same woman each time.

Some days, she smiles when I pull her to my chest after we both come. Others, she continues to scratch and claw at me until I release her.

Last night was one of those nights, one of the times that really made me believe she fucking hates me.

The change didn't happen with the sunrise, however.

She didn't seek me out in the kitchen naked with a mischievous smile on her face like she's done in the past. She stayed in bed, curled in a ball. I could hear her sobs through the closed bedroom door.

I fought the urge to go to her, to assure her she was fine because that's not what she's looking for, not what she needs when she gets that way.

I tried it the first time, and when she told me she was leaving, I believed her. But instead of walking out the front door after her shower, she went right back to bed where she stayed for the next day and a half.

The woman is truly fucking broken, and I feel helpless, trying to figure out how to fix it, terrified she's going to find the strength she's been punishing herself to find for so long. I can't fix her any more than she can fix me. I still struggle daily trying to silence the voices in my head that tell me I'm a fucking idiot for thinking I could ever be happy.

Her hair blows in the breeze, the jacket of mine she's wearing, whipping around her thighs, but instead of walking off the porch toward my truck, her shoulders fall. It's a classic sign of defeat, and her face is wet with tears when she turns around and walks back into the house.

She doesn't startle when she sees me watching her, and there's an apology in her eyes she'll never let escape her lips as she drops the keys back on the table near the door.

"I'll chase you if you run," I remind her instead of asking her if she needs somewhere to go.

Her eyes find mine, but there isn't a glint of challenge in them.

Today may be the worst of them all.

"I'm bored," she mutters. "I need to work."

"Home Depot is hiring."

She scoffs. "I'm not working at fucking Home Depot."

"And you aren't going back to what you were doing."

She runs her hands over her head before pressing her fingers into her eyes as if she's in pain.

"It's fucking dangerous out there, Lauren."

"It's fucking dangerous in here, Angel."

For a split second I think she means inside my house, but realization dawns on me that she means inside her head before I can argue that I'll protect her at any cost.

We get rough when we fuck. We both enjoy it, but she has to know by now that there's no real danger where I'm concerned... unless she runs.

"I have to work," she repeats.

"You don't."

Those two words encompass everything. I'll take care of any fucking need she has, but I'm not fool enough to think she's referencing money.

"What about you?" she growls. "Are you going to stop working?"

"Not a fucking chance," I say before I can really think about her question.

"You don't need to work," she argues. "I bet you have more than enough money to last this lifetime."

I clamp my mouth closed.

"Money isn't the issue. I'm not going to stop working."

She's somehow managed to turn this back on me, and I fucking hate the way it makes me feel.

"It's dangerous," she snaps.

"I can handle myself." I step closer to her, but she doesn't inch back.

It becomes very clear we aren't playing one of our games, but that doesn't keep me from picturing how I'll get her to change her fucking mind. It's instinctual to get the upper hand on her.

"If I'm meant to stay, if I'm meant to be *owned*, I can't risk losing that."

Her words make me freeze.

She's giving me an ultimatum, telling me exactly what she needs to agree to what I've insisted on.

I expect her sacrifice, but she expects mine in return.

"Do you really want me here twenty-four-seven?" The question carries an edge of menace because it's taking all I have not to fuck her right here.

She fucking wants this. This is her way of telling me so.

I'm asking her to give up on the idea of going out and getting herself hurt, and she's asking the same from me. She's asking me if I think *she's* enough.

"Fine."

Her eyes widen, but then she looks suspicious.

"Really? It's that easy?"

"That easy."

"I don't fucking believe you."

"Only because you've never met anyone you can fully trust until now."

She watches my face for a long moment before speaking. "I'll never fully trust you."

A wide grin spreads across my face. "Smart girl."

"I'll end up running," she confesses. "I won't be able to help myself."

I think I can appreciate her honesty, but it won't change anything.

"I can't fucking wait. I'll fuck you right into the dirt where I catch you."

Chapter 38

Lauren

That itchy feeling I've suffered all my life never leaves me, but I've gotten used to not scratching at it the last several weeks.

Instead of fighting the lows when they start, I give in to them. It's been taking less time to get past the darkness. I blame that fucking podcast Angel forced me to listen to for the suggestion.

Angel leaves me alone now. The first time he found me that way, he tried to fuck me through it. As much as I enjoyed the pain he offered, it did nothing to help. I thanked him by nearly clawing his eyes out. I was fucking rabid.

When he comes to find me in the morning now and I'm still in the bed, he walks right back out. He doesn't say a word or try to urge me to feel better. I don't know if he suffers from some of the same types of demons as I do, but it's clear he understands to a certain point.

I'll never tell him that I'm grateful for it, but I think he knows I need the solitude as much as I need the other elements of whatever it is we have. When I get back to feeling normal, I suck him off harder as a thank you for letting me live in my darkness. I'd never actually use the words because it still feels like handing him too much of me.

I press a finger into one of the bruises on my arm, smiling at the sharp burst of pain. His entire handprint is there, a kaleidoscope of reds, blues, and purples. I sigh with as much contentment as I can manage, but it never lasts long.

I haven't left since I arrived set on stabbing him in the chest. I literally haven't stepped off the front porch. I've thought about it many times, but that makes my skin crawl more than the darkness that sets in.

Angel runs the errands and grabs food.

I use nearly every second he's gone, which has only been a handful of times in the last couple of weeks, to search his house high and low for my sister's things. I've tried to convince myself that I'm only here for those two things, that when I find them, I can leave.

The first time I searched, I did it in his office. The man is smart enough to lock his computer system down but leaves the combination to his safe taped to the underside of his desk drawer?

Does he really think I'm that stupid? I know he isn't, and it didn't take long before I realized he's fucking with me. It's why I go back and search the same spots over and over. I wouldn't put it past him to keep moving the damn things around. It's a game I both love and hate.

He doesn't mention things being out of place despite him being so fucking OCD about where things go. Last time, he locked eyes with me as he put the handful of books he owns back in the correct order on the bookcase.

I've already checked the office. The code has changed, and the combination is no longer written down anywhere I can find. Although I'm certain the things are in the safe, I keep searching elsewhere because it could be a week before I get the chance to look again.

The closet is so organized, literally by style and color, it makes me freak out a little. He's so fucking meticulous it's annoying. I check every pocket, knowing they aren't big enough for the diary but that fucking necklace could be hidden anywhere. I kick at the shirt that falls off the hanger, making sure it's crumpled in the corner just to be annoying.

Next is the dresser. I start at the bottom because I know from digging in them before that they hold summer clothes, not that I can picture Angel in a pair of fucking cargo shorts, but he owns them, nonetheless.

The first three drawers prove to be fruitless, but I notice the items have been refolded from the last time I went through the drawer. The second drawer from the top, the sock drawer, looks like it was done by a professional. Each pair perfectly matched and in rows, also by color like the hanging clothes in his closest.

Feeling like a brat, I dig my hands in deep and start swirling them around. He may be extra rough tonight if he finds this before bed, and my body hums with the promise of more bruises.

Then my fingers brush over something hard.

I tell myself not to get too excited. I did that two weeks ago and ended up pulling out an old zippo lighter.

I turn the sock upside down, knowing how weird it is for something to actually be inside of it, but I wouldn't put it past Angel to do shit like that just to give me hope, only for it to crash to the ground. He's an expert in all things painful to me and delivers often.

The tarnished locket falls into my hand.

The world fucking stops spinning as I look down at the costume jewelry. I blink as if the thing will disappear, but it doesn't.

It's here, what I've been searching for this entire time.

I could leave, but then I remind myself that I can't leave. This is only half of what I'm looking for. Taking a chance, I fist the necklace and pull open the very top drawer. It's not even hidden. Right there on top is Liana's diary, the string that keeps it closed unwound.

He read her words.

I mean, I suspected he did.

I don't know a single person who wouldn't have it in their possession and not at least peek, but it feels like the ultimate betrayal.

Not because he knows in explicit details what she went through, but because he knows what kind of sick disgusting family I come from.

How am I still here with him knowing the truth?

How is he not disgusted with me?

I don't bother pulling the diary from the drawer, just like I don't bother closing the top two drawers before letting the necklace slide from my hand. It lands on the top. Because of Angel's nonexistent decorating skills, it's the only thing sitting there as I take two steps back, my eyes locked on what I considered the two most important things in my life.

This is part of his game.

The promises, the joy, the pain I love so much, has all just been a way to make me let my guard down, and fuck if it hasn't worked.

Just like with the hidden combination to his safe, he wanted me to find this.

I haven't mentioned these things by name at all, and only mentioned them in the abstract once when I came back. He knows I'm looking for them, knows I'll stick around until I find them. To find them so easily means another goodbye, just like when he cut me loose before.

My heart races as my hands sweep my lower belly.

Did he find out? Is he disgusted with what we created?

My hands tremble as I make my way to the front door, fear washing over me for still being here.

I took my time looking this time, certain I'd never find them.

I have no idea what will happen if he catches me here when he returns. My walking papers were as clear as day, sitting right on top in that drawer. If he wanted to, he could've made it harder. If he didn't want me gone, he could've destroyed the fucking things, or locked them in his safe.

He wanted this.

Tears sting my eyes, and it pisses me off. I've spent so much time trying not to feel settled, to not watch his every move, trying to catch him lying to me.

He said I was a smart girl for confessing I'll never fully trust him. He flat out fucking said it was a bad idea, that he was untrustworthy, but his actions over the last several weeks didn't make me suspicious.

I grab the jacket I've worn more than once when I stand on the porch, and shove my arms into the sleeves. I reach for a pair of boots that will be way too big for me just as I see the headlights coming up the long driveway.

Heartache freezes me right on the spot. I want to confront him, to confess how bad he's hurt me, but I won't give him the satisfaction. As he drives nearer, I decide to face him calmly, to tell him this is over, and I'd appreciate a ride into town so I can catch a bus out of state.

But then he slows, his headlights flashing over me.

Maybe I have it all wrong, I bargain as the truck pulls to a stop.

It doesn't take him long to climb out, the porch light reflecting off that sexy devious grin of his.

"Gonna catch cold out here, babe," he says as he closes the driver's side door before opening the one behind it to grab the groceries he went to get.

I thought things were great, and with the way he's acting right now, I try to convince myself I got it all wrong.

I was brave enough to request clam chowder and spicy chips. I woke up this morning with that on my brain and it sounded like the most amazing meal ever. He scrunched his nose but assured me he'd grab some.

I swallow, my entire body trembling, my nerves shot at having to make a decision.

Tears stream down my face when he turns around, both hands full of grocery bags. He stops in his tracks as he notices the pain on my face.

"Don't fucking do it, Lauren."

His words are like a gunshot, the beginning of the race.

"Goddamn it!" I hear him roar as I fly off the porch and run top speed in to the night.

Chapter 39

Angel

There's a very real chance I broke the jar of fucking pickles when I dropped the bags at my feet.

I knew she was going to do this eventually. Fucking leave it up to her when I'm most settled in, when I've let myself believe things were good.

I know why she's running. I know she's scared. I know she can't let herself imagine being happy and as healthy as her mind will allow her to be. It's my job to remind her, and unlike with most people, words don't fix shit for Lauren. She needs a different approach.

She's about to find out just how fucking serious I am about her safety.

We've had an early spring this year, and that increases the damn risk of snakes on the property as they wake up from their winter hibernation.

I'll spank her ass relentlessly if she gets her ass bit while pulling this shit.

My boots pound over the ground, and I'm torn between letting her run as far as she can before giving up, and worrying about each and every fucking step she takes.

I thought this was going to be fun. I've been anticipating fulfilling my promise after she guaranteed this would happen, but things are different now. I plan on making sure she knows it by the time I'm finished with her.

The jacket of mine she's fond of billows behind her in the moonlight, and it's a fucking gorgeous sight to see.

I've been worried about her the last couple of weeks. She's practically turned into a hermit. She won't leave the house. It started with her making excuses, to her yelling when I urged her to go with me to the grocery store. That's something else that's going to change after tonight. If she thinks I won't hogtie her and plop her ass in a shopping cart, she's very fucking wrong.

There's a difference in fresh air on the porch and getting away from the house for a few hours to recharge.

She's nearing the edge of the property, so I increase my speed, grabbing her about thirty yards from the ditch.

"Let go of me!" she screams.

Her breathing is ragged with exertion as I pull her against my chest.

"What did I tell you would happen if you ran, baby?"

"I'm not fucking playing, Angel. Let me go."

"You don't get to leave. I'll never allow you to walk away. You had your fucking chance when you stepped over my bleeding body in El Salvador." My voice is a low growl, every word enunciated so nothing gets lost in translation. "Do you know what happened after that day? Do you even care that the men who found me tortured me for weeks? That you made me the man I am today?"

I can tell she's giving the fight all her best, but even on a bad day for me, it will never be enough. Even with her skills there's no way to win against my size.

She attempts stomping on my feet, wincing in pain when her heel comes down on the steel toe.

When I lift her from the ground, she kicks and flails, but the pain in my shin hardly fazes me.

"Do you want the fucking dirty details, Lauren? I'll give them to you, baby. I can tell you all about how they cut me, burned me, electrocuted me, in retribution for the man that died because he raped that girl."

She looks pained, her eyes starting to shed tears, but I'm too far gone.

"You're my whore now," I hiss, our faces mere inches apart. "You created this monster. You're responsible for me now. Leaving will never be an option for you."

There is literally nowhere to set her down. We're too far from the truck for me to wait to get inside of her if I carry her there.

"Angel, don't."

I ignore her plea as I shove up the t-shirt of mine that she's wearing.

I nearly collapse on the ground with need at the feel of her slick cunt against my fingers.

"That's my dirty whore," I pant in her ear as I shove three fingers inside of her.

She whimpers. "Angel, please stop."

Please isn't a word she's used with me very often. It's too close to begging for her.

It's almost enough to make me pause, but I know that won't do either of us any good.

We both need this.

I know why she ran, just like I know she's been searching the house high and low for that stupid fucking necklace and the diary that doesn't mean shit. I don't how she's letting possessions from a dead girl rule so much of her life, but I'm tired of cleaning up after her searches. It took me ten minutes to put my fucking sock drawer back together last time.

I spin her around, pushing my body flush with hers before she can get any more leverage than pounding her fists on my back. In the next second, we're on the ground.

She claws at me, holding nothing back as I shove the t-shirt under her chin before pulling my dick out.

I wince when she catches me in the eye with her fist, and I bite her neck for it with a hand tangled in her hair.

"This what you wanted?" I snap as I slam inside of her. "This what you needed?"

She gasps at the intrusion, and it's the sweetest fucking sound she ever makes. I'm addicted, needing it more often than is probably healthy.

She needs it too or we wouldn't be rutting around in the fucking dirt like goddamned animals.

"You hurt me!" she wails, her arms falling to her side as if she's giving up the fight.

"Baby," I say, caressing her cheek.

I don't stop fucking her because I just can't.

"Don't," she sobs, turning her head away so I can't watch the pain on her face.

She has to know I need that as much as she needs all of this from me.

I urge her to look at me.

"You want me gone! Why won't you let me fucking leave?"

This stops the entire world.

"The fuck are you talking about?" Confusion explodes behind my eyes. Why is she saying shit like this after everything I just said to her?

"You wouldn't have left that shit for me to find if you wanted me here. You know I've been looking for it."

I tilt my head to the side as I watch the flood of tears coming from her eyes.

"We'll talk about this shit when I'm done," I growl, the pressure in my balls too much at this point to ignore.

Her mouth hangs open when I find the end of her, and I can tell this is going to be one of those times she's going to try and be fucking stubborn. But this is too much of an important moment. It's too pivotal to who we are together for me to just let her continue the bratty behavior.

With ease, I pull back and lock her legs in the crooks of my arms.

"You'll fucking come."

"I can't."

"If you can't come now, I may never let you come again," I threaten, my fingers finding her clit easily.

Her stubbornness doesn't last much longer, and I can tell how close she is by just looking at her face.

"Waited too long." I pull from her, the start of my orgasm beginning inside of her unintentionally.

I hiss my pleasure as I paint her lower belly with the rest.

"Angel!" she screams, and I fucking know how she feels.

Orgasm denial isn't fun at all.

"Beg for it."

"I will fucking not." She tries to scurry away, but I grab her leg, keeping her on the ground. "Let me go."

"Beg, baby."

She crosses her arms over her chest and if it weren't for the goosebumps on her skin I know is caused by the cool air and not the promise of my threat, I'd spend all night out here with her until she caved.

Instead, I swirl my finger around her clit, waiting until she lifts her hips from the ground an inch or so before pulling back.

"I'll kill you in your fucking sleep," she growls.

"Suck my cock first," I tease, my fingers going right back to her clit when she settles. "I can do this all night, baby."

She fucking knows I can.

"Make me come."

I raise an eyebrow, knowing she can see my face enough to know that isn't going to work with me.

"Don't demand."

"Make me come, please."

"Asking and begging aren't the same thing, Lauren, and you know it."

I stop touching her when she starts to quicken again.

"Goddamn it, Angel. Please make me come."

My smile is quick, rewarding, as I move my mouth to her pussy.

Our moans are simultaneous. I don't think anything in the world tastes as good as us combined.

I lick at her and nip her flesh when she grows silent. She's controlling this moment as much as I am, and I don't have a problem with sharing the power for a little while.

Her knees come up, squeezing at my ears just a few seconds before I feel the pulse of her cunt against my tongue.

I don't stop, but instead double my efforts. She's out of control with pleasure, but it turns into too much quickly.

She pushes at my head, resorting to pulling my hair when I refuse to stop.

She knows what it takes, but it takes her another orgasm and several long minutes before she relaxes her legs and releases my hair.

I don't let her linger on the ground. After zipping myself back up, I scoop her up and start the trip back to the house.

"What about the groceries?" she asks as we walk past the mess beside the truck.

"I'll get them after I get you bathed and in bed."

She tucks her face into my throat, and it makes me want to hold her like this forever. Lauren is quick to want to get fucked, but other displays of affection come very far and few between.

"Jesus fuck," I mutter as I walk into the room and see the top two drawers of my dresser in a mess.

I nudge her face until she pulls it back and point at the damn thing.

"That's why I hid the shit where you could find it. I'm tired of the fucking messes."

She bites the inside of her cheek as she stares at the sock hanging over the edge of the second drawer.

"I'm messy."

"And I'm going to make you scrub floors with a plug in your ass the size of a Coke can if it happens again."

Chapter 40

Lauren

It's still dark outside when I wake, and Angel doesn't even stir in the bed when I climb out to head to the bathroom.

He kept his promise. I ran, and he caught me.

It can't be this simple though, can it?

He left the things for me to find because I was messy?

I thought it was my walking papers, a way for him to tell me he was done.

It's been impossible to fall asleep, impossible for me to let myself believe that there's something real between us.

I've never depended on anyone since Liana. The letdown from that shaped my entire life from the rest of my horrible childhood with my grandmother to the profession I chose.

How can I possibly depend on him?

I'm terrified he's going to change his mind, and I'll be left alone.

I glance at my flat, lower belly. Well, not completely alone.

I'm fucking terrified of where my life is heading. That doesn't mean it has to be a bad thing, but it's impossible to shove down certain thoughts. Is there any way for me not to fuck up a child's life? Can I be a good mother? Will the child grow up hating me? Hating him?

I scan my body, smiling at the marks left behind from our roll in the field earlier. I don't know how long we can keep it up safely. That brings its own feelings of guilt because I don't want to stop what we do. How fucking selfish is that?

My eyes lock on the necklace dangling from my throat.

I must've fallen asleep at some point because it wasn't on me when we got into bed.

It feels foreign against my skin.

It's a token of horrific proportions. It's what I held onto so I never forget the pain I've been through.

I tug at it, easily breaking the chain. I've never worn the thing a day in my life. It's not a prize, not a sentimental possession I hold dear. It's how I've always hurt myself in the past.

Liana valued it. According to her diary, it was the apology gift my dad gave her to keep her mouth shut after raping her the first time. It was payment for abuse. It was the first of many, and as a child, I sort of hated my sister for the gifts she always got because I had no clue what they stood for. I didn't understand how some days, she was so proud of the trinkets, and others, she was burning them in the backyard while our father was at work. I thought she was wasteful, petty, and spoiled. I know now she was hurting with a pain so deep no one could help her.

The necklace clinks on the counter when I drop it there, but brushing my skin where it touched doesn't make the disgust go away. Angel has no idea how much I hate the thing, but I can't help but be a little angry for finding it around my neck.

I swallow down that disgust and take a true long look at myself.

For decades I've avoided any prolonged looks in the mirror. I've always hated what I saw there. It was always a reminder of the pain, of the failures, of the abuse I've been ashamed to admit to.

Maybe my dad knew he didn't have to hurt me the way he did Liana because I was going to be an expert at doing that to myself.

Today isn't one of my bad days, and I'm grateful for that. These contemplations would be dangerous on a bad day.

I find myself smiling at my reflection, and it's not forced. It isn't an attempt to practice fooling people I may run into.

It's real, true. It's happiness.

I'm not the type to have lightbulb moments. I pay too much attention to things going on around me to be genuinely surprised by much of anything.

But I'm hit in the chest with the fact that I want what Angel is offering.

I want the attention, the life we could have. I want the baby growing inside of me, and if he didn't want a child with me, he never would've cut my implant out of my arm.

He wanted it before he cut me loose, before I left.

He's said it so many times. I'm his. I'm never allowed to leave. He'll hunt me down and drag me back.

How am I only now seeing it?

Is it because I never thought I could find happiness? Because I deem myself unworthy of anything good?

My skin flushes pink with all the possibilities, my hands trembling a little as the thought puts a smile on my face.

I search my eyes in the mirror, afraid this is just another manic episode where everything is perfect, and tomorrow I'll suffer the crash.

I straighten, refusing to believe that. I'm so sick and tired of the apocalyptic thoughts that drag me down, the worry of what tomorrow will bring.

Angel would die to protect me, to protect us, and somehow it's taken me this long to fully understand it.

I feel lighter on my feet than I can ever remember as I make my way back into the bedroom.

He's asleep, his dark lashes fanned across his cheekbones, arm outstretched as if he is searching for me in his sleep, despite the standing rule that we don't touch each other during the night unless it's for him to wake me because he has needs.

I've spent so much time looking for the bad in him, I haven't paid much attention to the good. I see it. I'm not blind, but I convinced myself it was a manipulation.

The breakfast he cooks, the sporadic smiles he gives me, the way even when he's rough with me, his eyes are searching my face to determine if I'm hurting too much but refuse to tap out because of pride.

It has fucking been right in my face all along.

I don't know when the change happened, when his hatred for me dulled enough for him to begin to care, but it's there, and it has been for a while.

I'm cautious in my movements as I climb on the bed. He always wakes before me, and I've never done this before. After we're done playing, I pass out from exhaustion, so I've never woken him.

Even the time I snuck into his hotel room the first time, he was awake and just pretending not to be.

I know I'm at risk. I know he could startle awake and hurt me, but I can't not touch him.

His eyes slowly open when I brush his chest with my palm.

"Baby?" His voice is husky from sleep, so full of gravel. That's all it takes to light my skin on fire.

"I need you," I confess, and from the soft smile on his lips, I know he can tell I mean more than just sex.

My heart is racing as I straddle him. I've avoided all soft touches, anything that could be construed as loving, but I ache for that right now.

"You have me," he whispers.

"I have conditions," I say quickly before I lose the nerve.

"Of course you do." He doesn't say it in a way that makes me think he's annoyed. The words are spoken with humor.

"I need you to let me do this on my own." I roll my hips in an attempt to calm my nerves.

I need to know he's right here with me, capable of letting me see this through.

"Take what you need, baby."

There's a certain thrill in what he says, but it's also marked with apprehension. I'm not a fan of soft and sweet, and I know that has to do with meeting my own needs. Those needs more often than not have been my form of punishment. At some point in my life, the rough, painful, and hard were what I longed for, what I needed to get off, but I feel it in my bones that soft with him could bring me the same pleasure. I'm not foolish enough to think I'll want this all the time, but sprinkling it in every once in a while could be possible.

"You keep looking at me all sweet and cute, and I'm going to come the second you slide down my cock."

"How disappointing," I tease as I position myself higher on my knees.

He takes the initiative to stand his cock up for me, but leaves me with the decision of when to drop back down.

I don't see this as him relinquishing power. I know the tables could turn at any second, and the chance of that makes this all the more exciting.

We both groan with pleasure as I slide down the length of him, and that's all it takes for my legs to stop shaking.

I focus on everything—the feel of him inside me, the pleasure, the way he watches me with such adoration, and for the first time in my life, I let it all in. There's affection in his touch as his hands curve around my ass, and I know he isn't doing it to try to take control but because he just can't help himself.

He doesn't taunt or tease me when I try to lean forward, my mouth closer to his. He doesn't shy away despite me having bit him every fucking time he tries to kiss me. He isn't using the opportunity to deny me what I denied him so many times.

He leans up, situating himself in a sitting position, and lets me take charge.

I lick at his lips, a swarm of butterflies in my belly with the sound he makes the second my tongue sweeps over his.

It's a full fucking body experience, and I'm not scared. I'm not disgusted by the softness or the tender way his arms wrap around me.

We're a mess of swiveling hips, lapping tongues, and for the first time in my life, I feel that quickening, the warning signs I'm going to orgasm without an element of pain being attached to it.

It scares me, the vulnerability I'm showing him.

"Stay with me, baby," he begs, his hand cupping my cheek as he pulls back just to watch my face.

I nod, fighting the urge to close my eyes because I'm just too raw from it all.

When he licks his thumb, I almost don't need the feel of him teasing my clit, and soar the second he touches it.

Tears leak down my face as I orgasm because I feel free for the first time in my life.

I'm not unreasonable. I know this feeling won't last forever. I have bad days ahead of me, but I choose to live in this very moment. Right now, nothing else matters.

"That's my girl," he says, the praise still sounding awkward but not ungenuine. "Make me come."

I smile at his command as I come down from my orgasm. There's the guy I could see myself spending my life with.

He helps because I'm just exhausted, by cupping me under the ass and helping me rise and lower onto him, and when he reaches that point of no return, he locks eyes with me. I can read what he's saying without him even opening his mouth, and it titillates every part of me.

I feel the pulse of him inside of me as he groans his release, and when he leans in to kiss me, I don't back away. I was worried the crash after the orgasm would have me running from anything soft, would have me backing away or taunting him until he showed me that rougher side of him I'm used to.

I kiss him back, my hands on his face as I we take just a moment to enjoy the other.

When I pull back and look down at him, he smiles again, but then it's there, that wolfish grin that's more teeth and threatening than anything else.

I squeal when he pinches my ass hard enough to leave a mark.

It has me climbing from his lap immediately, but he doesn't let me get far.

In a second, I'm on my back with him between my legs. He watches my face as he pins my arms over my head.

It makes me want to run, not because I'm afraid, but because he has that we-need-to-talk look, and it makes my skin itch.

"Thank you."

"For what?" I ask.

"Everything. For being who I need, for letting me be who you need. I know it comes with sacrifices on your part."

I swallow thickly. Going slow and enjoying each other that way was easier than actually hearing the words from his mouth.

"Do you think we hurt the baby?"

I tremble.

"Earlier when we were outside," he clarifies when I remain silent.

"How did you know?" I finally manage.

He doesn't answer me, and it doesn't surprise me at all.

"Do you think the baby is okay?" he asks again, and I know I have to be honest with him.

"I don't think the baby will ever be okay with us as parents."

He considers my response for a long moment before speaking.

"I'm going to have so much fun proving you wrong."

With that declaration, he presses another kiss to my lips before slipping beside me in the bed and pulling me to his chest.

It lasts all of five minutes before I have to pull away and get some distance.

His laughter at my insistence follows me into a dreamless sleep.

Chapter 41

Angel

"Keep sitting there with that look on your face and I'll fuck you against the window."

Testing my patience, Lauren rolls her eyes.

She's doing it for attention. She's become a professional over the last six months of thinking she can call my bluff.

My cock threatens to thicken, giving a little kick in my jeans.

"You think I'm playing," I warn. "I don't care who—"

I snap my jaw closed, drawing a tiny chuckle from her when the door opens after a quick knock.

"Good to see you two again," the doctor says when she enters.

Lauren smiles at her, and it's not one of the fake ones she struggles through in public these days.

"I wanted to start the visit with your test results."

Dr. Taylor hands each of us a piece of paper, and we each studiously look down at the results.

I smile when I see my results, looking up at Lauren to find the same look on her face.

Nothing would change for us no matter what the results were, but I know she was worried about the health of the baby if the STD panel came back with different results.

She's felt guilt for a while about what she put her body through and what that could mean for our unborn child.

"We're clear?" Lauren asks.

"A hundred percent," Dr. Taylor confirms. "The baby is healthy."

"Our son," I clarify, bringing a grin to the doctor's face.

"The baby," she counters.

Lauren chuckles again. She didn't want to know the sex of the baby, but it hasn't stopped me from trying to get the doctor to slip since our twenty-week ultrasound.

We work through scheduling the next appointment before the doctor starts asking the hard questions.

"Have you been to one of the meetings?"

Lauren holds her head high, refusing to let the guilt from not going to one of the support group meetings that were recommended after she was blatantly honest with the doctor, during her first appointment win.

Lessons Learned | 224

"I made it to the parking lot," Lauren answers.

"That's a start," Dr. Taylor commends.

The woman has never judged her or our lifestyle when uncomfortable questions were asked.

Lauren explained what she considered selfish thoughts about still liking things rough where sex was concerned.

"What about the dizziness?" Lauren asks.

Dr. Taylor gives her a knowing look that makes me wonder just what this woman is into that keeps her from questioning what we like.

"No more prolonged time lying flat on your back. The baby's weight has gotten to the point that he's pressing against something to cause it."

"He's getting pretty big, huh?"

Lauren rolls her eyes, but Dr. Taylor doesn't fall for my trick.

"I can direct you to a website for other positions that won't cause—"

"No back lying. Got it, Doc."

I can't sit in here, minutes after threatening to fuck my woman against the window, and listen to a conversation about positions to fuck her in without popping wood.

Lauren and Dr. Taylor both chuckle, and it causes me to send a glare Lauren's way. She's well fucking aware of what's going on, and I'll be happy to correct her behavior soon enough.

"And before you ask," she begins, looking directly at me. "I have more clients coming in so no you can't have a few private minutes in the room."

"Jesus Christ," Lauren mutters.

"You're sure?" I verify.

Dr. Taylor laughs, but she doesn't take the chance as she stands in the open doorway while I help Lauren off the table.

"Cockblock," I mutter to the doctor as we walk past her.

Laughter follows us out of the office.

"Why do you always try to embarrass me?"

I smile as I keep my eyes scanning the parking lot as we make our way to the truck.

"There's nothing embarrassing about you being so irresistible that I want my dick in you all the time."

She doesn't argue, and I know as much as she's annoyed with what I said, her pussy is wet with the implication that I'd fuck her in the exam room.

"Before you get any wild ideas," she says as I cup her ass a little too long as she climbs in the truck. "We have that meeting back at the office."

I close her inside the truck, grumbling as I make my way to the driver's door.

We've kept our promise to each other about not returning to work, but it's left both of us bored.

Lauren suggested opening an office, a home base of sorts for the men I've been sending out on jobs.

I hate the idea, but I don't hate her, so now we have office space in town.

"I think we need to turn the phone off," she mutters as we pull up to the front of the building we're renting space in.

"People will just keep knocking on the door if we do that."

The company line to the public is that we're private detectives and private security. We also happen to be booked out for the foreseeable future because all of my scheduling is still done with the guys through the dark web. We look legitimate, but honestly it's dirty business as usual.

"Maybe a voicemail system?" she suggests. "My patience is wearing thin on people calling to get quoted a price for someone to follow their cheating spouse around."

"You wanted this," I remind her, pointing to the fucking logo on the front glass. "I was content to just sit at home with you on my cock all fucking day."

She smiles but keeps her eyes locked on the Mission Mercenaries sign on the glass door. The skull is a true representation of who we are. The two birds are poetically us and the freedom we found in each other. The flowers? I see them as a waste of space, but Lauren said it looked too fucking macabre without them.

Finnis mali, the end of evil in Latin, is our promise that when the guys go out to work, they are judge, jury, and executioner, no questions asked.

"Do you think we have time to fuck?" Lauren asks as I open her door and help her out of the truck.

My hand immediately goes to my son growing inside of her.

I never thought I'd find a pregnant woman so fucking irresistible, but I think I may keep her knocked up forever with how much she turns me on this way. The idea of my seed inside of her, growing a child in there, makes me a territorial bastard.

"We always have time to fuck, baby," I promise.

She tries to get away from me, but I don't allow it until she clears the curb of the sidewalk. She almost face-planted the other day, and although it scared the shit out of me, I made sure to show her the error of her ways once we got inside.

Fighting the lock is a huge pain in the ass, but the second the door is open, I'm on her.

She's learned that dresses are better suited for anytime out of the house because I've ripped too many of her clothes.

"If you take those panties off yourself, I won't let you come."

Lauren freezes with her hands under her dress, indecision in her eyes.

She knows what she wants, but she also likes begging for it.

A pinch of disappointment hits me when she pulls her hands free.

"That fucking needy, huh, baby?"

I'm unbuckling my belt, working my zipper down as I walk to her.

"Fucking whore," I pant when she turns her back to me before bending over the desk at the back of the office.

She rolls her body for more attention when I flip her dress up and slowly pull her panties down.

Jesus, the scent of her arousal is the sweetest thing I've ever smelled in my life.

I grip a handful of her ass, relishing the marks left there from before our office visit with Dr. Taylor. She winces from the bite of pain before it turns into a moan.

I want to tease her, to torture her with waiting, but every second since the last time I was inside her a couple of hours ago has been my own form of punishment.

My jaw clenches in an effort not to show my hand when I slide inside of her. It's pure fucking heaven.

"Fucking move," she growls, demanding more when I attempt to spend a few seconds of bliss just enjoying the warmth and tightness of her.

"Greedy bitch," I hiss, pulling my hips back and snapping them forward.

I'm going full force, my balls high and tight as she moans and screams my name. She is the perfect fucking woman, taking it all and begging for more.

Reaching around, I squeeze her tits, wishing she was facing me so I could get a mouthful. I'm rougher, annoyed with missing out on seeing her face, when she comes on a cry.

As always, she takes me right over the edge with her, an orgasm so strong my vision turns blurry for a second.

A throat clears behind me, and I'm forced to spin in that direction, my cock just open to the air.

"Whoa!" Liam says from his spot by the fucking door, but he's looking past me.

Looking over my shoulder, I see Lauren pointing a gun directly at him. She isn't embarrassed that we got caught fucking. She's making sure we're safe. Even seven months pregnant, the woman is efficient, still capable of using those honed skills she learned in the FBI.

"Didn't mean to scare you. I'm sorry, Mrs. Guerra."

Lauren growls again.

"That's one way to get shot," I mutter.

I haven't had to ask Lauren to marry me. She's been very vocal about not wanting that, and I thought hearing it would upset me, but it doesn't.

She's mine, now and forever, and I don't need a piece of paper tying us together. I know she feels the same way.

"Call me anything but Lauren and I'll have your balls."

Liam nods his agreement, and he's smart enough not to smile when he does it.

"You're early," I mutter, my eyes darting from the clock on the wall and back to him.

"I came to tell you I fucked up."

Lauren mutters under her breath about all of this being a big fucking mistake, and I have to agree with her. Things were so much easier when I was dispatching these assholes from the comfort of my home office.

"We don't offer insurance," I remind him. "There's no liability on my end."

He nods, his throat working on a swallow, his eyes darting between me and Lauren who still has her gun trained on him, still undecided if shooting him is the wrong choice.

I place my hand over the top of the weapon, and despite looking annoyed that I'm taking her choice away, she lowers it.

"Can't risk the police getting called," I tell her before turning my attention back to Liam.

"I can explain. Well, I'll do my best to explain," he says.

The front door opens at his back.

"We're closed," I snap as a young woman steps forward.

"Jesus Christ," Lauren says at the exact same time I realize I recognize the woman.

The other woman looks up at Liam for answers.

"What the fuck is going on?" I snap. "Why is the senator's missing daughter in my fucking office right now?"

Liam swallows again, and I know Lauren is getting ready to make good on her promise, with no regard to whether the police get called or not.

Raya, the twenty-two-year-old recent college graduate and daughter of Texas Senator Thomas Reed, steps forward with the entitled air of someone who grew up being handed everything in life. She's been missing for the last several weeks, and the manhunt for whoever took her has been on every news station daily, from here to the fucking Canadian border.

She hitches a thumb toward Liam. "He's the one who kidnapped me."

THE END

Liam's story is next in Mistakes Made!

OTHER BOOKS FROM MARIE JAMES

Newest Series
Mission Mercenaries
Lessons Learned
Mistakes Made
Bridges Burned
Depravity Delivered
Redemption Refused
Confusion Cleared

Blackbridge Security
Hostile Territory
Shot in the Dark
Contingency Plan
Truth Be Told
Calculated Risk
Heroic Measures
Sleight of Hand
Controlled Burn
Cease Fire
Crossing Borders
Blackbridge Box Set 1
Blackbridge Box Set 2

Standalones
Crowd Pleaser
Macon
We Said Forever
More Than a Memory

Cole Brothers SERIES
Love Me Like That
Teach Me Like That

Cerberus MC

Kincaid: Cerberus MC Book 1
Kid: Cerberus MC Book 2
Shadow: Cerberus MC Book 3
Dominic: Cerberus MC Book 4
Snatch: Cerberus MC Book 5
A Very Cerberus Christmas Novella (1.5)
Lawson: Cerberus MC Book 6
Hound: Cerberus MC Book 7
Griffin: Cerberus MC Book 8
Samson: Cerberus MC Book 9
Tug: Cerberus MC Book 10
Scooter: Cerberus MC Book 11
Cannon: Cerberus MC Book 12
Rocker: Cerberus MC Book 13
Colton: Cerberus MC Book 14
Drew: Cerberus MC Book 15
Jinx: Cerberus MC Book 16
Thumper: Cerberus MC Book 17
Apollo: Cerberus MC Book 18
Legend: Cerberus MC Book 19
Grinch: Cerberus MC Book 20
Harley: Cerberus MC Book 21
Landon: Cerberus MC Book 22
Spade: Cerberus MC Book 23
Aro: Cerberus MC Book 24
Boomer: Cerberus MC Book 25
Ugly: Cerberus MC Book 26
Bishop: Cerberus MC Book 27
Cerberus MC Box Set 1
Cerberus MC Box Set 2
Cerberus MC Box Set 3
Cerberus MC Box Set 4
Cerberus MC Box Set 5

Ravens Ruin MC
Desperate Beginnings: Prequel
Book 1: Sins of the Father
Book 2: Luck of the Devil
Book 3: Dancing with the Devil

MM Romance
Grinder
Taunting Tony
Snatch
Tug
Landon
Crossing Borders

Westover Prep Series
(bully/enemies to lovers romance)
One-Eighty
Catch Twenty-Two

Made in the USA
Monee, IL
29 April 2023